BLOOD ISLAND

T0017135

ALSO BY H. TERRELL GRIFFIN

Matt Royal Mysteries

Longboat Blues

Murder Key

Wyatt's Revenge

Bitter Legacy

Collateral Damage

Fatal Decree

Found

BLOOD ISLAND

A Matt Royal Mystery

H. Terrell Griffin

Longboat Key, Florida

ISBN: 978-1-933515-70-0

Published in the United States of America by Oceanview Publishing, Ipswich, Massachusetts
www.oceanviewpub.com

2 4 6 8 10 9 7 5 3 1

PRINTED IN THE UNITED STATES OF AMERICA

Miles J. Leavitt, Jr.

1946–2007

This one's for you buddy

For zeal's a dreadful termagant,
That teaches saints to tear and cant

— Samuel Butler

ACKNOWLEDGMENTS

Writing, for me, is a team sport. I have the good fortune to have a brain trust that keeps me on track, provides plot suggestions, criticisms, editing, and a prod now and then when I get lazy. Peggy Kendall, Debbie Schroeder, and Jean Griffin are the brains behind the writing. I could not do it without their help, and for that I am very grateful.

Peggy's husband, Dave Kendall, has patiently listened to my ramblings about plot and structure at the same time that he was defeating what John Wayne once called "the big C." Cancer. Dave has fought this terrible scourge with grace and humor and determination, and awed me with his courage.

John Allred, the oil man from Houston who was once a boy from Sanford, lends me his persona and his prodigious brain. My oldest buddy is still my best buddy.

Jay Davis is an idea man. One of the thoughts that bubbled to the surface of his overworked brain fueled this book. Dudley Brown, Patrick Gray, Demetra McBride, and Paul Roat are inveterate supporters of writers in general and me in particular. Thank you, my friends.

Some of my friends from college and law school days sneak into my writing at the oddest times. You know who you are, and I'm grateful for your willingness to allow me to use you.

Debby Stowell, bookseller par excellence, has been my great supporter. This book would not be in circulation without her devoted efforts on my behalf. Thank you, Deb.

Bob Gussin and Patricia Gussin gave me a chance. Thank you. Your dedication to publishing, your confidence in the written word, and your always pleasant and upbeat demeanor have given a number of writers, including me, the confidence to keep writing. Pat's ideas and help with the manuscript of this book have been invaluable.

The gang at Oceanview Publishing, particularly Susan Greger and Maryglenn McCombs, have been more accommodating than I would have imagined. You all make me a better writer. Thank you.

I trust that my Key West friends and readers will forgive me a few indiscretions with the geography of their lovely island and will not think I overstepped the bounds of literary license.

Finally, Jean Griffin, the woman who, in a lapse in judgment, married me when I was a college student so long ago. You brighten my life more than the morning sun.

BLOOD ISLAND

CHAPTER ONE

The body lay on its back, nude. Its eyes and parts of its face were gone. Chunks of flesh had been torn from its torso, its genitals mutilated.

Vultures sat impassively on the limbs of the tree that grew from the center of the tall cage. They were used to humans standing around, talking, watching, eating peanuts, their kids laughing at the funny looking birds.

I dialed Vince on my cell phone. "There's a dead guy in your vulture pit," I said.

"I'm on my way."

Vince Delgado was the director of the Pelican Man's Bird Sanctuary, which clung to the edge of City Island in Sarasota, Florida. Sick and injured birds were brought in for treatment and rehabilitation. Those who were too badly compromised to return to the wild after treatment were kept in cages spread around the sanctuary.

Vince was a drinking buddy from Tiny's, a bar on Longboat Key, the island just across New Pass from City Island. The night before, I had mentioned that I'd never visited his sanctuary, and he'd invited me to come down early in the morning, before the tourists showed up.

I'd been walking idly through the area, drinking from the cup of Starbucks I'd bought on St. Armand's Circle, enjoying the early morning of a bright April day. I didn't expect to see one of our citizens turned into vulture food.

Vince was chugging up the path from the office, his short arms pumping, his pumpkin-size belly jiggling as he ran. He was a short fat guy with curly black hair and a face that was overshadowed by a huge nose. His dark eyes had a look of panic as he slid to a stop at the vulture cage.

"Oh shit," he said. "This isn't going to look good in the papers."

"Call the police, Vince."

"Yeah." He took out his cell phone and dialed 911.

"Do you know him?"

"I don't think so, but it's hard to tell with his face all chewed up. I'd better get to the front to let the cops in."

I stood there, alone with the vultures and the dead man. Nearby, gulls were screeching for their breakfast, calling to whomever fed them, demanding service. A siren wailed in the distance, growing louder as the police cruiser turned onto Ken Thompson Parkway and headed for Pelican Man's. The car skidded to a stop on the parking lot, its siren abruptly dying, leaving only the sound of agitated birds.

A Sarasota patrolman trotted up, followed closely by a winded Vince. The young cop was my height, six feet, but he probably weighed twenty pounds more than my one eighty. His uniform hugged a body that had spent many hours in a gym. He was hatless, and his close-cropped hair resembled that of a military recruit. He introduced himself. Vince was bent over, hands on his knees, breathing heavily.

"I'm Matt Royal," I said, shaking the officer's hand.

"Did you find the body, Mr. Royal?"

"Yes."

"What can you tell me about this?"

"Nothing. I was just strolling by and saw the dead man."

"Why are you here when the place isn't even open yet?"

"Mr. Delgado invited me."

Vince found his voice. "I asked Mr. Royal to come by before we opened so that he could get a good look at the place. I'm hoping he'll give us a chunk of money."

It was an open secret that the sanctuary was in financial trouble. It depended on donations and admission charges for the daily tours, and the just-ended winter season had not been kind to the birds. Donations had dried up.

The policeman turned back to me. Vince winked, signaling that he knew I wasn't a donor.

The cop looked closely at me, a small scowl on his face. "Did you touch anything?"

"No."

"Don't run off. The detectives will want to talk to you." He pulled his radio mic from the Velcro tab on his shoulder and called for the detectives and a crime scene unit.

Vince had regained his composure; his breathing was back to normal. "We'll be in the office," he said, and we left the policeman to wait alone for his colleagues.

CHAPTER TWO

The next day, early, I was enjoying my morning ritual, sipping coffee and reading the newspaper on my sunporch overlooking Sarasota Bay. The sun was tentatively peeking over the mainland, as if trying to decide whether to show itself. A flats fishing boat sped by out on the Intracoastal, the high whine of its outboard competing with the cries of diving gulls. The phone rang.

"Hello, Matt."

The soft voice pierced my brain, resonating of joy and regret and loss. Images flashed. A tall brunette clad in the white garb of a nurse, her hazel eyes bright with humor. A smile that could make a man weep. Lips that once caressed mine, lightly, like the fine hair of a butterfly's wing. And sometimes, hungrily, drawing me into her in bursts of passion that singed my soul. My hand tightened around the phone.

"This is Laura."

"I know."

"Are you well, Matt?"

"Yes. You?"

"No. I need to see you."

"When?"

"Soon."

"Where?"

"Breakfast. I'm at the Hilton."

"I'll be there in twenty minutes," I said.

She hung up.

Longboat Key is a small island, about ten miles long and a quarter-mile wide. It lies off the southwest coast of Florida, south of Tampa Bay. I live on the north end in a condo facing Sarasota Bay. The Hilton Hotel sits on the Gulf of Mexico about three miles south of my home.

We'd met soon after Laura finished her degree in nursing. She was standing in my cubicle in the emergency room, grinning. I had just finished law school and begun practicing in Orlando. A pick-up game of football in a city park had landed me in the hospital with a twisted ankle.

"What's so funny?" I asked.

"Nothing. You just look kind of bedraggled. Not as spiffy as you were when I saw you at Harper's last night."

"Harper's?"

"Yes, the bar. I was there watching the beautiful people hang out."

"I'm not one of them."

"Oh? Could've fooled me."

"I was there with a client who *is* one of the beautiful people."

"Well, here you are now. I have to get some blood from you."

"Why blood for a twisted ankle?"

"Don't know. The doctor ordered it."

"You'll be gentle?"

She grinned again. And stuck the hell out of me.

Within a year, we were married.

I walked through the Hilton lobby and out to the deck overlooking the Gulf of Mexico. Laura was sitting at a table, a cup of coffee and a glass of water in front of her. A large banyan tree provided shade, and lines of twine were strung across the area to discourage the gulls from joining the guests for meals. The sun was behind us, rising over the bay, and a soft morning glow suffused the air. The scent of the sea surrounded us. She sat quietly, staring out at the turquoise water. She was not aware of me.

I stood for a moment, drinking her in, remembering. She'd left me ten years before, but I couldn't see any changes in her. She was still beautiful, her dark hair swept back over her ears. Just the way I liked it. Did she do that for me this morning? She was wearing a pink tank top and white shorts. Her feet were in sandals, toenails painted pink, her ankles crossed under the table.

Her face was still unlined, except for a few laugh wrinkles at the edges of her eyes. She was staring out to sea, her face locked in a grimace. A glint of sun slipped through the banyan branches and reflected off her water glass. She raised the coffee cup to her lips.

She put it down without taking a swallow. She turned toward me, as if some silent signal had hinted at my presence. She smiled and melted my heart. She stood, arms out, as I strode toward her. She wrapped me in an embrace that was more than friendly. Her hair was redolent of lilacs, and the scent of vanilla tickled my nose. She still used the same shampoo and body lotion.

"I've missed you," she whispered. "More than I should."

"Me too," I said, choking back a wave of emotion, wary of saying more.

She stood back, her arms still on my shoulders. She had a quizzical look on her face, and a smile played on her lips.

"You don't have any gray," she said. "Your hair's still dark."

"Good genes."

We parted, and she said, "I ordered you coffee."

We sat, and the waiter arrived with my drink.

"I need help, Matt," she said, without preamble. "My stepdaughter Peggy is missing."

Laura had left me with good reason. I had been too caught up in being a lawyer and an occasional drunk to give her the family she wanted. She'd met a good man, a widower with two children, and she had married him and moved to Atlanta.

I'd spent the first part of my life doing what I thought I was supposed to do. The military, college, law school, the practice, politics, the climb up the ladder of success. It didn't work out. I was unhappy and drinking too much. I couldn't quite figure out where I was supposed to be in the world. Laura was unhappier than I knew, and after she left, my life spiraled downhill faster than a falling meteor.

I'd been a good lawyer, a trial lawyer, a believer in the system and the nobility of my profession. I worked hard and cared about my clients. I told them the truth, and never took on a case just for the fee. If a client's cause was unwinnable, I told him so at the beginning; told him he didn't need to throw away money on a lawyer who couldn't help him. And I refused the case.

The profession changed. Money became the Holy Grail. The law became a business, and I hated it. I stayed in it because I didn't know anything else. Then Laura left and a fog of despair settled over me like a dark night. There were days when I couldn't find my way through the void.

Laura took nothing from our marriage but my heart. I kept working for a couple of years, trying to salvage a career I no longer cared about, and then said the hell with it. I sold everything I had and moved to Longboat Key. I had enough money to live a modest life without working.

I was enjoying myself. I'd made a lot of friends, and occasionally I used my legal skills to help out someone who needed a good lawyer. I never charged any fees. I didn't need the money as much as the people I helped did.

"Tell me about it," I said.

"She came to Sarasota on spring break, and we haven't heard a word from her since."

"How long?"

"Three weeks."

"Maybe she's just not communicating."

"No. She's had a bad time lately, but she always checks in with her father. She wouldn't just fail to call."

"Her cell phone?"

"It goes straight to voice mail, and now we're getting a recording telling us that her box is full. She's not returning anyone's calls."

"Have you talked to the police?"

"They won't do anything. She's eighteen and is considered an adult. Unless I have some proof that she's been kidnapped or something, the law isn't interested."

"What can I do?"

"I don't know. You're a lawyer. You know this area, know people. Maybe you can help find her."

"I don't practice anymore."

"I know. I keep up with you. Jock and I talk."

I was surprised. Jock Algren was my oldest friend, and I didn't know he'd maintained contact with Laura after the divorce. I felt a little betrayed.

"I didn't know that," I said.

"Don't be angry. I call him sometimes when I'm missing you a lot. That's all."

"You miss me?"

"I've always loved you. I've always wondered if we could have made it work if I'd been a little tougher."

"No, you did the right thing. I'd still be in Orlando drinking myself to death if you hadn't left. It took losing you to get my life back on track. Are you happy?"

"Yes. I love Jeff. He's been a great husband. We have a good life, but that doesn't mean I have to stop loving you."

"I take it you're talking platonic love here."

She laughed. "Not really, but that's the way it'll be. I'm a one-man woman."

"I know. Damn."

She laughed again, and reached out and touched my hand. "We'll always have Paris," she said.

I laughed now. We must have seen *Casablanca* a hundred times, and she still couldn't get the accent right.

We ate breakfast, chatting and enjoying the soft breeze off the Gulf. She told me about Peggy, a troubled teen who had dropped out of the University of Georgia after her first semester. She moved into a house near the campus in Athens with several other disaffected former students. Her father had pleaded with Peggy to come home to Atlanta until she was ready for college, but the girl was staying put. Laura and Jeff suspected that Peggy had gotten mired in the drug culture that often grows up around college campuses, but they were powerless to do anything about it.

Peggy was not completely lost to that underworld culture, and she called home every Sunday to chat with her family. She had never missed a week, until she'd come to Sarasota for spring break.

Laura sighed. "We didn't think too much about it the first Sunday she missed calling," she said, "but after the second week we tried to track her down."

"Did you check out the house in Athens?"

"That's the first place we went. There were some kids living there, but they told us Peggy had moved out. They didn't know where she'd gone."

"Do you know where she was staying in Sarasota?"

"No. She told us she would be at the beach, but that's all."

"So, you don't even know if it was a hotel or a rented condo."

"No. Sorry."

"How long are you going to be here?"

"I'm leaving today. I came in yesterday and talked to the Sarasota police, but they're no help. I came out here last night, and finally worked up the nerve to call you."

"I'm glad you did. You can't stay for a few days?"

"Afraid not. My other stepdaughter Gwen is so upset about her sister that I don't want to leave her alone for too long. Jeff tries, but she needs her mother. Me."

Laura had moved on into another life that didn't include me. I understood that, but I felt left out. She was still part of me, and yet she wasn't. I was used to that, and my life had moved on as well. What might have been will never be. Somebody ought to write that on a tombstone somewhere. Maybe someone had.

"It's moving too fast," she said.

"What is?" I asked, puzzled.

"Time."

"What're you talking about?"

"We're on a collision course with death you know."

"From the moment we're born."

"Yes, but it's coming closer now. Closer than I want to think about."

"We've got a lot of years left, Laura."

"Do you remember when we were young, the day we got married?"

I remembered every moment of it. Sometimes, at night, when I couldn't sleep, I'd retrieve those memories from back where they live, hidden away like precious gems in the vault of my mind. I'd wade into them, take myself back to that warm spring day in Orlando, smell the flowers in the church and the slight vanilla aroma of her skin as I leaned in to kiss her at the altar. I'd hear the swell of the organ as we strode up the aisle into the rest of our lives. And because I'd be overwhelmed by regret for what might have been, I'd quietly store them away again, to be brought out and caressed when my soul demanded a visit with Laura.

"Yes," I said. "I remember."

The waiter appeared and poured us more coffee. The sun was higher now, its rays more concentrated, heating up the patio. A gull cried in the distance, a chair scraped away from a nearby table. Then there was quiet.

I said, "I'll see what I can find out about Peggy."

Laura gave me a picture of her stepdaughter taken in a garden on the day she graduated from high school. "This was taken in June, in our yard at home."

There was no point of reference that would give me her height, but she was a lovely girl. Five feet seven, Laura said. Peggy was wearing her graduation gown and holding her diploma. She was smiling. She had blonde hair reaching to her shoulders, a nose that might have been a little too perky for my taste, and good legs below the hem of the robe.

I took the picture and told Laura I'd do what I could. "You realize this is a long shot," I said. "I'll show the picture around here on Longboat and the other islands, but the chances of anybody remembering her are slim."

"I know, Matt. But I don't know what else to do. I'll keep trying to get the police involved, but I don't think they're going to help. Maybe you'll get lucky."

We talked a while and drank another cup of coffee.

She looked at me, staring at my face for a long time, long enough that I was getting uncomfortable. Then she shrugged, as if snapping out of a trance.

"I've got to go," she said. "I've got a plane in a couple of hours."

"I'll be in touch."

We hugged each other and she left. I watched her walk across the deck with the languid movements that had always been Laura. She'd never understood how beautiful she was, and she didn't posture with any intent of evoking desire in men. Her movements were as natural to her as breathing. She was the most desirable woman I'd ever known, and I'd let her slip away.

We were connected now, if for just a little while. And even if it was a connection born of her life without me, I would enjoy being a small part of her universe, like a distant planet circling a warm and seductive sun.

I didn't know it was the last time I'd ever see her alive.

CHAPTER THREE

I drove straight to the Longboat Key Police Department's new headquarters building on Gulf of Mexico Drive. My buddy, Bill Lester, was Chief of Police. I wanted to file a missing persons report.

"Not possible," Lester said. I was sitting across the desk from him, sipping the coffee his secretary had brought me.

"Why not?" I asked.

"By definition, she can't be a runaway. She's legally an adult. The fact that she doesn't call home while she's on spring break just isn't enough to indicate foul play."

"Bill, this girl is in some sort of trouble or she wouldn't be out of touch with her parents."

"I don't doubt you, but we have to follow protocol. I need more than the fact that she stopped calling her daddy. Is there any evidence of foul play?"

"No."

"Then I can't do anything."

I knew he'd help if he could. I thanked him and changed the subject.

I said, "Do you know anything more about the body I found at Pelican Man's yesterday?"

"No, but let me check with Sarasota PD."

The morning paper didn't have much information. Just a big story on the front page about the body being found. No identification or cause of death.

Bill reached for his phone, and after a short conversation hung up and turned his attention back to me. "They don't know much," he said. "The autopsy is scheduled for today, but they think he was shot once behind his right ear. It looks like an execution. His prints don't match anybody on file."

"I thought you could just about find anybody today if you had fingerprints."

"You can. If they're in the system. But if the person never served in the military or got licensed in some occupation that required prints or was never arrested, he wouldn't be on file. There're a lot of reasons why some people might never have their fingerprints taken."

"Let me know if you hear anything," I said, and left.

At my condo, I scanned Peggy's picture into my computer, cropped it so that I had a good head shot, and ran off several 4 x 6 prints. I'd start at the northern end of Anna Maria Island and work my way south to the southern end of Siesta Key.

Bartenders have good memories for attractive young women, so I'd start there. If that didn't turn up anything, I'd try hotels and then the condos that rented by the week. Maybe I'd get lucky.

I called my friend Logan Hamilton. "Want to do a little barhopping tonight?" I asked.

"Absolutely," said Logan.

He'd recently retired from his executive position with a financial services company, telling anyone who asked why he'd quit early, that he had all the money he needed, and Matt Royal needed a playmate. I explained why we were going.

We started at the north end of Anna Maria, an island connected to Longboat Key by a drawbridge spanning Longboat Pass. Our first stop was The Sandbar, a restaurant and bar hugging the beach near Bean Point. One drink and no luck later, we headed south, stopping at each bar, having one drink, and striking out.

We left the last bar on the south end of Anna Maria, planning to head home and to bed. Logan suggested that we stop at Pattigeorge's on Longboat for a nightcap. We drove across the bridge heading south to mid-key, where the restaurant overlooked Sarasota Bay.

The dinner crowd had cleared out, and we were alone at the bar with Sammy, the bartender.

"What're you guys doing out so late?" Sammy said, as we sat down.

Logan grinned. "Looking for a needle in a haystack."

Sammy put Logan's Scotch in front of him and reached into the cooler for my Miller Lite. "You trying to get laid again?"

Logan laughed. "Go to hell, Sam. We're trying to find a missing girl. Matt's ex-wife's stepdaughter."

Sam set my beer on a coaster. "What's that all about?"

I told him about my conversation with Laura. "Peggy was probably on one of the islands in this area, but we didn't have any luck on Anna Maria."

"Got a picture?" Sam asked.

I showed it to him. "Good looking girl," he said, handing it back. "I'd like to meet her."

"Sam," I said, "she's young enough to be your daughter."

Sam grinned. "Everybody I date is young enough to be my daughter. Let me see that picture again."

He took the photo to the back of the bar and held it under the light that hung above the mirror. "You know," he said, "I think I did see her in here one night. She was with a group of people who sat at the high-top right behind you."

"When?" I asked.

"A couple of weeks ago, maybe. There were five people, I think. One was an older guy, and there were two girls and two young men together. I assumed they were couples out with somebody's dad."

"What else do you remember?" Logan asked.

"Not much," Sam said. "They seemed to be having a good time. The girls didn't have IDs and were drinking cranberry juice. The guys were old enough and were drinking mixed drinks. I don't remember what."

"Stretch your brain," I said. "I need anything you can remember."

"I'm not sure why, but for some reason I got the impression they were staying across the street at the Sea Club. You ought to talk to Chris, the manager. She'll know if they were there."

CHAPTER FOUR

The Sea Club is a small condominium complex that rents by the day and week. It sprawls along a stretch of beach across from Pattigeorge's and hosts the same guests year after year. During the off-season, Longboat Key is a small place, and most of the year-round residents know each other. Chris and Bill, the husband and wife team who managed the resort, are friends of mine.

"Matt, how've you been?" said Chris, as I walked into the small air-conditioned office the next morning.

"I'm fine, Chris. Kind of glad the season's about over."

"I know what you mean. What can I do for you today?"

"A young woman named Peggy Timmons stayed here a couple of weeks ago. She's the daughter of a friend, and she's missing."

Chris turned to her computer, stroked a few keys, and said, "I don't have her in the system. Are you sure she stayed here?"

"Sam Lastinger over at Pattigeorge's said she did."

I handed her a copy of the Peggy's picture.

"Sure," said Chris. "I remember her. But she was using a different name. Came here with a group of people. They took one of the two bed-room units."

"How many people?"

"Five, total. I figured them for two couples and one older guy, maybe somebody's dad."

"How long did they stay?"

She stroked the computer keyboard again.

"Three days," she said.

"Names?"

"Matt, if it wasn't you, I wouldn't give these names out."

"This is important, Chris. The girl is eighteen and her parents are worried sick."

A few more strokes.

"Linda and Larry Olsen, Yvonne and Patrick Walsh, and Jake Yardley. That was the older guy. He paid for everything in cash."

"Do you remember which name this girl used?" I asked, tapping the picture.

"No. Sorry."

"Addresses?"

"Yeah, but they're probably as bogus as the names."

"Got to check them out."

"I guess so."

She stroked the keyboard a few more times and the printer next to it came alive, spitting out a single sheet of paper.

"Here you go," said Chris. "The young people all have the same address in Athens, Georgia, and the older guy gave a Tampa address. The phone numbers are there too."

"Thanks, Chris. You've been a big help."

I left the office, stopping for a moment on the shell parking lot. The Gulf was turquoise and still, stretching to infinity. A lone pelican soared overhead, rising effortlessly on an air current, heading to the Gulf for breakfast. High cumulus clouds drifted lazily, and the smell of frying bacon rode the onshore breeze. I could almost hear it crackle in the quiet of the early morning.

This was truly a paradise. How could anything bad happen here? But bad things did happen in beautiful places, and we usually didn't see them coming.

There's a darkness lurking deep in the souls of us all. Our parents instill in us a modicum of civilized behavior and that usually keeps our baser instincts at bay. But sometimes that blackness seeps to the surface and a monster walks quietly among us. Because we are not attuned to evil, we don't see it rise up until it strikes us down without warning. I was afraid that Peggy Timmons had stumbled into the darkness and met the beast.

CHAPTER FIVE

I went home and called Laura in Atlanta. She confirmed that the address in Athens was the house in which Peggy had lived with her friends. The phone number was Peggy's cell. Laura had never heard any of the names I got from the Sea Club, and she couldn't imagine why Peggy would be with a man of Yardley's age. I told her I would keep looking and keep her posted.

I called the number in Tampa, not expecting much. A man answered.

"Is this Jake Yardley?" I asked.

"Yes."

I was surprised. I didn't expect to get a working number, much less Jake Yardley.

"Mr. Yardley, my name is Matt Royal. I live on Longboat Key. Were you here about three weeks ago?"

"Yes. Why do you ask?"

"Did you stay at the Sea Club?"

"Yes. Who are you?" He had a southwestern accent, probably Texas.

"I'm sorry, sir. I'm trying to find a young lady who has disappeared. I've heard that you were with two young couples at the Sea Club."

"I was. What's the missing girl's name?"

"Peggy Timmons."

"Don't know her."

"She was using a different name. May I come see you in Tampa?"

"Sure. Coffee's always on."

He gave me directions to his house.

•   •   •

I called Logan to tell him what I had discovered, and that I was going to Tampa.

"Give me a few minutes and I'll go with you," he said.

We headed out to I-75 and north to the Lee Roy Selmon Crosstown Expressway. We exited in downtown Tampa and drove onto Harbour Island, a dredged up spoil island that bordered the ship channel. Over the years, condominium apartment buildings that blocked the sun had sprouted from this recycled bay bottom. Jake Yardley lived in one of the penthouses.

He was a big man, maybe six foot four, and had the parched skin of one who made his living outdoors. He wore faded jeans, a plain white T-shirt, and boat shoes. His graying hair fell to the top of his ears. He was a handsome man who appeared to be in his mid-fifties.

I introduced Logan and myself, and Yardley invited us in. The condo was large, with an expansive view over Davis Islands and the Tampa General Hospital, to the bay beyond. The St. Petersburg skyline shimmered in the distance, the haze rising from Tampa Bay making it slightly opaque.

Yardley pointed to a sofa, and said, "Have a seat."

Logan and I sat.

"Can I get y'all a drink?" Jake Yardley asked.

"Not for me," I said.

Logan shook his head.

Yardley sat in a stuffed chair facing the sofa and waited.

"Mr. Yardley," I said, "I'm a lawyer on Longboat Key, and one of my client's daughters has disappeared. We have information that she may have been staying with you at the Sea Club about three weeks ago."

I handed him the picture of Peggy.

"Sure, that's Linda Olsen. She was there with her husband Larry."

"Did you know them from somewhere?"

"No, I'd just met them."

"Would you tell me how you ended up in a resort with them?"

Yardley readjusted himself in his chair. "Yeah, but I guess this'll sound a little weird."

He was quiet again, sitting there, rocking a little against the back of his chair. I was about to ask him again when he spoke.

"I'm a petroleum engineer by training. I worked the oil fields in Texas and Oklahoma for thirty years. And I got rich and retired to Florida. The American dream."

He smiled, but something crossed his face. Sadness, maybe, or regret. He continued. "Two months after my wife and I moved in here, she had a stroke and died. She'd just had her fiftieth birthday."

"I'm sorry," I said.

"We never had any children, not in thirty years of marriage. I've got no family to speak of, and no friends within a thousand miles. So, sometimes I go hunting for company. I find young couples that want to keep me company for a few days. I pay for everything. I know they're just humoring me and spending my money, but it gives me a reason to get up in the morning."

Logan stirred on the sofa. "Ever go hunting for young women alone?" he asked.

"No, sir. I always find couples. I'm not there for sex, and I don't want the women to feel like they're being hustled. The men either, for that matter."

I leaned forward, "Where did you find Peggy and her friends?"

Yardley was quiet for a moment. His silent stretches were a little disconcerting, but I was getting into the rhythm of it, and waited him out.

"In a bar in Sarasota. I overheard them talking. They were looking for a place to stay, so I bought them a drink and made the offer. They took me up on it."

"Just like that?" I asked. "Isn't that a little dangerous?"

Yardley smiled ruefully. "You have to understand. These kids are the lost ones. Most of them are on drugs of some kind, or they're drinking a lot, and their judgment isn't very good. Offer them a freebie and they jump at it."

"Then what?" Logan said.

"Then nothing. We went to Longboat Key and got the condo. I bought their meals and booze, and we spent the days on the beach. Then I dropped them off and came home."

"Where did you drop them off?" I asked.

"Robarts Arena. In Sarasota."

20

H. TERRELL GRIFFIN

"Why there?"

"I don't know. That's where they said they wanted to go."

"What were their plans?"

"I don't know. They didn't mention anything."

"Did they say where they were going from Robarts?"

"No. I assumed they were going to hitch back to Georgia, but they didn't say."

"Did they have any money?"

"Don't know. I didn't ask."

Logan leaned forward on the sofa, his arms resting on his thighs. "Let me get this straight," he said. "You pick up four young people in a bar, wine and dine them for three days, don't have sex with any of them, and then drop them off without knowing where they're going or whether they have any money to get there."

"That's about it," said Yardley, his voice rising. "You can believe me or not. I don't really give a shit."

Logan stood. "Let's get the hell out of here," he said, and started for the door.

I rose from the sofa and shook Yardley's hand. "Thanks for your time," I said, and followed Logan to the elevator.

Logan suggested that we treat ourselves to one of those delicious slabs of meat at Bern's Steak House. We drove south on the Crosstown Expressway and followed Howard Avenue to the restaurant. We each ordered a steak.

The waiter took our order and left. Logan said, "What now?"

"I don't know. We're sort of at a dead end."

"I don't like this Yardley guy. I think his story is bogus."

"Maybe. Or, maybe, he's just weird."

"Did you notice how sterile his condo was?"

"What do you mean?"

"He talked about his wife like she was the center of his life, but there weren't any pictures of her anywhere. There were no knickknacks, artwork, or anything. Even I have some of that crap lying around."

"I didn't really notice," I said. "Maybe he just doesn't want reminders of his other life."

"Or maybe," Logan said, "he's bullshitting us."

"There's that," I said.

We drove back through St. Petersburg, and across the Sunshine Skyway Bridge. The sun was setting into the Gulf, giving a glow to the waters of Tampa Bay. Egmont Key sat in the middle of all the splendor of colors, like a drop of ink splotched onto a brilliant canvas.

Thirty minutes later, we crossed onto Anna Maria Island, and drove south toward Longboat Key, enjoying the slight chill of the spring evening. I saw headlights in my mirror, coming faster than the speed limit allowed. I slowed to let him pass, and as the car came abreast of me, I saw an arm holding a large revolver reach out of the passenger side window. I hit my brakes just as the pistol fired, the bullet passing over the hood of my car.

Logan sat up abruptly. "What the hell?"

I swerved to my right, still braking. The brake lights on my assailant's car flash on. He wasn't finished. We were at the south end of Anna Maria Island, driving along Coquina Beach. No other cars were in sight. I kept to the right, trying to turn around and head back toward Bradenton Beach, where there would be people on the sidewalk.

The car in front of me came to a stop. I pulled the steering wheel to the right and drove into the parking lot that edged the beach. I was turning back north when I saw the car coming at us again. A second car had come into the parking lot, blocking my exit.

I brought my Explorer to a stop at the edge of the beach.

"Get out!" I shouted. "Now."

Logan was already unbuckling his seatbelt and opening the door. The window on the hatch of the Explorer exploded, pieces of glass flying into the front seat. I heard Logan grunt in pain as he dove out the open door.

I followed, diving for the ground. More shots were fired. I crawled to the front of the Explorer, putting it between the shooters and me. Logan was already there, breathing hard.

I touched him on the shoulder. "Are you all right?"

"Yeah. Who are these assholes?"

"I don't know. Who've you pissed off this week?"

"Nobody that I can remember." He pulled his cell phone from the pocket of his shorts. "We need to get out of here," he said.

I heard the sound of men moving up, cautiously. The voices were low, restrained. They didn't know if we were armed, so they were being careful.

"Let's go," I said.

We inched back toward the beach, keeping the Explorer between the bad guys and us. Human shadows flickered in the glow of the sparse security lights from the nearby snack stand. Four men had spread out, trying to get an angle on us.

Logan was murmuring into his phone, trying to get help, as we inched backward on hands and knees. As we neared the dunes, he closed his phone and said, "Help's coming."

We reached the dunes and rolled behind the nearest one. We got to our feet and began to run, crouching so that we were not visible above the sand hills. We headed north, keeping low. Gunfire erupted behind us. We'd gained a lot of space, but now they were coming on the run. We were too far away for an accurate pistol shot, but we certainly weren't out of danger.

The shrill sound of a siren cut through the night, getting louder, coming our way. One of our pursuers shouted something, and the shooting stopped. I glanced over my shoulder as the men scrambled over the dunes, back toward the parking lot.

The police wouldn't know exactly where we were. The beach parking area is a half-mile long, and all Logan had been able to tell the 911 dispatcher was that we were at Coquina Beach. The sirens had spooked the shooters, so we were safe for the moment. On the other hand, I didn't want an overzealous cop to start shooting at us.

I motioned to Logan. "Let's stay here until the cops have the area under control," I said.

We sat on the sand and waited. A quarter-moon hung over the Gulf, a shaft of light illuminating the dark water. The sea air carried a hint of dead fish, the result of the red tide that had left us the week before. The sand was still warm from the sun, and the only sound was the voices of the officers in the parking lot, punctuated occasionally by the static of a police radio.

Blood was running down Logan's forehead, looking black in the moonlight. "You're hit," I said.

"I took a piece of your rear window. No big deal."

After a few minutes, a loud voice erupted from behind the dunes. "Bradenton Beach Police. Is anybody here?"

I shouted. "Matt Royal and Logan Hamilton. We called this in. We're coming over the dunes, hands up. We're unarmed. Okay?"

"Come on, slowly."

We rose and crossed the dunes, hands in the air. One cop kept his weapon trained on us as another frisked us. He took our wallets.

"They're clean," he said.

Another cop, wearing lieutenant's bars on his uniform shirt, walked up. "The Explorer is registered to Matt Royal," he said. "Is that one of you?"

"I'm Royal," I said.

He took my driver's license from the cop who had frisked us, looked at it, nodded, and handed it back to the officer. "What the hell happened out here?" he asked.

"Don't know, Lieutenant. We were on our way back to Longboat, and somebody started shooting at us." I told him how it had happened.

A paramedic arrived and put a bandage on Logan's brow as I talked. He asked us if there were any other injuries, and then went back to his ambulance.

The lieutenant had a skeptical look on his face. "We'll have to process your vehicle for evidence," he said. "I'll have one of my men take you to the station for statements. Somebody will take you home from there."

CHAPTER SIX

The Bradenton Beach Police station was small. It nestled between a boat-yard and the approach to the Cortez Bridge. The waiting room was tiny, with a couple of green vinyl and metal armchairs sitting next to a table that held year-old magazines. The walls were painted in light beige, a color intended to soothe the fears of those who visited. A civilian sat behind a partition near a glass-enclosed opening, working on something on his desk that I couldn't see. The room was chilly, the air conditioning cranked up too high for this time of year. A large round clock on the opposite wall told me it was nearing nine o'clock.

The lieutenant had escorted Logan into the back of the station to take his statement. He told me he would be with me as soon as he finished with my friend. I assumed he wanted to make sure that I wasn't influenced by what Logan had to say.

Time moved slowly. The room was quiet. The occasional crackle of a police radio slipped from behind the glass of the receptionist's area. The faint sound of a siren came from the bridge, a signal to motorists that the span was about to open for boat traffic. Probably a large trawler coming from the north, heading for the fish houses that lined the bay next to the Coast Guard station.

When the clock read nine thirty, the lieutenant appeared with Logan, and asked me to step back to his office. Logan grinned and winked as he passed me. The lieutenant caught it and looked a little miffed. Maybe he thought Logan wasn't taking this thing seriously enough. He didn't know that Logan seldom took anything seriously.

The lieutenant's office was small, with barely enough room for a desk and two chairs. The top of the desk was cluttered with loose documents, a couple of wanted posters, and a framed picture of a pretty young woman holding a blonde girl of about three years old.

"Why would someone try to kill you on my island, Mr. Royal?" he asked.

"I wish I knew."

"I know who you are."

"Is that good?"

"I know about some of your escapades on Longboat," he said.

"Then you know I'm one of the good guys."

"Yeah. I already called Chief Lester. He vouched for you."

"He always does," I said, smiling.

"This happen a lot?"

"No. But when it does, I can always count on Bill Lester."

"I know you've been involved with law enforcement in the past," he said, "and that you killed some bad guys. Is this shooting tonight related?"

"I don't see how it could be. There wasn't anyone left from the last fiasco to come after me."

"Did you ever think that practicing law might be safer than your retirement?"

"Lately, I have. But I don't go looking for trouble. It just seems to have a way of finding me."

"Where were you today?"

I told him about our visit with Jake Yardley, and what I had learned from Chris at the Sea Club. I explained why I was looking for Peggy, and told him I didn't think there was any reason for anybody to try to kill me because I was looking for a teenager.

He agreed. "Maybe it was some sort of mistaken identity," he said. "If you find out anything different, you let me know."

An officer drove us home, dropping me at my place and going on to Logan's. I didn't sleep well that night, and I didn't think the shooting was random. It must have had something to do with Peggy. I'd have to take a good look at Jake Yardley. He had to be part of the riddle.

And I was going to start carrying a pistol. You never know when you might need one.

CHAPTER SEVEN

The next day, I did my morning run along the sidewalk that borders Gulf of Mexico Drive. The sun was just coming up, and the usual coterie of runners and walkers were already out. Wild parakeets were chattering in the trees that bordered the walkway, and a cooling breeze blew anemically from the north. Traffic was light, but steady, the kind of day when nobody in his right mind would take a shot at me on a busy road in broad daylight.

I got home safely, showered, shaved, put on clean shorts and a T-shirt, and went to Isabelle's Eatery for breakfast. The morning paper was full of bad news of people all over the world killing and maiming each other. It all seemed a long way from our quiet island at the edge of the Gulf of Mexico.

There was a tingle of alarm rolling around in the back of my mind. It was a gut reaction to something I'd seen or heard or sensed about Yardley. Something was off about him and his story of meeting Peggy and her friends. Logan's observation about Yardley's living quarters only added to my sense of unease. And, my gut was usually right.

I spent the rest of the morning trying to find out something about Yardley. His name didn't pop up on Google or any of the other databases I could access. I hadn't come up with anything and decided to go see Chief Lester the next day. Maybe he could help.

At noon, the Manatee County Sheriff's crime lab called to tell me that they were finished with my car, and I could pick it up anytime. Logan came and got me, and I went from the lab to an auto-glass shop where they replaced the rear hatch window while I waited.

I drove back to Longboat Key and met Logan at Tiny's, a little bar on the north end of the island. It was a neighborhood watering hole, and at five thirty on a weekday afternoon, it was packed with locals enjoying themselves, savoring the winding down of the day.

Word had spread of the shooting the night before, and everybody wanted to know what had happened. The more Logan told the story, the bigger it got. Four Scotches into the evening and he was a hero.

The people of Tiny's knew Logan was kidding. He was a war hero who never talked about it, and he'd pulled my butt out of the fire just a few months before over in the center of the state. He was a self-deprecating guy, and was much loved on the key.

We finished our evening at Tiny's. I ordered a pizza to go from A Moveable Feast, a small restaurant that shared the parking lot with the bar. Logan was going to drive to St. Armand's, at the other end of Longboat, for Chinese food.

CHAPTER EIGHT

The ringing phone jangled me out of sleep early the next morning. I eased my eyes open, ruing the beers I'd had the night before. Over served. Again. Light was just beginning to make its way through the opening in my drapes. The clock read six a.m. This had better be good, I thought.

I reached for the receiver. "Hello." I think I groaned.

"Matt, there's a body in Durante Park. I need you down here." It was Bill Lester.

"Sure, Bill, but why?"

"I think you know the dead guy."

"Who?"

"Jake Yardley."

"I'll be right there."

"Park at the end of Gulf Bay Road. Take the trail to your right, and you'll find us."

Durante Park takes up thirty-two acres on Longboat Key, about three miles south of the north end of the island. It is a haven of wetlands, mangrove forest, and salt marsh. Various species of waterfowl and shore birds make their homes there. Trails and boardwalks snake through the area, and unobtrusive little signs are placed at intervals, describing the plants and birds.

I parked the Explorer next to two police cars, and began walking down a shell-topped trail. The sun was still rising out of the bay and light filtered through the mangrove branches. The air was cool, the sky clear. It was quiet, and I could hear a dove coo in the distance. The breeze off the Gulf brought the soft hum of tires on Gulf of Mexico Drive.

I came to a boardwalk and bore to my left. The bay stretched to my right, the early morning sun reflecting off its still surface. A mullet jumped and splashed loudly as it fell back into the water. Was the fish trying to escape a predator or was it just imbued with the joy of living? Who knows?

I heard voices ahead. I rounded a turn and saw two Longboat cops standing in front of a line of crime scene tape anchored to the rails of the walkway. They were talking quietly, almost whispering.

"Morning, Matt," the one nearest me said. "The chief is waiting for you. Don't touch anything. We're waiting for the sheriff's crime lab people."

I ducked under the tape, walked around another curve, and stopped at a gazebo that faced the water. There was a bench across the back of it. There was an emergency phone attached to the wall next to a plastic rack holding brochures. A sign on the phone said that it connected directly to the Longboat Key Police station.

Bill Lester was standing in the middle of the gazebo, his back to me, talking into his cell phone. Jake Yardley was sitting on the bench, his arms spread across the rails behind him, his chin on his chest. He looked like a man catching a catnap, perhaps resting from a walk around the park. He was wearing shorts, a golf shirt, and running shoes, all white. A large splotch of red across his chest added a touch of color. Blood.

Just past the gazebo, an older woman stood on the boardwalk, holding a leash tied to a golden Lab. The dog was lying on the walk, apparently bored with the drama surrounding him. The woman looked pale, scared, and distracted, as if she would rather be anywhere but here, sharing her slice of paradise with a dead man and a police officer.

Lester turned to me, snapping his phone shut.

"Thanks for coming, Matt," he said. "Is this your buddy?"

"He's not my buddy, but that is Jake Yardley."

"That's what his driver's license says."

"How did you know I knew him?"

"The Bradenton Beach Police Chief sent me the statements you and Logan gave the other night. He knows you guys are friends of mine. It was a courtesy."

"What happened?" I asked.

"Don't know. Mrs. Johnson was walking her dog at first light and found him," he said, pointing to the distressed woman with the dog. "Called us on the emergency phone."

"It looks like Jake was posed after he was killed. I don't get that."

"Neither do I. Maybe we'll know more when the crime lab guys get finished."

"Chief?" It was the cop at the tape. "CSI's here."

"About time," Lester said. He turned and went up the boardwalk to meet them. "Take Mrs. Johnson back to the station and get a statement," he said to the officer. "Matt, can you and Logan meet me for lunch at Mar Vista?"

The Mar Vista restaurant, known to locals as The Pub, is in the Village at the north end of Longboat Key. This was the original settlement on the island, and a place where working people and poorer retirees could still afford to live. It had been a thriving community for many years before the developers discovered our island and began to build bigger and bigger condominium projects for wealthy refugees from the Midwest and New England.

The Mar Vista hugs the shoreline of a little lagoon that meanders off upper Sarasota Bay. Tables and chairs are arranged on a patio overlooking the water. Servers were trudging back and forth between the kitchen and the tables, delivering lunch to the patrons.

Logan and I sat on the patio and ordered soft drinks. Logan told the server we were waiting for one more person. The noon sun was warm and a light breeze blew off the water, rustling the fronds of the palm trees that provided sparse shade to the diners. A large yacht, gleaming with white paint and polished bright work, cruised the Intracoastal, heading north toward Tampa Bay. A go-fast boat bounced over the yacht's wake, and with unmuffled engines roaring, passed to port.

Chief Lester arrived, walking among the diners, stopping to say hello to some of them. Bill was mid-forties about five foot eight, and while not overweight, sported a little paunch that didn't quite hang over his belt. He was wearing the same clothes as that morning: a navy blue golf shirt with a Longboat Key Police badge embroidered over the left breast, khaki pants, and black athletic shoes. No weapon was visible.

He took a seat at our table, grinned, and said, "You guys get into more trouble. I don't know how you do it."

Logan laughed. "It ain't easy," he said. "Not at all."

"What'd you find out about Yardley?" I asked.

"First off, he's not Yardley," said Bill. "His real name is Clyde Varn. He's got quite a rap sheet. Fingerprints confirmed it."

"What else?"

"He didn't live in that condo in Tampa, where you met him. His driver's license, the one with the name Yardley, had an address in Brooksville, but Varn hasn't lived there in years."

Logan leaned forward, his elbows on the table. "Who is he?" he asked.

"He used to be hired muscle for some of the drug rings that work out of south Florida. Apparently, he was some kind of a freelancer; worked for whichever group needed him. He's been arrested a dozen times, but only convicted once. Possession of marijuana. Did thirty days in the county lockup in Miami-Dade."

I said, "What about the condo in Tampa?"

"Owned by a Bahamian corporation. We're trying to find out who the shareholders are. That could take a while."

Logan took a sip of his cola. "Did the crime lab people find anything?"

The chief shook his head. "Not much. He'd only been dead about an hour when Mrs. Johnson found him. He was shot on the boardwalk, about fifty feet from the gazebo where we found him. There was blood splatter in the area, and they found scuffmarks on the boards. Looks like the killer dragged him to the gazebo and propped him up."

"Why?" I asked.

"Who knows? Why kill him on Longboat? Maybe they were trying to send a message to somebody. Maybe to the two of you."

I shrugged. "If somebody was, I don't understand the message."

We sat quietly, sipping our colas. The waiter came, brought Bill a glass of iced tea and took our food orders. Logan asked for scallops, the chief chose a burger and fries, and I ordered a salad.

Bill said, "Tell me more about this guy and your meeting the other day."

Logan and I filled the chief in on what we knew about Yardley and why we went to see him. While we talked, the waiter brought our food and refilled our drinks.

Bill said, "It's got to be connected to Peggy somehow."

I chewed a bite of salad. "What in the world was he doing with Peggy?" I asked.

The chief looked up from his burger. "I wondered about that myself. I did some checking on missing young people in this area. Manatee and Sarasota have had reports of about twenty people missing in the last year. All of them were late teens or early twenties, all over eighteen. Male and female."

Logan speared a scallop with his fork. "Why wouldn't somebody get interested in that many disappearances?"

"Nobody put them together. There were one or two or three in various jurisdictions, both counties, Bradenton, Sarasota, Venice, North Port. They were all adults in the eyes of the law, so nobody got excited about them."

"I bet their families did," I said.

"You know what I mean, Matt," said Bill. "Cops have a lot better things to do than look for kids old enough to make their own decisions."

"I guess," I said. But I was thinking that Peggy's disappearance might be more than it seemed. I didn't like that thought.

CHAPTER NINE

"Why do you think Varn told us he dropped Peggy and her friends at Robarts Arena?" I asked Logan.

"Maybe he did."

We were driving down the key, heading for my condo. The salad had not done much to fill me up, and I heard a faint rumbling from the area of my stomach.

I said, "That doesn't make any sense, unless he had nothing to do with her disappearance. That's a pretty big coincidence to get my arms around. He admitted to spending the three days with them at Sea Club, and then he lied to us about who he was. The kids seemed to have dropped off the earth when he left them."

"Why don't we see what was going on at Robarts the day he says he dropped them off?"

"Good call. The arena probably has a Web site."

We pulled into my condo complex and parked next to a huge bougainvillea, its blood red blooms dancing in the breeze off the water. We took the elevator, sharing it with one of my neighbors, and got off on the second floor.

I had enclosed my balcony the year before, making it into a sunporch. I also put an air-conditioning duct out to the area. Florida is hot in the summer. My computer was set up there, giving me a magnificent view over Sarasota Bay as I surfed the Internet.

My new twenty-eight foot Grady-White walkaround sat sedately in its slip in front of the condo, bobbing slightly when a wake rolled in over the sandbar that separated our little harbor from the bay proper. The sun was high and the cerulean sky was dotted with puffy clouds. The Sister Keys, uninhabited mangrove islands, defined the eastern edge of the Intracoastal Waterway across from my home. Several elderly ladies were doing water aerobics in the pool that took up most of the space between my building and the docks.

I Googled Robarts Arena and came up with a list of events for the entire year. I scrolled down to the period three weeks before.

"Looks like a revival ended the same day that Peggy checked out of the Sea Club," I said, pointing to the highlighted event.

"I can't see how that would be of interest to a guy like Varn."

"We'll have to check it out. Let's see if the evangelist has a Web site."

He did. I found it, and clicked on the tab that detailed his schedule.

"They moved on to Venice," I said, "and they've been there for three weeks. Last night was the last evening for saving local souls. Maybe somebody's still there."

"Probably a waste of time. Let's go."

We drove to the mainland and took Highway 41 to Venice, about fifteen miles south of Sarasota. The address given on the Web site turned out to be a large undeveloped lot on the highway south of the city limits, about halfway to the town of North Port.

The lot wasn't empty. A sea of canvas covered the ground, a tent being disassembled for transport. A crew of about ten men was rolling up the canvas. A small forklift stood nearby, ready to put the tent into the white semi parked nearby. The trailer's aluminum side was emblazoned with red letters spelling out REVEREND ROBERT WILLIAM SIMMERMON MINISTRIES, WORKING FOR JESUS. Next to the sign was a painted picture of a handsome gray-haired man, whom I assumed to be the evangelist. A sleeper cab was backed up to it, but had not yet hooked on. It looked as if they were about ready to leave. A forty-foot motor home was parked nearby.

We stopped next to the trailer, got out of the Explorer, and walked around to the other side, near where the men were working with the canvas. As we cleared the rear of the truck, a woman stepped out of the door of the motor home. She came up short when she saw us.

"Can I help you?" she said. Her voice was soft and held the inflections of the southland. She was about five seven and her high-heeled sandals added another two inches. Her auburn hair was thick and hung below her shoulders. She had the body of a woman who would do a bikini proud. I'm not much on fashion, since I usually wear a T-shirt, cargo shorts, and boat shoes, but I could tell that her clothes were expensive. She had either a large diamond or a beautifully cut piece of glass on her right ring finger. Several gold chain bracelets concentrated around her left wrist and clinked quietly when she moved her arm.

"I'm looking for Reverend Simmermon," I said.

She smiled, showing me teeth that were so perfect they must have been the work of a very good cosmetic dentist. "I'm afraid he's not here. I'm Michelle Browne. I'm his administrative assistant. Can I help you?"

"Do you know a man named Clyde Varn or maybe Jake Yardley?"

She was quiet for a moment, screwing her face into a little moue, as if thinking was not something she was used to doing. "Can't say that I do. Who are they?"

"Same guy," I said, "but he uses both names."

"I wish I could help." She smiled again, and turned to a man who had just walked up, in effect dismissing me. The truck driver, I thought.

I interrupted before she spoke to him. "When do you expect Reverend Simmermon?"

"Oh, he's already gone," she said, turning back to me with a shrug and a smile. "On to the next stop. The work of the Lord never stops, you know."

"Where's the next stop?"

"Key West. Sorry I couldn't help."

Logan and I thanked her and returned to the Explorer.

As Logan snapped his seat belt closed, he said, "Mighty helpful little southern gal, don't you think? Did you notice that the last time she said 'help' it came out 'hep'?"

"I did. That's a little more country than she'd like us to believe she is. She's been working on that accent."

"I think so. And she's mighty pretty to be a minister's assistant."

"A little overdressed too."

We sat quietly in the vehicle for a few moments before I cranked up and headed back north.

"Didn't Bill Lester say that some teenagers had disappeared from the North Port and Venice areas?" asked.

"Yeah, but he didn't say when. Aren't you reaching a little on this?"

"Probably so. But I'd like to check with the chief anyway."

CHAPTER TEN

The traffic between Venice and Sarasota was brutal. The snowbirds hadn't yet gone back north, and the spring breakers were descending upon us. It took us more than an hour to go the twenty miles between the site of the revival and the approach to the John Ringling Bridge.

By the time we cleared the bridge and drove onto St. Armand's Key, it was dusk. Too late to find the chief at the station. We parked and walked to Lynches Pub and Grub for a drink. St. Armand's Circle is one of the more upscale shopping areas in Florida, a rival to Worth Avenue in Palm Beach. As we walked to the restaurant, I could see the area coming alive with the evening visitors. It was dinnertime, and the restaurants and bars would be full of vacationers. Foot traffic was picking up, people window shopping, enjoying the quiet evening in a gentle climate. There was a fresh-ness in the air, and people were smiling, nodding hello to each other. Our barrier islands provide a sense of permanent vacation, even to those who live here year round.

We took a table on the sidewalk and ordered beer. I watched the passersby for a minute, many of them red from the spring sun that sur-prised them with its strength.

"What do you think?" Logan broke into my reverie about a twenty-something female tourist from Ohio, who wore shorts and a halter top. Or maybe she was from Arkansas. I couldn't tell, and it didn't matter. I en-joyed the view.

I shrugged. "Why would Varn use his real name, or at least the name he was known by, and the Tampa address at the Sea Club if he was up to no good? Maybe he told us a partial truth. He was just having a good time getting to know young people. All that bullshit about his wife may have just been a cover. Maybe he's just a little hinky, and was embarrassed to be found out."

"Could be, but why would a muscle man for the drug mob be entertaining young couples?"

"Maybe he was taking a vacation."

"I'd like to know who owned the condo he was living in."

"I'd like to know why he was killed, and why on Longboat," I said.

"Lots of questions and no answers."

Logan had finished his beer.

"Want another one?" I asked.

He nodded. I signaled for the waitress.

"Two more, darling," I said, wagging two fingers at her.

We sat quietly, sipping beer and watching the people on the sidewalk. Night had fallen. It was pleasant, the temperature in the low seventies and none of the humidity that we'd get by mid-May.

"Best time of the year," I said.

"Without a doubt."

"Another one?"

"No, thanks. Time for me to get home. I've got a refrigerator full of Chinese food to eat."

I laughed. Logan's late-night forays to the Chinese food restaurant were the stuff of legend. They always left him with enough food to last a week.

I paid the tab and we left. We drove in silence across the New Pass Bridge and onto Longboat Key. A short way down the island, we turned into the drive leading to Logan's condo. The gate guard stopped us and then waved us through when he recognized Logan.

We stopped in front of Logan's building. I said, "I'll call Bill Lester in the morning and see if he can tell us anything about those disappearances in North Port and Venice."

"Let me know what you find out."

"See you tomorrow," I said, and drove the Explorer home.

CHAPTER ELEVEN

The day begins slowly in our latitude. As the sun starts its morning trek from behind the mainland, the bay takes on a gray color, lightening slowly until the sun's rim rises above the horizon. Color seeps into the world, and the eastern sky turns deep blue with bright orange streaks. Soon, the whole round ball of fire is hanging above the mainland horizon, and another day has begun.

I was sitting on my sunporch, drinking a cup of coffee, watching the morning unfold. Nature's display never failed to arouse a feeling of contentment in me. I was where I wanted to be, living on an island separated from much of the world's troubles by a wide bay.

The day's lead story told of a trial going on in the courthouse in Sarasota. It was about complex civil issues growing out of the building of a major hotel downtown. I smiled, relieved to be on the sunporch drinking coffee. The trial was in its third week and was expected to last two more. I knew what those lawyers were going through. They weren't getting enough sleep, they were eating on the run, they had abandoned their families for the duration, and their ulcers were burning in their guts.

I'd been a trial lawyer in Orlando for a long time. The pressure on those who go into the pit to do battle is enormous, and too many of them turn to alcohol. I did. That was a big part of Laura's decision to end our marriage, and it eventually ended my career. I wasn't run out of the profession; I just gave up and moved to Longboat Key.

A good man talked me into taking one last case, to right a wrong done him. I beat the alcohol problem, regained my self-respect, won the case, and not incidentally, made some money. I had enough to live modestly for the rest of my life, and I was content.

At seven thirty, I called Bill Lester. I explained what Logan and I had found out the day before, and asked him whether the North Port and Venice young people had gone missing recently.

"I don't think you're going to find any connection between Simmermon and the missing kids," he said. "Varn was probably lying when he said he dropped them at Robarts."

"I know, but I'd like to satisfy my curiosity. Will you check on it?"

"I'll check on it and let you know. By the way, I got a note on my desk overnight about that body you found at Pelican Man's."

"Did you get an ID?"

"No, but the body disappeared yesterday. From the county morgue."

"How in the world does something like that happen?"

"Somebody from a funeral home showed up with papers signed by the family, directing the morgue to turn over the body. Only problem was, after the hearse left, a supervisor looked at the papers and thought they were a little hokey."

"Hokey?"

"Yeah. You know. Not right somehow. How would the family have known the body was there if it hadn't even been identified yet? Anyway, the supervisor called the funeral home, and nobody there had heard anything about the body or its being picked up."

"Weird. What's Sarasota PD doing about it?" I asked.

"Investigating. Whatever that means. They're also keeping the whole thing under wraps. The detectives think it might be some sort of death cult that uses bodies in their rituals. If the body was unidentified, no family would be looking for it, and they could get it with minimal fuss."

I laughed. "This place gets kinkier and kinkier."

"I hear you, Matt. Everybody's living the dream. I'll call you later about the missing people."

The chief called an hour later. "No go," he said. "Those kids in North Port and Venice disappeared months ago, long before Simmermon came to town. It's a dead end, Matt."

"I'm not really surprised," I said. "There's no reason to think a traveling evangelist is kidnapping people. What about another connection, though? Young people disappearing. Can you think of any reason?"

"The word I'm getting is that in each case there was some family trouble going on. Probably nothing more than kids growing up and getting out of a bad situation. Two of those reported missing turned up on their own.

"I checked with Sarasota PD about the vulture pit guy."

"Anything?" I asked.

"Nope. Not a trace. It's as if the body disappeared from the face of the earth. No leads, no clues, nothing."

"What about the death cult idea?"

"Didn't go anywhere. The gang unit has never had a whiff of that sort of thing going on around here."

"Bill, I know you don't have a lot of manpower. I wonder how you'd feel about me showing Varn's picture around the key. See if anybody else remembers seeing him."

"Not a problem. Stop by the station and I'll give you a print of his driver's license photo."

CHAPTER TWELVE

After getting the picture of Varn, I spent the rest of the morning cleaning my boat. I showered and went to Moore's Stone Crab Restaurant for lunch. I ate in the bar, talking idly with Debbie, the bartender. I hadn't been in for a while, and we were catching up about mutual friends. I also told her about Peggy.

Cracker Dix came in as I was finishing my burger and onion rings. "Hey, Matt," he said. "Heard you found that body down at Pelican Man's the other day."

"Yeah. Great way to start the day," I said.

Cracker was an expatriate Englishman who had lived on the key for many years. He was about fifty, medium height, and bald as a billiard ball. He sported a close-cropped beard, a Hawaiian shirt, beige shorts, and flip-flops. A small gold stud was planted in his right earlobe, a thin gold chain around his neck. He ordered a beer and took the stool beside me.

"You catching any fish?" he asked.

"No. I haven't even been out this week. Too much wind."

Debbie was back with a glass of dark beer. She set it in front of Cracker and put her elbows on the bar, leaning into it, joining the conversation.

We were alone in the lounge, but I could hear low voices coming from the dining room, the clanging of utensils on plates punctuating the conversation. Stone crabs were in season, and the snowbirds were taking their fill of them before going home for the summer. Somewhere in the back of the restaurant, a plate fell and shattered on the tile floor.

The bay outside the large windows was rippled by the northerly wind blowing down the channel. Two sailboats were anchored in the cove, swinging gently on their anchor lines. The sun was high, still hanging in the southern sky, waiting for summer before it angled directly overhead and heated the island, bringing our annual bath of humidity.

A waitress came to the service bar and called a drink order to Debbie. She left to fill it.

"Cracker," I said, placing the picture of Varn on the bar, "you get around a lot. Did you ever see this guy?"

Cracker looked closely at it for a moment, chewing on his lower lip in concentration. "Yeah," he said, finally. "I've seen him a couple of times with Wayne Lee, over at Hutch's on Cortez Road."

I frowned. "Wayne Lee," I said. "Where do I know that name from?"

"You've met him at Tiny's. He comes in now and then. He works the boats out of Cortez when he's sober."

"Right. Comes in some with Nestor Cobol."

"That's him."

"Where can I find Lee?"

"I don't know, but Fats Monahan, the bartender at Hutch's, probably knows."

Hutch's had been there as long as I'd been coming to the key. It hunkered down next to Cortez Road, just over the bridge that spanned the Intracoastal between the mainland and Anna Maria Island. Because of its proximity to the fish houses and commercial docks, it had a rowdy reputation, fueled by the men who fished the sea for a living. I'd never visited the place.

The building was concrete block covered by a layer of stucco, some of it sloughing off. I could see bare blocks under the beige exterior. A glass door gave entrance to a dim recess of ugliness and body odors, tinged with the smell of fish, cigarette smoke, and stale beer. A bar took up one wall, with tables situated about a small linoleum-covered floor. Bare concrete showed in the spots where the covering had been ripped up. No sunlight penetrated this dark space. A fat man in a white T-shirt with no sleeves leaned on the bar, talking to the lone customer. It was two in the afternoon.

I'd brought Cracker with me. He knew this world and I didn't. The regulars whispered secrets to each other that they would never divulge to an outsider.

We walked in. The bartender gave me a bored look through hooded eyes. He saw Cracker, and his mouth turned up in what could be taken for a smile. I wasn't sure.

"Hey, Cracker," the bartender said. "Beer?"

"Sure," said Cracker. I'd never known Cracker to turn down a beer, no matter the time of day.

"Fats," said Cracker, "this is a friend of mine, Matt Royal."

"Beer?" asked Fats, looking at me. I assumed that was his idea of a pleasantry.

"Miller Lite, if you have it."

He bent to the cooler behind the bar and came up with a can of Budweiser for Cracker and a bottle of Miller Lite for me. He set them on the bar. No coasters.

"Fats," said Cracker, "I'm looking for Wayne Lee. Do you know where he lives?"

"Not exactly. He got kicked out of his trailer over at the park when he stayed drunk a few days and didn't work. The manager said he was tired of putting up with that."

"Do you know where he went?" asked Cracker.

"Pretty much. Why?"

Cracker looked at me, and I nodded my head. "I think he's in some trouble, and Matt here is a lawyer. We want to help him out."

"I know he ain't got no money for a lawyer," Fats said.

"It's a freebie," I said. "For Nestor Cobol."

"Nestor's still trying to take care of him, huh?" asked Fats, a sneer on his face.

I had no idea what that was about, and I didn't want to find out. Maybe Nestor and Wayne had had a falling out, and sooner or later, Fats would mention my visit to Nestor. Well, no harm. I'd know what I needed to know by then.

"I guess so," said Cracker.

Fats took a swipe at the bar with a paper towel, moving a little dust around. "He'll be drinking somewhere by now," he said. "I don't know where he goes. He moved over to the Tamiami Trail area a couple of weeks ago. He's only been in here once since then. He can't get a ride, usually."

"Do you have an address?" I asked.

"No, but I can give you directions. I took him home the last time he was here." And he told us the block on which Wayne lived.

CHAPTER THIRTEEN

There are parts of Bradenton into which one does not venture alone at night. Wayne Lee lived in one of those areas. I took Logan and my nine millimeter along for company.

"What are we doing?" he asked. "I wouldn't even come here in the daytime."

"We're looking for a guy."

"What guy?"

"Wayne Lee."

"Who's he."

"Just a guy."

"That doesn't make any sense."

"It will," I said.

"Why are we looking for this guy?"

"He may know something about Peggy."

"Okay. I give up. What?"

"Varn used to hang out at a dive called Hutch's on Cortez Road. He was usually with a guy named Wayne Lee, a deckhand on fishing boats out of Cortez. I know Lee. The bartender at Hutch's said he lives up here. On this street. In this block. I don't know which house, but you can always count on Lee being drunk by ten and stumbling home from somewhere. Maybe we'll get lucky."

"What if we don't?"

"We'll come back tomorrow night."

"Wow. I can't wait."

The neighborhood was quiet and dark. No streetlights, although the fixtures were still present. The city had stopped replacing the lights when some bureaucrat determined that his department couldn't stay ahead of the street thugs shooting the lights out. It's easier to deal drugs in the dark.

We sat. The street was lined with bungalows built for returning servicemen at the end of World War II. A neighborhood built on the G.I. bill. It was once a pleasant place to raise a family, but it was now a testament to urban blight; a warren of drug dealers and dope addicts, a decaying ruin that would continue to deteriorate until the city bulldozed the whole damn place.

We watched a car approach the corner, blink its lights twice, and pull to the curb. A hooded figure darted from an alley, passed a small package through the window of the car, took a wad of cash in return, and slithered back into the darkness. The late-model Mercedes sped off.

Over the next hour, several more cars stopped, made their buys and left. The kid in the hooded sweatshirt was doing okay.

I saw the lone figure walking up the sidewalk, weaving a little as drunks do, staying upright by sheer will. He was not tall, about five eight, and skinny. I'd met him at Tiny's a couple of times, brought there by Nestor Cobol, a fishing boat captain who had married one of the local girls. Lee was affable, if quiet, and took his drinking seriously. His tattooed arms were ropes of muscle, his hands calloused and scarred, the result of working the nets on the fishing boats. He was missing several teeth, and his blond hair was cropped short; a buzz cut that grew out over the weeks until he could afford another haircut. He was in his early thirties and looked fifty.

I turned in my seat. "We're going to take him when he gets to us," I said. "He's strong, so don't get careless."

"You're the lawyer," Logan said, "but wouldn't this come under some kind of kidnapping statute?"

"Probably. But he won't know who we are, and we'll let him go as soon as he tells us what we want to know."

"Okay. Give the word."

Lee was at the back bumper of the Explorer.

"Now," I said.

We both opened our doors. I ran around the rear of the car as Logan confronted Lee. The specter of two men jumping out of a car at him didn't seem to cause any great surprise to Lee. He stopped when he saw Logan, and then turned to face me. He must have heard me coming.

"Matt," Lee said. "What're you doing here?"

"So much for anonymity," said Logan.

I stopped, stuck out my hand to shake. "Hey, Wayne. Got a minute?"

"Sure. You got anything to drink?" he asked, shaking my hand.

"Get in," I said, motioning to the front passenger door. "We'll find a bar."

Logan got into the backseat, and we drove two blocks to Tamiami Trail and turned south toward Sarasota. No one spoke. It was as if Lee was used to people picking him up in the middle of the night and taking him for a beer.

In the second block, on the right, I saw a small concrete block structure with a blinking neon sign advertising Budweiser beer. I pulled into the gravel parking lot and we entered the building.

The air was permeated with the smell of stale beer and unclean air-conditioning filters. A faint hint of urine floated out of the open restroom door. There was a bar along one side of the room with three men sitting on stools, hunched over their drinks, not talking. They all turned as we entered, and then returned to staring into their glasses.

The bartender sat on a stool, smiling at a girlie magazine. "Help you gents?" he asked reluctantly, raising his head.

"Beer all around," I said, making a circular motion with my index finger. We sat at one of the tables.

Lee looked at me and smiled. "I ain't got no money, Matt."

"Beer's on Logan," I said.

Logan raised his head, a resigned look on his face. "What the hell. I'll buy."

The bartender brought three bottles of Bud and placed them on coasters on the scarred tabletop. "That'll be nine bucks," he said.

Logan dropped a ten on the table, and said, "Keep the change."

"Wayne," I said. "Do you know a Clyde Varn?"

Lee chugged half his beer, set the bottle down on the coaster, and wiped his mouth with the back of his hand.

"Nope."

I showed him the picture of Varn.

"Sure. That's Jake Yardley. He's an old buddy."

"From where?"

"I don't know. Just around."

"Around where?"

"Around here." His voice was taking on a whiny quality. "I don't remember a lot sometimes."

"Wayne," I said, "it's important that you remember where you first met Yardley."

"Oh, I first met him at his house."

"In Tampa?"

"No. At the trailer park on Cortez Road, out near the fish houses."

"He lived there?"

"Yeah, with some young girls."

"Girls? How many? How old?"

"There was two of them. Probably twenty or so. Well developed, if you know what I mean." He held his hands in front of his chest and tried for a leer, but didn't quite make it.

"Who were they?"

"I don't know. He never said."

Talking to drunks is difficult. Logan often complains about it after I've had too many.

"How did you meet Yardley?" I asked.

"I help out in the trailer park sometimes, raking stuff up when the boats ain't running. I was working out there one day last summer, and Jake invited me in and offered me a beer."

"And the girls were there?"

"Yeah, but they didn't stay long. They was gone within a couple of weeks."

"Do you know where they went?"

Wayne took another long swallow of his beer, shook the bottle, and held it up to the sparse light from the bar. He stared pointedly at its emptiness.

"No. He never said. I figured they got tired of hanging out with an old man and took off."

"I heard that you and Yardley go out drinking together a lot."

"Yeah, when he's around. Which ain't much anymore. He moved out of the trailer park. Can I get another beer, Matt?"

"When?"

"Now."

Logan stood. "I'll get it," he said, and walked toward the bar.

"What I meant," I said, "is when did Yardley move out of the trailer park?"

"Months ago."

"Where'd he move to?"

"Don't know. But he shows up sometimes and buys me beer."

"How does he know where to find you?"

"Don't know. He just comes into the bars where I like to go."

Logan returned with another beer for Lee. Mine was still untouched.

"Who'd want to kill Yardley?" I asked.

"Nobody. He's a nice guy."

"Somebody killed him yesterday. Planted him in Durante Park."

"You're kidding."

"Nope. He was shot."

"Wow."

"And his name's not Yardley. It's Clyde Varn."

"Son of a bitch," Lee said, taking another long pull on his beer.

"What else do you know about him?" I asked.

"Nothing."

"Did he ever say where he was from?"

"Not really. South Florida, I think. Maybe the Keys. He used to talk about the fishing down there."

"Did he ever say anything about the girls who were living with him?"

"No. But they were sisters."

"How do you know that?"

"Because they always called each other 'sister.' "

"And you don't know where they went?"

"No," he said. "One day they just weren't there anymore."

CHAPTER FOURTEEN

"That's a spooky guy," said Logan.

We were driving back to Longboat Key. It was near midnight and the streets were quiet. A rain squall had moved through the area while we were in the bar with Wayne Lee. The streets were wet, the lights reflecting off the sheen on the asphalt of Cortez Road.

"I feel sorry for him," I said. "He's a drunk, and he's getting worse. Pretty soon, they won't let him work the boats anymore, and he's going to end up on the streets."

"He's almost there now."

"That's why Captain Cobol tries to take care of him. He won't jeopardize his boat with a drunk, though. When Nestor won't take him out anymore, it'll be over for Wayne."

"What do you think about what he said about Varn?" Logan asked.

"Not much to go on. Who were the two girls living with him last summer, and where did they go?"

"Yeah. And if Varn was hired muscle for the drug runners in Miami, what's his connection to the Keys? Maybe Wayne will remember something else and call you."

I'd left my business card with him in case he sobered up enough to dredge more information from his booze-soaked brain.

"I'm not counting on it," I said. "I think I'll ask our friend Debbie to see what she can find out about Varn on the Internet."

"Debbie? From Moore's?

"Yeah. She's been taking computer classes. She swears she can find anybody or anything. I think she's figured out how to hack into a lot of databases."

•   •   •

I called Debbie at home early the next morning. She was a night owl, and I knew I'd wake her up, but I needed information. She'd forgive me. Sooner or later.

"Deb," I said. "Matt Royal."

"Do you know what time it is?"

"Yeah. Almost eight."

"Geez. This better be good, Royal."

"Can you get on your computer and see what you can find out about a guy named Clyde Varn?"

"Call me back this afternoon. It's way too early."

"This is important, Deb."

"Who is he?"

"I think he may have something to do with the missing girl I was telling you about yesterday."

"Okay. I'll get back to you in an hour."

"Bill Lester tells me Varn was convicted on a marijuana charge some years ago. The FBI files don't show anything else. Maybe that'll help you find the right guy. Check out Jake Yardley while you're at it," I said, and hung up.

I was drinking coffee on my sunporch, reading the morning paper. The wind was up, and the bay was roiled and gray, punctuated by little white caps. The sun was shining, and in the quiet I could hear the moan of the wind as it cut through the palm trees and around the building.

My phone rang again.

"Matt, Bill Lester."

"Morning, Bill."

"Do you know Wayne Lee?"

"Yeah. Why? Is he in trouble?"

"He's dead."

"What?" I was shocked. "I saw him last night."

"Bradenton PD found your business card in his pocket. They called me. I'm calling you. Talk to me."

I explained why Logan and I were with Wayne the night before and how we came to find him. "We left him at the bar, drinking. I gave him a twenty for more beer, and Logan and I left."

"He just had some pocket change on him. He probably drank up the twenty."

"How did he die?"

"Shot through the heart. Small caliber, maybe a .38. The same caliber that killed Varn."

"Same weapon?"

"We don't know yet. The crime lab will compare it and let us know."

"Where did they find him?"

"On the street, about a block from where he lived."

"Bill, why is it that two people I just talked to about Peggy turn up dead?"

"That's what I'd like to know," he said, and hung up.

I called Logan to tell him what had happened.

"The poor bastard," Logan said.

"We've got two dead guys that you and I are connected to. All within two days. They have to be involved somehow in Peggy's disappearance. That's the only common thread between us and them."

"Stay safe, Matt. I don't know what we've stumbled into."

"I'm beginning to think the shooting at Coquina Beach wasn't random. It must be connected somehow to Yardley and Lee, and to Peggy. You got your gun?"

"Nearby at all times."

"Mine too."

My day was not off to a good start. I couldn't concentrate on the morning rag. No good news anyway. Curiously, there was nothing on the missing body from the vulture pit. Sarasota PD was keeping a lid on it. I put the paper down and poured myself another cup of coffee.

If the placement of Varn's body was supposed to be a message to me, it would be clear to the killers that I didn't get it. I had spent time with Wayne Lee. Would they be coming for me next?

That was not a pleasant thought, but I was pretty confident I could take care of myself. I'd stayed in shape, and the Army had long ago taught me a lot about self-defense. Those lessons are drilled into the soldier with such intensity that they're not likely to be forgotten. The memory resides in the muscles, and reactions become automatic, instinctive, and violent. Plus, I knew how to use my nine millimeter.

The phone rang. Debbie.

"Got some stuff for you, Matt, but it's a little confusing."

"Talk to me."

"Clyde Varn was born in Brooksville, up just north of Tampa, graduated from high school there, got drafted, fought in Vietnam, honorable discharge, and then a string of petty-crime charges. A lot of those are in Monroe County, down in the Keys. He was convicted once in Miami on pot possession, and that's it.

"Seven years ago, he testified against some drug runners in federal court in Miami. Then he dropped off the radar and hasn't been seen since."

"How long ago did he disappear?"

"Right after he testified."

"Isn't that a little odd? Could he have been in jail somewhere?"

"No. I would've found those records. Plus you said that Bill Lester's search of the FBI files didn't show any convictions other than the misdemeanor pot thing in Miami some years ago. And I found that one."

"Where has he been for the past seven years?"

"That's the interesting thing. About the time Varn dropped off the planet, Jake Yardley shows up. He gets a couple of credit cards, a Kansas driver's license, and he's living in an apartment in Topeka. He doesn't seem to have a job, so I don't know what he was living on. I can't find any history on him before he showed up in Topeka. It's like he dropped in when Varn dropped out."

"Maybe that's what happened," I said.

"Then about a year ago, Yardley shows up in Tampa and trades his Kansas driver's license for a Florida one with a Brooksville address. The same one where Varn grew up. From then on, there's nothing on him. No credit cards, no traffic tickets, nothing. He must've been paying cash for everything he bought."

"Thanks, Deb," I said, and hung up.

CHAPTER FIFTEEN

I was reaching for the phone when it rang. Again. I answered, expecting more bad news. I got it.

"Matt, Cracker Dix here. Fats Monahan just called me. Said he needs to see you as soon as possible."

"What about?"

"He said to tell you he knows who killed Wayne Lee. I didn't even know he was dead."

"Last night. Where is Fats now?"

"At Hutch's. He lives above it, so he's always there."

"Thanks, Cracker. I'll go right over."

I crossed the Longboat Pass Bridge and drove north a couple of miles, turning right onto Cortez Road. I had to wait on the Cortez Bridge while a tall-masted sailboat moved slowly under power through the open span. Pelicans were diving into the bay like Stuka bombers, hitting the water and then bouncing back up, floating as they raised their heads and swallowed the hapless fish they'd caught. A gull landed on the back of a pelican and tried to snatch breakfast before the bigger bird could swallow it. No luck.

The bridge siren sounded. The span was going back down, and when it was locked in place, the barricade rose from the roadway, signaling me to move on.

I drove less than a mile and pulled into the shell parking lot of Hutch's. The front door was open, and the place seemed deserted. I walked in, stopping for a moment to let my eyes adjust to the darkened interior. I could smell the place. An almost overpowering stench of unwashed bodies, cigarette smoke, and stale beer lingered from the night before. It was so quiet I could hear the air shuffling through my nostrils.

"Fats," I called out.

Nothing.

"Fats." Again, louder.

Nothing. I pulled my nine millimeter from the pocket of my windbreaker. I pumped a round into the chamber, and held the pistol down by my leg, pointing to the floor.

I noticed a partially open door across the barroom. It led to another room, perhaps a storeroom or a bathroom. I couldn't be sure. The interior was pitch dark.

I eased toward the door, my pistol in front of me, held in a two-handed grip. I pushed the door all the way open with the barrel of the weapon. I reached in with my left hand, fumbling along the wall next to the door, trying to find a light switch. My hand closed on a plastic cover with a round knob, like the controls of a rheostat. I pushed the knob in, and light flooded the small room.

I was standing in a dusty vestibule, with stairs leading upward. There were cases of whiskey stacked around the little room and under the stairs. The space was unpainted, and dust covered the boxes of booze.

I saw a door at the head of the stairs and started climbing, slowly. Light was seeping from around the door, casting a faint glow on the area. I stayed to the edge of the steps, hoping not to cause one to creak and give me away. I pointed my gun upward. I wasn't sure why I was being so careful, but it seemed like a good idea.

I reached the door and slowly turned the knob. It wasn't locked and I carefully opened it. Light poured through the crack between the door and the jamb. As the opening widened, more sunlight splashed out.

I swung the door all the way open and at the same time stepped back down a couple of steps, crouching. I wanted to make as small a target as possible.

Nothing. No movement. No sound.

I stood and moved into the room, gun pointing forward. No one was there. It wasn't much of a room. A single bed was positioned under the window across from the doorway in which I stood. This was the source of

the sunlight that flowed into the room. The bed was unmade, the sheets
tangled, a pillow on the floor. An overstuffed chair was positioned at the
foot of the bed, a reading lamp next to it. The walls were an institutional
gray, the paint peeling in spots. I could see a brown blotch on the ceiling
where the roof had leaked. On the wall across from the bed, someone had
built a floor-to-ceiling bookcase. It was filled with books. A quick glance
told me that the reader's interest ran to history and biography. A closed
door bisected the wall to my right.

"Fats," I called again.

The door opened, and a naked man stood there, shaving cream covering his face, a safety razor in his hand, a startled look on his face, dis-
solving quickly into fear.

"What the fuck?" said the naked man. It was Fats.

I angled the gun toward the floor. "Sorry," I said. "I didn't mean to
startle you."

"Startle? You scared the ever-living shit out of me, Counselor. What
the hell are you doing?"

"The door downstairs is open and nobody was in the bar. I wasn't
sure what I was going to find. Sorry."

"That door should be locked. You sure it's open?"

"Wide open."

"What are you doing here?"

"You said you wanted to see me."

"I never said that."

"Didn't you call Cracker Dix and tell him you wanted to see me about
Wayne Lee?"

"No. Why would I?"

He reached into the bathroom and grabbed a towel, wiped his face
and then put it around his considerable girth.

"About his murder," I said.

"Wayne's murder?"

"Yes. Last night."

"Damn."

Fats moved to the chair and sat down heavily. He put his hands to
his face, almost prayerfully. "What happened?"

"He was shot in the chest. Over near where he lives. That's all I know."

"Shit. Poor guy. He never hurt nobody."

I had moved into the room, keeping an eye on the door leading to the stairs. Somebody had called Cracker and told him to get me here. Why? Why was the door downstairs open? Was somebody else in the building?

Then I heard it. A step creaking. I turned to Fats, putting a finger to my lips, the universal signal for quiet. I raised my pistol, sighting on the open door to the stairs. Another creak, and then the door was thrown all the way back, bouncing against the wall.

A big man pushed into the room. He was about six feet tall, but he must've weighed three hundred pounds. I didn't think any of it was fat. He wore a black ski mask, and he had a shotgun in his hands, leveled at me. I saw his eyes squint in anticipation of the shot. His finger was pulling back on the trigger, whitening under the pressure. His lips, visible through the mouth hole of the mask, were beginning to part in a grin, or a grimace.

I shot him in the face. He went over backward, the shotgun discharging into the ceiling. I rushed the body, ready to pump another round into him. It wasn't necessary. His eyes were open just above the entry wound to the right of his nose. Some air escaped through his open mouth, a gurgling sound emanating from his throat. The death rattle.

I positioned myself beside the doorway, waiting to see who else was coming up the stairs. Fats was sitting in the chair, a yellow stain spreading across the white towel draped over his lap. I didn't blame him. That shotgun scared the piss out of me too. His breathing was irregular, his eyes wide in fright.

Feet pounded the floor of the room below. It sounded like one man running. The front door slammed, and a moment later tires careened over the shell parking lot. A car coming off the street, fast. A door slammed, and the vehicle screeched out of the parking lot, its tires loudly grabbing the pavement.

I ran to the window over the bed and looked out. A green sedan was on Cortez Road heading east. It was too far away for me to see its license plate or to even determine the make of car. It was gone.

I turned to Fats. "You okay?"

"Not really. What the hell's going on?"

"I don't know, but somebody got me over here to kill me. Looks like they wanted to kill you too."

I took out my cell phone and called Logan. I told him where I was and what had happened. "Stay inside," I said. "If they came for me, they may come for you too. Call Bill Lester and tell him what's going on. I'm calling 911."

After I told the emergency operator where I was and why I needed the police, I turned to Fats. He was still breathing hard, but he'd gotten himself cleaned up and put on a pair of shorts.

"Why would somebody want to kill you?" I asked.

"Don't know."

"Look, Fats. Somebody's out to get me and probably you as well. Once the cops get here they're going to separate us and you're not going to be able to tell me what's going on. Do it now, and maybe I can figure out how to save our asses. Does this have something to do with Jake Yardley?"

"Probably. There's a lot I can't tell you, Mr. Royal, but I'll tell you what I can."

"Call me Matt."

"Okay, Matt. I knew Clyde Varn from way back. I recognized him right away, the first time he came in here. He said his name was Jake Yardley, but I knew better."

"Where did you know him from?"

"Down in the Keys, and later, Miami."

"How did you know him?"

"We worked for the same outfit."

"Come on, Fats. We don't have all day. Spell it out."

"We worked for Javier Savanorola. He was in the drug business. Clyde was hired muscle. I handled the books and kept the IRS off Javier's back.

"The feds came down on us hard six or seven years ago. Clyde and I both testified for the government. He disappeared, and I figured Javier had him killed. I left town, changed my name, and bought this place."

"Didn't Clyde recognize you when he came in?"

"No," Fats said. "I've gained about a hundred pounds, and when we worked together I had a full beard. I don't think anybody from those days would recognize me."

"What was your name?"

"Can't tell you, Matt. Sorry."

"Did you spend much time with Varn?"

"For a while. He lived up the street in the trailer park and would come in most days. We'd sit here at the bar and talk."

"About what?"

"Sports, mostly. He did tell me that he came here from Kansas, but he never told me anything else of a personal nature."

"How did he make his living?" I asked.

"I don't know. He never said anything about a job."

"Could he have been doing work for the drug guys in South Florida?"

"I doubt it. They put a contract out on him after he testified against them. I figured that's why he changed his name."

I heard sirens in the distance, drawing closer. Tires crunched onto the shell parking lot. Car doors slammed. Feet ran on the cement floor below, the leather boot soles making slapping sounds. Leather equipment holders creaked, and I heard a rifle chambering a round.

"Up here," I called out. "We're unarmed."

There was quiet for a beat, two, and then a voice, strained with tension, came from below. "Come to the door where I can see you. Hands over your head. Come out slow."

I lay my gun on the bed and eased over to the door, hands raised. I stood by the jamb and said, "I'm coming out. Here are my hands." I stuck them into the doorway. If some trigger-happy cop was going to shoot, I'd rather he hit my hands than my chest.

"Show yourself," came the voice from below.

"I'm coming out," I said, and slipped into full view in the doorway, hands high.

"Anybody else up there?"

"One live and one dead guy," I said. "The live one's coming over now."

I looked back at Fats. He was standing with his hands up. I nodded. He started walking slowly toward me. Heavy footsteps were bounding up the stairs. Just as Fats got to me, a sheriff's deputy came through the doorway and shoved a rifle into my gut.

"Move back," said the cop.

I did, being careful not to step on the body.

Another deputy came through the doorway, pistol drawn. He looked at the dead guy, stopped, reached down, and felt for a pulse in his neck. He stood back up, shaking his head, and looked at me. "Who're you?"

"I'm Matt Royal. I live on Longboat Key. I have identification. The gun on the bed is mine. I shot this guy with it."

The cop nodded, then looked at Fats.

"I'm Fats Monahan. I live here."

The deputy took a deep breath. "The detectives will be here in a minute," he said. "Let's just sit tight until they get here. Don't touch anything."

He signaled us to put our hands down. He walked over to the bed and stood by it, not touching the nine millimeter lying on the tangled sheets, but making sure that neither Fats nor I could get to it.

The other deputy turned and yelled down the stairs. "We're cool up here. Send the detectives in when they get here."

We stood silently for a few moments. I could hear traffic whizzing by out on Cortez Road. Somewhere in the building, an air-conditioning unit clicked on. Cool air rushed out of a vent in the ceiling that I hadn't noticed. A car horn, the short squeal of brakes, a diesel engine accelerating, the ambient noise of early morning in a quiet neighborhood.

I heard another car coming to a stop on the shell parking lot. In a minute a voice from below said, "Detective coming up." The deputies in the room seemed to relax; glad someone was here to take control.

A man of about six feet, slender with a small belly, dark hair going to gray, and a bald spot that would eventually claim his head, stepped into the room. He wore a beige sports jacket with brown pants, white dress shirt, and a red tie with small white polka dots. A gold badge was held in place over his jacket pocket by its leather case. "I'm Detective David Sims," he said. "What the hell happened here?"

The deputy who had entered the room first said, "We just got here, Detective. We secured the area, but we haven't talked to the witnesses. This is Mr. Royal and that's Fats Monahan. I haven't seen their IDs yet."

The detective looked at me. "Let's see," he said, holding out his right hand.

I reached for my wallet and handed him my driver's license. He looked at it and handed it back. He looked at Fats.

Fats pointed to a wallet lying on the table beside the bed. "Mine's in the wallet."

The detective made a "come on" move with his fingers, and Fats crossed to the table and picked up the wallet, extracted his license, and handed it to the detective. Sims glanced at it and handed it back.

"What happened?" Sims asked quietly.

I shifted my weight, looked at the detective. "A friend called and said Fats here wanted to see me," I said. "I came over. Fats hadn't asked to see me. We were discussing it when this guy came through the door with that shotgun leveled at us. I shot him."

Sims stared at me for a long beat. "That's a very short story. You can do better, Mr. Royal."

I was about to open my mouth when Bill Lester walked into the room. He was wearing his usual attire, but this time he had a sidearm strapped to his belt.

Sims turned. "Chief," he said, "what brings you to our side of the bridge?"

"I heard one of my citizens shot one of yours," Bill said.

"Royal's one of yours, but I got no idea who the dead guy is."

"Do you think it'd help if you looked at his face?" asked Lester.

"Might," said Sims.

He walked over to the body, pulling latex gloves out of his jacket pocket and putting them on his hands. He bent over and pulled the ski mask up off the corpse's face. He studied the dead man for a few moments, rose and said, "Don't know him. We'll run his prints through and find out who he is. Guy like this is bound to be in the system."

A voice from downstairs announced, "CSIs coming up."

Bill Lester started for the stairs. "I'll get out of your way, Detective. I'd appreciate it if you'd keep me in the loop."

"Chief," said Sims, "what's your interest in this?"

"I think this might be connected to a homicide I'm working on Longboat, and maybe to one that Bradenton PD is working from last night."

"Shit," said Sims. "About two too many jurisdictions in that mix. Why do you think they're connected?"

"Because my friend here seems to be connected to all of them." Lester was pointing at me.

Sims grinned. "I'll make sure to get a long statement from him. Do you know anything about a friend calling him this morning to tell him to come over here?"

"Yeah," said Bill. "That would be Cracker Dix. He's out in my car waiting for you to talk to him."

Sims waved his arm in my general direction, motioning me to follow him down the stairs. Fats brought up the rear.

CHAPTER SIXTEEN

The parking lot was crowded with police cruisers and crime-scene vans, all bearing the colors and logo of the Manatee County Sheriff. An unmarked police car was parked near the entrance. Cracker Dix was leaning against it, his arms folded, a bored look on his face.

Detective Sims and Chief Lester had stopped walking after leaving the building and were huddled in the shade of the roof overhang. Lester was talking, gesturing, Sims listening.

Fats and I went to join Cracker.

"Morning Cracker," said Fats. "That wasn't me talking to you earlier."

"That wasn't you who called me this morning?"

"Wasn't me," said Fats. "Matt like to have scared the shit out of me when he came busting into my place this morning. If I'd called, I'd have met him in the bar."

"Sure sounded like you."

"Cracker," I said. "Where's Logan?"

"Home, I guess. The chief came by my place this morning and said I needed to go with him. He didn't say anything about Logan. I thought I was being arrested again. Then he told me about you having to shoot that guy. I told him what I knew and he told me to come with him. Here we are."

I called Logan on my cell phone.

"You okay?" I asked.

"Yep, sitting here with a bowl of oatmeal, the paper, and a nine mil."

"Logan, keep an eye out. If that dead guy was after me, somebody's probably after you."

"What in the hell is going on?'"

"I don't know. We must have kicked over a hornet's nest somehow. Maybe we'll know more after the cops get through comparing notes."

"Hope so," said Logan.

I hung up.

Sims and Lester came over. Sims didn't look happy. "Mr. Royal," he said, "you have fouled my nest."

"Sorry, Detective," I said. "I sure didn't mean to."

Bill Lester was grinning. "Matt has a way of doing that. Never means to, either."

This was not helping.

The chief snorted with what passed for a laugh. "The detective wants statements from all three of you," he said. "We can do it at the Longboat station. Save you a trip downtown."

It was lunchtime when we finished with the statements. I drove Cracker back to the village and met Logan for lunch at Mar Vista.

"Somebody went to a lot of trouble to take you out," he said, when we were seated on the patio.

"There has to be a reason. Somebody tried to kill us on Coquina Beach, and now this. I wonder if somebody thinks we know something that we don't."

"Let's look at this logically. We're looking for Peggy. We talk to Varn and he's murdered. The same night somebody tries to take us out. Then we go to see Wayne Lee and within a few hours, he's killed. Next morning, they come for you again. It's got to be about Peggy."

"Not necessarily," I said. "Maybe it has something to do with the body I found at Pelican Man's."

"Has anybody been in contact with Vince Delgado?"

Vince, the curator at Pelican Man's, had left for Michigan to visit family the morning after we found the body. "He won't be back for a couple of weeks. He's in the Upper Peninsula of Michigan."

"I'm not sure it makes sense to try to tie these murders to the vulture pit guy. All you did was find a body. How would that tie you into anything that'd get people killed?"

"Suppose somebody thought I knew more about that body than I was supposed to, and they thought I was getting Varn and Wayne Lee involved in it somehow. Maybe they just took them out as a precaution, and they figured to do the same with me."

"That's a little far-fetched. The cops don't even know who the vulture pit guy is."

"Did you know that his body disappeared from the morgue?" I asked.

"You're kidding. How?"

I told him the story of the fake funeral home pick up, and the fact that the police had no leads.

"That's weird," said Logan. "Maybe you have a point. Have you discussed it with Bill Lester?"

"Not yet."

I brought Logan up to date on Debbie's research on Varn.

He shrugged. "Sounds like he was hiding out from the drug folks."

"But why show back up now? Even with a different name, you wouldn't think he'd get within a thousand miles of Florida. Not with a contract on his head."

"Did Bill ever get any info on the owner of the condo where Varn was living?"

"Sort of. I talked to him this morning about that. It seems that a Cayman Islands corporation, whose shares are held by a Cayman bank, owns the Bahamian corporation that owns the condo. Cayman banks are more secretive than those in Switzerland. Bill thinks we may have hit a dead end."

"Lovely," said Logan. "And somebody's trying to kill us."

CHAPTER SEVENTEEN

I'd been staying in touch with Laura by e-mail, and I wanted to run some names by her. I doubted she would have ever heard of Wayne Lee, Fats Monahan, or Clyde Varn, but it was worth a try. Truth to tell, I just wanted to hear her voice.

I called her after lunch. Her husband, Jeff, answered the phone. I identified myself and asked if Laura was available.

"Matt, I've been meaning to call you all morning. Laura's missing." He was agitated, talking too loud, a little out of breath.

"What do you mean, missing?"

"I came home for lunch yesterday and she wasn't here. She hasn't been back."

"Police?"

"When she didn't come home by suppertime, I called them. Her purse was here, her cell phone, her car was in the garage. There was no note, nothing. That's not like her. If she was going out unexpectedly, she'd always leave a note."

"What are the police telling you?"

"Nothing, so far. They didn't even start looking until she didn't come home all night."

"They're doing something now, I hope."

"Something, I guess. But I don't know how serious they're taking this. They keep asking me if we're having marital problems. I think they think she just took off."

"Any chance that's the case?" I asked.

"None. Certainly not now, not while Peggy's missing. Have you found out anything?"

"Nothing more than what I've told Laura so far."

There was no reason to alarm him further with the deaths that may or may not be connected to his daughter. He had enough on his plate right now.

I said, "Did you tell the police that Peggy's missing?"

"Yeah, but they don't see any connection. Laura was here and Peggy was in Florida. I was trying to call you to find out if Laura had contacted you. I guess not."

"No, but if she does, I'll call you right away. Keep me posted."

"I will, Matt. And thanks. Oh, before you go, there is one other thing that's kind of curious. I got a call this morning, but the caller hung up before I could get to the phone. My caller ID had a three-oh-five area code number, so I called it back. It was a pay phone in a bar in Key West called the Sharkstooth. Nobody knew who had called. And, my home phone is unlisted."

"Maybe it was just a wrong number," I said. I didn't believe that, but why worry a guy more than he already was?

As soon as I hung up, I called Bill Lester. "Bill," I said, "can you call the Atlanta PD and find out about a missing person?" I filled him in on Laura's disappearance.

"I'll see what I can do," he said.

I paced my living room. This thing was getting out of hand. Peggy had been missing for four weeks, and now Laura drops off the planet. There had to be a connection, but I couldn't see it. None of it made any sense. Why were dead people cropping up all over the place? And why was somebody trying to take Logan and me out of the picture?

I was trying to make sense of my day. I'd killed a man, and even though he'd left me no choice, I was in some sort of a state of mourning. I didn't know the guy, and the world was better off without him, but the taking of a human life alters you forever. I'd killed before, in war and in self-defense, and each time the same awful feeling of regret ate at my soul. John Donne famously wrote that "any man's death diminishes me, because I am involved in Mankind." Maybe he was right. Especially when I'd caused the death.

On top of this, Laura was missing. Where had she gone and why? Did she go on her own volition, or were there sinister forces at work?

Laura would never leave without letting some one know where she was going. Her disappearance was troubling. Was it connected to Peggy? There was no other reason for Laura to go missing. The fact that Peggy had been in Florida and Laura was in Atlanta didn't mean the two things weren't connected.

I called Detective Sims's cell phone. He'd given me the number in case I came up with any good reason for why people were trying to kill me.

"Did you get any ID on the guy I shot this morning?"

"Yeah. He's an ex-con named Brad Bartel. Did five years in Raiford for assault down in the Keys. Before that, he did a deuce for possession of cocaine with intent to sell. That was another Monroe County bust in the Lower Keys, Stock Island. He was released from Raiford two months ago."

"Any idea what he was doing up here?"

"None. A detective I know in Key West said this guy was suspected in a couple of murders, but they couldn't get the evidence to pin them on him. He was a pretty bad dude and Key West is glad to be rid of him."

"Anybody know where he's been since he left prison?"

"Went back to Key West. Seemed to have a little money and spent most of the time drinking on Duval Street."

"His drinking days are over," I said.

"You don't seem too broken up over the whole thing."

"I'm not, Detective. He's not the first man I've killed."

"So I heard." He hung up.

Why would anyone in our area hire a hit man from Key West, if that's what Bartel was? I was sure there were any number of out-of-work bad guys in Tampa. On the other hand, both Fats and Varn had worked for drug runners in South Florida. Maybe that was the connection. Maybe Bartel wasn't after me at all. Just Fats.

But if that were the case, why would someone lure me to Hutch's? Maybe Fats was the target, and somebody thought they might as well take me out while they were getting Fats. Just in case I knew something I wasn't supposed to know.

But what was I supposed to know?

My phone rang. It was Logan.

"Matt, you'd better get over to my place. We're in a heap of shit."

CHAPTER EIGHTEEN

The gate guard recognized me and waved me in. I drove into the parking lot of Logan's condo and found three police cruisers, blue lights rotating in their light bars, a fire department ambulance, and a group of residents standing around chatting with each other.

Logan was standing off to the side, talking to one of the Longboat Key officers. I parked at the edge of the lot and walked over.

"What's going on?" I asked.

"There's a dead man on my balcony," said Logan. "Shot through the head."

"Who?"

"I don't know. There was a mop on the floor beside him, so he may be part of the cleaning crew that was supposed to come in today. I hired a new company to do the maid work. I don't know any of them."

"What's going on in your condo?"

"Bill Lester's up there with a couple of cops. They're waiting for the Sarasota County CSI people."

Our island is divided at its middle, with the northern half lying in Manatee County and the southern half in Sarasota County. Logan lived on the southern end of the key, and thus, in the jurisdiction of the Sarasota County Sheriff.

We watched a van with the Sarasota County Sheriff's logo on the door drive into the lot. Two men and a woman got out, went around to the back, and unloaded three large evidence kits. They walked to the door of the building and were let in by the Longboat Key officer stationed there.

I turned to Logan. "Did you notice anything missing from your condo?"

"I didn't take time to look. I saw the dead guy and left in a hurry and called 911 and then you. The cops got here about five minutes before you did."

Bill Lester was coming out of the building, striding toward us, a hard look on his face. He motioned for the officer, who was still standing with us, to leave.

"I think somebody was after you, Logan," he said. "Did you take a good look at the body?"

"No. I saw the bullet hole in his head and got the hell out of there."

The chief looked at me. "From a distance, the dead guy would look a lot like Logan. He's balding and about five foot eight. The slug that got him was large, maybe from a sniper rifle. Went right through his head and lodged in the wall."

There were two buildings near Logan's that could have given a shooter a sight line. I looked at both of them, but didn't see anything out of the ordinary. I didn't expect to.

"The shot could have come from either of those buildings," I said, pointing.

"I agree," said the chief. "The dead guy had an immigration green card on him. He was from Poland and worked for the Tidy Lady's Maid Service. Are they yours, Logan?"

"Yeah. I just hired them to come in once a week. Today was their first day."

"And that guy's last day," said the chief. "We'll know more when CSI gets through with the crime scene."

"We've got to stop meeting like this," a voice behind me said.

I turned to look into the cold eyes of Detective David Sims.

The chief introduced him to Logan and said, "Thanks for coming, Dave. This has got to tie in to the Lee and Varn killings. I thought you'd be interested."

"I am," said Sims, pointing at Logan and me. "I just don't see any connection, except these two. They keep showing up at murder scenes."

"My thought exactly," said the chief. He turned to me. "Why don't you take Logan to your place, Matt? Stay out of sight. I'll send a patrolman if you like, but I want you guys safe until we get a better handle on this. I'll come over as soon as CSI finishes up here."

"We'll be at my condo," I said. "The patrolman isn't necessary. We'll be okay." I wasn't too sure about that, but I didn't want my neighbors to get antsy about a cop at my door.

Logan and I were back in my condo by mid-afternoon, sitting on the sun-porch idly watching a pontoon boat with a maroon Bimini top make its way south. An easterly breeze lightly rippled the bay, and clouds were moving in, obscuring the sun. The sliding glass doors were open, and the sound of an idling outboard engine drifted up from the marina. The air smelled of rain and seaweed drying in the sun.

"That could've been me," Logan said.

"Yes."

"Why?"

"Don't know."

"We've got to figure this out or we're going to be dead," he said.

"I know."

I told him about my earlier conversations with Sims and Jeff Timmons. "Everything seems to be pointing to Key West. I'm going down there," I said.

"To do what?"

"I'm not sure. I think the starting place is the bar where the pay phone is."

"Why?"

"The call to Jeff's house is just too coincidental. Maybe it was Peggy. Or maybe she called earlier and talked to Laura. Maybe Laura's in Key West."

"She wouldn't have left without her purse or credit cards or clothes," Logan said.

"There's that."

"And you said her car was in the garage at home."

"I know. But we've got too many signs pointing to Key West. At least the bar gives me a starting point."

"I can go with you."

"I think I'd be better off alone. Besides, I need to have you here to help me stay in touch with the police. I don't think you ought to be too conspicuous on the island, though."

"Dave Kendall has an extra room at his place. I can stay there and keep my head down. I'll even use his motor scooter to get around."

"Stay out of your usual haunts."

"Yeah. I don't want any more holes in my hide."

We worked out a plan for me to get to Key West and to stay in touch with Logan on a regular basis. I called Cracker Dix and asked him to stop by the condo. I needed a favor.

Cracker showed up about four and sat sipping a beer while I told him where I was going and why.

"Didn't you tell me a while back that you still had contacts down there from your old days?" I asked.

"Sure do," said Cracker. "I was a stand-up guy, and they appreciate that sort of thing."

"What do you mean?" Logan asked.

"I took a run from Key West to Los Angeles for them. They were going to pay me fifty large to take a load of coke in the side panels of a rental car. I got busted the first time out by some highway cop in New Mexico."

"What happened?" I asked, not sure I wanted the whole truth.

"They got me in a roadblock looking for illegals. I had my green card and my passport, so that was fine. They were looking for Mexicans anyway."

"How did they find the drugs?" I asked.

"My friend Paco was asleep in the backseat. He's Cuban, but was born in this country, so he didn't have a green card or any other form of ID except a driver's license. They thought he was a Mexican. While they tried to sort that all out, I went over to the side of the road to pee. When I came back the coppers were taking the car apart."

"Why?" I asked, my lawyer brain thinking about all the defenses to a search, such as lack of probable cause.

"While I was taking a piss," said Cracker, "one of the cops asked Paco if they could search the car. Paco didn't know about the drugs. He was just along to keep me company, and he told them to go ahead. Next thing I know, I'm in the Las Cruces jail with a high bond."

"How long did you get?" I asked.

"I was there for about three months, and when we went to an evidentiary hearing one of the cops testified that he'd asked Paco for permission to search the car, not me. My lawyer argued that since I was the one who rented the car from Avis, I was the only one who could legally give permission for the search. The judge agreed and cut me loose."

"You got lucky," I said. "Did you make any more runs?"

"No, but the big guy in Key West gave me the fifty K anyway and told me he appreciated my not ratting them out. Said if I ever needed anything to give him a call."

"If I need a guide for the Key West underworld, will he help me? As a friend of yours?"

"I'll call him and find out."

Cracker finished his beer and left just as Bill Lester was coming in my front door.

"We found where the shot came from," he said. He dropped onto the sofa and rested his feet on my coffee table. "An empty condo in the building just across the courtyard from Logan's was broken into this morning. The balcony would have given the shooter a straight line to Logan's place."

"Any evidence as to who the shooter was?" I asked.

"No. The place was clean. No cartridge shells, no prints. There were some footprints in the carpet, but they were too faint even to get an impression. We assumed they were from the shooter, since the carpet was vacuumed yesterday by the maid service."

"You're sure that's where the shot came from?" Logan asked.

"About as sure as we can be. The CSI team confirmed the angle of the shot, and that was the only condo in the building that wasn't either occupied or locked up tight."

"You think he was after me?" asked Logan.

"I don't think there's any doubt about that," said the chief. "The Polish guy was your size and had a hairline similar to yours. From that distance, anybody would have assumed it was you."

I couldn't sit around Longboat Key and wait for somebody to finally get lucky and kill me. Plus, I had to find Peggy. Laura's disappearance had spooked me more than I'd let on to her husband. She was dedicated to Jeff and their children, and as concerned as she was about Peggy, Laura would never have left Jeff and Gwen at such a critical time.

Apprehension was settling over me, slipping ominously into the crevices of my brain, whispering softly of impending loss. Fear, my old nemesis from the war, was lurking on the edge of my consciousness, its stench percolating into my soul. Laura was my heart, and the thought of losing her was almost paralyzing. That's the way fear works. It sneaks in and builds in intensity until it takes over, and at that moment it wins. It had never beaten me, although it had tried mightily, and on occasion it had been a close thing. If it beat me now, Laura was lost, and I couldn't live with that.

I shook myself out of my macabre reverie. "I'm going to Key West," I said.

Bill shrugged. "Can't hurt, I suppose. By the way, the Atlanta cops aren't taking Laura's disappearance too seriously. They think she just took off. They're going through the motions, though. Maybe something will turn up."

"Tell me about Sims," I said.

"Good guy. I've known him for years and worked with him from time to time. He's a good detective. I'm glad to have him working with me on this one."

After Bill left, I called Sims. I told him about Laura's disappearance and the phone call from Key West. I told him I was going down there. I asked for the name of the detective friend of his in Key West.

"His name's Paul Galis. I'll call him and tell him you're coming," Sims said, and gave me a phone number.

CHAPTER NINETEEN

Early the next morning Logan drove me to the Tampa Airport, where I caught a commuter jet to Miami. A taxi took me to the Miami Arena. I walked the three blocks to the Greyhound station on Northwest 1st Avenue, bought a ticket, and sat down to wait for the bus to Key West.

I was flying under the radar. I didn't know what kind of surveillance anyone had on Logan and me, but I didn't want them to know I was on my way to Key West.

Logan was staying with his friend Dave on the mainland. He'd stay out of sight and be in touch with me by cell phone. He'd be okay, I thought, if he didn't get careless.

When you travel by airplane, you have to show identification. Not when you go by bus. I also thought that if anyone saw me arrive at Key West Airport, I would have company sooner than I wanted.

The bus was another matter. I didn't need an ID to board one, and if anybody was looking for me, they wouldn't expect a preppy lawyer to travel by Greyhound.

I had a .38-caliber snub-nosed pistol in my backpack. I'd checked it through in Tampa so as not to upset the security people and get myself arrested. Bus drivers didn't make you go through a metal detector before you boarded. I'd have the gun with me.

I had a Florida State ID card identifying me as Ben Joyce, a friend who lived on Anna Maria Island. He'd lost his driver's license as the result of a DUI conviction, and had gotten the card for identification. He'd gotten his license back after a year, and he didn't need the ID card anymore.

Ben and I didn't look that much alike, but we had the same coloring and hairline. It was good enough to fool anybody who didn't look too closely. I also had a credit card in Ben's name. I'd promised I would repay him for any charges.

I bought the bus ticket with the credit card. If anyone was curious, or anything showed up on somebody's computer, it would show that Ben had bought a one-way ticket to Key West, and paid for it with his credit card. That would dovetail with any use I had to make of the card while in the Keys. I was probably being too cautious, but, as the old saying goes, even paranoiacs have enemies.

I kept the credit card, ID, and two thousand dollars in twenties and hundreds in a money belt under my shirt. I'd get by on cash in Key West, but I had the credit card if I got into a pinch. My backpack also held toiletries and a couple of changes of clothes.

My bus was called, and I grabbed a seat toward the rear. There were only a few other passengers, and we started the five-hour trek south. We picked up several people at Homestead, mostly Hispanics who daily commuted to work in the Keys. At Florida City, the last stop on the mainland, more passengers crowded onto the bus. There were not enough seats and some stood in the aisle.

The Keys had become the playground of the wealthy. The people who cleaned the hotels and mansions and worked on the roads could no longer afford to live there. They'd found affordable housing in Florida City and Homestead, and would make the daily trip by Greyhound to their jobs in the Keys. Now, even those mainland towns were in danger of being overrun by the middle class who had been displaced from the Keys. Soon, there would be no place for the workers to live. There were no solutions in the works. One day the rich people would wake up and figure out that they either had to do the work themselves or move back to wherever they came from. Most would leave, and maybe the Keys would get back to what they used to be; funky islands peopled by oddballs who appreciated the paradise they'd been bequeathed.

U.S. 1 is known as the Overseas Highway as it makes its way from island to island. It was built over the bed of the railroad that was washed away in the great hurricane of 1935. Some of the ancient bridges still supported the road, but much of it was now bottomed on new structures spanning the water between the keys.

I watched the ever-changing colors in the seas surrounding us. It went from turquoise over sand bottoms to brown coral heads to blue in the deeper holes. It was magnificent, but like much of the world's greatest scenery, it finally becomes boring. Perhaps we can only drink in so much beauty before it all pales into mediocrity. The human condition. Even great beauty finally bores us.

A few of the domestic workers got off at each stop, and by the time we arrived in Marathon, about halfway to Key West, the bus was virtually empty. We took a rest break, and I went inside the tiny terminal to use the bathroom. When I came out, there was a large group of senior citizens milling about in the parking lot, waiting to board the bus.

I retook my seat, and the driver told the new passengers to board. A wizened old gentleman sat next to me, stuck out his hand, and said, "I'm Austin Dwyer."

I took his hand. "Ben Joyce," I said.

"Headed for Key West?"

"Yes."

"Vacation?"

"Looking for work."

"I'm on vacation," said Dwyer. "A whole bunch of us from Connecticut are seeing Florida. Our tour bus broke down, and they put us on this one to Key West. We'll have another bus waiting for us down there."

"Hope it works out," I said, thinking that I had to end this conversation.

"Where're you staying down there?"

"Don't know. I'll get a room somewhere."

"What kind of work do you do?"

"I work the fishing boats."

"Well, good luck," he said and turned to talk to the lady sitting across the aisle from him.

I lay my head on a pillow against the window and pretended to sleep.

CHAPTER TWENTY

Key West is a big coral rock that hosts a small city. The place is a state of mind as much as a geographical location, and it's undergoing drastic change. The old stores along Duval Street have given way to T-shirt shops that are now being replaced by major chain stores usually found in shopping malls. The town is schizoid, the residents resenting the tourists, but unable to survive without them. Stasis is never attained, balance never found. Change is constant, turmoil a part of daily life.

Cruise ships dock daily, disgorging midwestern tourists in guyabara shirts and Bermuda shorts. They fill the bars, especially the ones made famous by Ernest Hemingway, and leave before dark to take their ship to the next island destination. Then the locals and the tourists who fill the hotels and bed and breakfast establishments come out to take their places at the bars. Key West never sleeps.

It's a small island, about a mile wide and four miles or so long. It covers a little over eight thousand acres and houses twenty-five thousand locals, who like to call themselves Conchs.

Its history is full of robber barons, pirates, thieves, wreckers, sailors, and whores. Bad people doing bad things made fortunes in every decade. In the eighties it was the drug runners based here at the end of the country, and many of the bad guys who were lured here stayed.

The Greyhound station in Key West is on the south side of the island near the airport, about as far away from the downtown section as you can get. It was going to be a long hike. I couldn't afford to be seen in a cab. A guy looking for work on the fishing boats wouldn't have the cab fare.

The elderly crowd exited the bus and began to fill up vans with the

Hyatt Hotel logo on the doors. I'd started my walk toward town when one of the vans pulled up beside me. Austin Dwyer stuck his head out of the window and said, "Ben, you going downtown?"

I nodded my head.

"Get in. We're going to the Hyatt."

It beat walking. I got in. The conversation was mostly about what they were going to do over the next few days in Key West. When we pulled into the Hyatt, I thanked the driver and Austin, hiked my backpack onto my shoulders and started up Duval Street.

I went several blocks and turned onto a side street near the Garrison Bight. I entered a neighborhood that hadn't yet seen urban renewal. The houses were old and dilapidated, and they wouldn't last long. The guys with the money would tear them down and build monuments to themselves and their successes. They'd spend a few weeks each winter in their new acquisitions and have the maids take care of it the rest of the year.

I found the house I was looking for. One of Cracker's fisherman friends from Cortez told him about this rooming house where nobody got too nosey. It was bigger than the others in the block, but just as unprepossessing. It had once been painted white, but most of that had peeled off, leaving bare clapboard. There was a large porch running along the front of the house, with a few rocking chairs placed haphazardly. They were all empty.

A screen door with rusty hinges guarded the entrance. I opened it and went in. In what had been the entrance hall in better days, there was a desk piled high with newspapers. A bulletin board took up space along one wall. It had newspaper clippings pinned to it, that I realized were help wanted ads from the local mullet wrapper. Nobody was in evidence, but a little round bell with a plunger on top sat on the desk. I hit the plunger, and in a minute a stooped elderly woman came out of the back, wiping her hands on a dishcloth.

"Help you?" she said.

"I need a room."

"How long?"

"I don't know. Can I get it from day to day?"

"Yeah, but you got to let me know by ten every morning if you're planning to stay another day."

"That's fair. How much?"

"Thirty a day. Share a bathroom."

"Okay." I pulled two twenties from my pocket and set them on the desk.

"Got to register," she said. "City ordinance." She handed me a registration card and ten wrinkled one-dollar bills in change.

I filled it out with Ben Joyce's name. "I don't have an address," I said, putting the pen down.

"Where did you come from?"

"Tampa."

"Put your last address in there. That'll do."

I made up a street address and wrote it on the card.

The old woman gave me a key. "Up the stairs, second door on your right, room eight."

I went to the room and called Logan to tell him where I was.

CHAPTER TWENTY-ONE

The Sharkstooth Bar was without atmosphere. It was a dim and dirty place where hard men came to drink themselves into oblivion. They came here early, chased by the demons that infested their lives, bringing body odor and a monumental thirst. They sat quietly, drinking their poison of choice, occasionally acknowledging each other with a joke or an observation. This was the bar from which the call to Jeff had originated the day before.

The place was small. A chipped and scarred bar of some indeterminate wood took up one side of the room. A few tables were scattered about a concrete floor. A single pool table sat across from the bar. Two men were playing a desultory game, drinking from green bottles of beer, not talking. A forlorn neon sign advertising a brand of beer I'd never heard of sputtered over the lone window, its dirty panes diffusing the light from outside. A few dim light fixtures hanging from the ceiling created a brownish glow in the room. The smell of dead fish wafted in from the nearby commercial docks.

I saw the pay phone in the corner, under a sign advertising the unisex restroom. I reached into the pocket of my cargo shorts and fingered the cell phone button that I had programmed to ring with the number on Jeff's caller ID. The pay phone rang once, and I fingered the off button. A couple of heads turned expectantly toward the phone, but returned to their drinks when it didn't ring again. Right phone, right bar.

In addition to my cargo shorts, I was wearing an old T-shirt with the faded logo of the Tampa Bay Bucs on the front. Reeboks, no socks. I sat at the bar and ordered a Miller Lite from the ancient bartender. He had a shaggy head of gray hair, bloodshot eyes, and a face so wrinkled it was hard to make out its features. He didn't say a word.

I sat quietly, nursing my beer. The customers ignored me, no one acknowledging my presence, not even the bartender. When my beer was gone, I held up the bottle and wagged it at him. He bent to the cooler and brought me another one.

"Barkeep," I said. "I'm looking for a woman who was here yesterday."

"Can't help you." he said.

I put the pictures of Peggy and Laura on the bar next to a twenty dollar bill. "Just take a look," I said.

He bent over the photos. His gnarled hand, quick as a snake, grabbed the twenty and transferred it to his pocket.

"Nope," he said. "Never saw either one of them."

I put another twenty on the bar. "Would you be kind enough to show the pictures to your customers?"

The gnarled hand made another quick swipe and the bill disappeared. He nodded his head and picked up the photos. I watched him walk the length of the bar, showing the pictures. Heads shook in the negative.

The bartender shuffled over to the pool table and held out the pictures to the two men. One of them, a big man about thirty years old, with blond hair, craggy face, and skin ruined by the sun looked over at me, locked eyes, and then looked away, shaking his head.

The bartender brought the pictures back to me. "Nobody saw them. I ain't surprised."

"Why aren't you surprised?"

"Mister, this is the kind of place where everybody takes care of his own business and don't pay no attention to anybody else's troubles. If a woman had been here, either somebody would have noticed and remembered or just not give a shit, if you know what I mean."

"What about you?"

"What about me?"

"Do you remember or just not give a shit?" I put another twenty on the bar.

The old man stared at the bill for a moment, as if making up his mind about something important. He wanted the money, but he wasn't sure what or how much he should tell me.

Finally he said, "Who are they?"

"They're my wife and daughter." The lie slid easily from my mouth.

"I used to have a wife and a daughter," he said. Something passed over his face, maybe an emotion, maybe sadness. "They left me twenty years ago. Never heard from them again."

"I'm sorry. That's tough."

"The young one was here yesterday," he said, pointing to Peggy's picture, still lying on the bar. "She came in here late in the morning, started to make a phone call, and ran out the back door when some guys came in the front door. They went after her."

"Did you know the men who came after her?"

"No. Never saw them before."

"I appreciate the help."

He took the twenty and moved to the other end of the bar.

I finished my beer, thinking about what little I had found out. Peggy had been here, and that meant she was in Key West. But, who was after her, and why? Not much to go on, but it was more than I had when I got here.

I had to assume that the men chasing her had caught her. I didn't know what that meant. Was she okay? No. Not if grown men were chasing her through a grungy bar. Maybe she'd escaped from whomever was after her, and had come to the nearest place with a phone. Tried to call her dad, but the men showed up before she could complete the connection. I'd have to try some other places in the area, see if she had been seen by anyone else.

I left money on the bar for the beer and started for the front door. One of the pool players was blocking my way. It was the big man who'd locked eyes with me before. His feet were planted firmly on the floor, spread slightly in the stance a man often assumes when he's about to knock the crap out of you. He had about four inches and fifty pounds on me. This wasn't shaping up as one of my better days.

I walked toward him, thinking he might move out of my way. He didn't. I stopped about a foot in front of him, and said, "Excuse me."

He looked mildly surprised. "Who the fuck are you?" His voice was a deep rumble tinged with the accents of the Everglades, southern, but not quite.

"Just a guy looking for his family," I said.

"I don't believe you."

"I'm sorry, but that's who I am."

I saw it in his eyes first, before his hands moved. I was a little slow as the punch came toward my face. I ducked, but not quickly enough. His fist had been heading for my jaw, but it caught me in the head, just above my left ear.

I staggered back on my right foot, stunned slightly from the blow. He was still in his flat-footed stance, but was shaking his big right paw. My head was harder than his knuckles, and I thought he'd probably busted one or two.

When I was in high school, I was trying to become a punter on the football team. This seemed to be a safer job than running with the ball and having bigger boys tackle me. The coach soon decided I was hopeless, but he tried to teach me the rudiments of kicking.

"Follow through, Royal," he'd say. "Kick the damn ball to the moon."

A nanosecond had passed since the big guy swung on me. I took aim with my right foot and kicked his family jewels to the moon. The coach would have been proud of my follow through. It raised my attacker onto his toes.

A scream escaped the big man's lips, and his face turned blood red, the pain starting to erode his features. Both hands went to his crotch, bending him forward. I turned 360 degrees, pivoting on my left foot, and brought the right foot in a soccer-style kick to his left kidney. This straightened him up some, and I ducked my head and butted him in the face.

As I backed off, I could see blood and mucus flowing from his busted nose. He fell to the floor moaning, writhing in pain. I started to kick him again, but as suddenly as it had appeared, the blood lust that had saturated my brain ebbed.

I stood there, breathing through my mouth. The whole thing had only taken a couple of seconds. I looked up to see three men coming my way. One had a pool cue held like a bat. He was lanky with roped muscles running up his arms. His unwashed hair hung to his shoulders. A scar ran from his nose back to his right ear.

I pulled the pistol out of my pocket and pointed it at them. "The guy with the cue will go first."

They stopped dead in their tracks. They were bullies and weren't used to someone else having the upper hand. They didn't know what to do. I thought I'd help them out a little. "Get on the floor, on your stomachs," I said, motioning with the pistol.

The man with the cue stick dropped it and sank to his knees and then onto his stomach. The other two followed suit.

"Who are you guys?" I asked, quietly, putting an edge to my voice.

The bar was dead silent, the bartender standing still, his hands on the bar. The two men remaining on their stools sat like statues, not moving, not even blinking. They wanted no part of this fight.

The big guy moaned and rolled over on his side. No one spoke.

"I'm going to shoot you one at a time until somebody talks," I said, and pointed the pistol at the one who'd brandished the pool cue.

"Wait," he said. "We didn't mean no harm."

I laughed. "Okay, do these jerks know who your next of kin is? Where to send your body?"

"Don't shoot," he said, his voice shaky, pleading now.

I aimed the pistol at his head. "What do you know about the woman who was here yesterday?"

"Not much. I just know the guys who were after her."

"Names."

"Charlie Calhoun and Crill somebody. I don't know his last name."

"Where can I find them?"

"I don't know. They sometimes hang out at the Mango Bar. That's all I know. Honest."

"Why in the hell did you attack me then?"

"Big Rick," he said pointing to the prostrate man who'd swung on me. "He said we could probably make a couple of bucks if we took you down and gave you to Charlie and Crill."

"Brilliant plan. Next time I see you assholes, I'll shoot you. Understand?"

"Yessir," they all said together.

The world is full of people who live their lives in a miasmal world of pure meanness. They prey upon the weak and don't know how to react when confronted by someone stronger. They figuratively adopt the canine surrender posture, rolling onto their backs, feet up, showing their vulnerability to the aggressor. They have no sense of shame in their behavior, because they see themselves as part of a pecking order. The strong devour the weak. Some days they're the stronger, and some days they're the weaker. It all works out.

I backed out of the door and left in a hurry.

CHAPTER TWENTY-TWO

I walked at a quick pace, not running, not wanting to attract attention, but in a hurry to put some room between me and the Sharkstooth Bar. I looked at my watch, a cheap one bought at the Wal-Mart in Bradenton. It was only a little after five. The sun hadn't really begun its descent yet. The tourists wouldn't be heading for the sunset show at Mallory Square for another couple of hours.

I was tired. It had been a long day, and I still had a lot to do before I could claim my bed in the rooming house. I had no idea how to identify Calhoun or Crill. I didn't think asking around in the Mango Bar made a lot of sense. I decided to call Detective Paul Galis.

I walked until I came to a church. There was a walled garden abutting the building, and a gate with a small sign announcing its availability to anyone in need of serenity. That was me. Serenity and a beer would just about revive my spirits.

I went through the gate and found a cement bench under a bougainvillea tree. Its red flowers were etched against a blue sky and surrounded by green bushes. It reminded me of Vietnam for a moment, and then I pushed that thought back to where my dark memories and even darker fears reside.

Laura wasn't with Peggy. I didn't know if that was a good sign or something worse. If she hadn't left Atlanta to find Peggy, where was she? Had she been taken by the same people who took Peggy? Was there a connection? I couldn't see one, and I thought that made Laura's disappearance even more menacing. Fear was slipping out of its chains, threatening me again with the sense of foreboding and loss that I felt whenever I'd thought about Laura over the past few days.

I pulled out my cell phone and called the Monroe County Sheriff's office. I identified myself and asked to speak to Detective Galis.

A pleasant voice came over the line carrying a faint echo of the hills of West Virginia. "David Sims said you might be getting in touch. How can I help you?"

"Did you ever hear of anybody named Charlie Calhoun or Crill, no last name?"

"Never heard of Calhoun, but a guy named Crill used to bartend over at Louie's Backyard. I heard he got into the booze pretty bad and fell on hard times. Crill isn't a name you hear very often. Might be him."

"Wouldn't know where I could find him, would you?"

"No, but I'll check around. He's hard to miss. Got a head full of red hair that he wears in spikes. Lots of gel. He has a blue birthmark that pretty much covers his right temple. How can I get ahold of you?"

I gave him my cell number and told him to leave a message if I didn't answer. I said, "Do you know where the Mango Bar is?"

He gave me directions, and said, "Be careful in there. That's a bad-ass place. If we could close it down, our crime rate would drop by fifty percent."

"I'll watch my back. I appreciate the help."

"No sweat. Sims says you're good people." He hung up.

I was a little surprised at Sims' recommendation, but maybe he'd been talking to Bill Lester and decided to help me. I'd take it where I could get it.

I dialed Jeff Timmons in Atlanta. I needed to know about Laura, and Jeff needed to know what I'd found out about Peggy. In the end, neither one of us was much help to the other. Jeff had no word on Laura, and the police were still not putting much effort into finding her.

I related what I knew about Peggy, and told him to try not to worry too much. If the men chasing the girl had meant her harm, they could have shot her in the Sharkstooth Bar, and nobody would have seen a thing.

He promised to call me as soon as he heard anything about Laura.

The Mango Bar was a step up the pecking order from the Sharkstooth, but it was a small step. It was located near the Key West side of the bridge leading to Stock Island, in an area of town that catered to the fishermen who manned the commercial boats that worked out of the nearby marinas. The bar was housed on the first floor of an old two-story building that was not aging gracefully. The second floor seemed to be empty, with several of the windows broken out. Wide double doors were open to the sidewalk. A small parking lot was next to the building. A rusting pickup truck and a beat up Mazda sedan were parked there.

I'd walked about two miles to get to the bar. I was sweaty and dusty and probably smelled like Bigfoot. I'd fit right in at a place like this.

I walked through the doors into the dim space. I stood for a moment, letting my vision acclimate to the lack of sunlight. I saw Crill at the far end of the bar, sipping from a shot glass of dark liquid. A cigarette smoldered in the ashtray in front of him. The spiked red hair and the birthmark were unmistakable. He was the only customer. The space was narrow, with four booths lining the wall across from the bar. A large fan sat atop a stand in the corner, barely stirring the sultry air in the room.

I sat at the near end of the bar, ordered a Miller Lite from the bored barmaid and paid her cash. I sipped the beer slowly, catching a steely glance now and then from the bar lady, wondering, I guess, how long I was going to sit there nursing one beer.

Crill raised his glass, and the barmaid poured him another shot from a bottle of Old Grandad. I motioned to her with my beer bottle, ordering another. I sipped some more, glancing occasionally at Crill. He seemed to be in deep contemplation, savoring his whiskey, drinking it in small swallows, wiping his mouth with the back of his hand after every taste.

An hour went by. Crill didn't move, except to raise his glass or his cigarette and wipe his mouth. He stared into his whiskey, moving only to drink or inhale or to order another shot. I wondered what he was thinking, or even if he was thinking. He drank with the single-minded dedication of the true alcoholic. I ordered another beer.

Another half hour elapsed. Crill jerked upright on his stool, as if he had felt an electric shock. His gaze swept the room, a look of consternation clouding his face. He stubbed out his cigarette, tipped the glass back, and gulped the remaining contents. He got off his stool and headed for the door. He was tall and rangy, with long arms and big hands. A tattoo of a dragon wound up his right arm, its tail trailing to his wrist, the snout covered by his shirtsleeve. He wore cutoffs, a T-shirt, and flip-flops. I let him get by me, and then followed. I planned to stay with him until I could get him alone.

As I stepped out the door, I saw the Mazda leaving the parking lot. Crill was driving it. So much for my grand plan. I was on foot and had no way to follow him.

I walked to the corner and used my cell to check for messages. Galis had called and left me an address for Crill. And a last name. McAllister.

I pulled out the city map I'd bought at a tourist stand on Duval Street earlier in the day. The address was only about a mile from where I was standing.

Darkness was descending on the town. Lights were winking on in the homes and businesses as I walked toward Crill's place. I was in an area of small clapboard houses. Most seemed to be of the shotgun variety; narrow with the rooms situated one behind the other. There was no grass to speak of in any of the yards. Chickens pecked at the dry earth, clucking their displeasure at the paucity of food. They were protected by city ordinance and roamed at will through the town. Every July there was a festival in honor of the stupid birds. Only in Key West.

By the time I found the right address, full darkness had cloaked the city. The streetlights were few in the neighborhood, and they put out scant illumination. That suited me just fine.

I was going to wring Crill dry, but I didn't look forward to it. I didn't like violence, even though I'd seen more than my share of it. Sometimes the blood lust took over, as it had at the Sharkstooth Bar. That always scared me, but it didn't happen often. I was usually in control, but sometimes I frightened the hell out of myself.

If Crill was the right guy, and I was almost sure he was, he didn't deserve much compassion. He'd chased down a scared teenager with the tenacity of a wolf, and if I had to do him violence, I would. And I would control the blood lust. If that made me a cold bastard, so be it. I just didn't want anybody to witness the act.

CHAPTER TWENTY-THREE

The house was like every other one on the street. It sat on a narrow lot with a small front yard. The Mazda was parked at an angle to the front steps that led to a porch that ran the width of the house. The green paint was peeling, and the roof had been patched with different colored shingles. Two window air-conditioning units jutted from the side of the house. Probably the bedroom and living room. A streetlight sat at the front edge of the property, giving me enough light to see the house clearly.

I climbed the three steps and knocked on the door. I had my .38 in my hand.

"Who's there?" The flinty voice of a heavy smoker.

"Key West Fire Department, Mr. McAllister," I said. "We've got a gas leak in the area and need to check your house."

The door flew open. Crill was standing there barefoot, shirt gone, wearing just the cutoffs. He had a beer in his hand.

"I ain't got no gas service here," he said. Then, realizing I wasn't the fire department, "Who the fuck are you?"

"People keep asking me that," I said, holding the pistol up so that he could see it. "Invite me in."

He stepped back from the door, raising his hands. "Be cool, my man."

"Put your hands down," I said, and walked into the house.

He backed up, keeping his eyes on me. We were in the middle of a small, sparsely furnished room. An old easy chair sat in the corner, stuffing coming out of tears in the fabric. A sofa took up one wall, a bedspread thrown haphazardly across it. A small black-and-white TV rested on a scarred table, rabbit ears drawing in a game show. The sound was turned low. The window air-conditioning unit chugged cool air into the space and made a noise like a deranged elephant.

A door led off the living room into a hallway. I knew the layout of these houses. There would be a kitchen off one side of the hall, a bedroom on the other. At the end would be a bathroom. A door at the rear of the kitchen would lead to the back yard.

The house was quiet, except for the noise from the air conditioner and Crill's heavy breathing.

I waved the gun at him. "Anybody else here?"

"No."

"If anybody comes through one of those doors, I'll shoot you."

"Nobody's here, man. Honest."

"Where is Charlie Calhoun?"

"Charlie who?"

I raised the gun, pointing it at his face. "You can do better than that."

"Okay, okay. I don't know where he is. I see him sometimes at a bar I go to."

"The Mango," I said.

"Yeah."

"Why were you chasing Peggy Timmons yesterday?"

"Who?"

"Look, dickwad, either you start talking straight to me or I'm going to start shooting you in the foot." I aimed the gun at his dirty feet.

"Okay. That the girl at the Sharkstooth?"

"Right."

"I don't know. I was drinking with Charlie at the Mango when he got a call on his cell. He offered me a hundred bucks to go with him to get the girl."

"How did you know she was at the Sharkstooth?"

"We didn't. Whoever Charlie talked to said she was walking down Benefit Street. We went over there and saw her just as she ducked into the bar."

"What happened?"

"She went out the back door and we caught her just down the alley.

Charlie put her in his car and took off. I had to hitch a ride back to the Mango to get my car."

"Did you hurt her?"

"No. She scratched the shit out of Charlie's face, though."

Good for her, I thought.

"Did you get your hundred?" I asked.

"He said he'd give it to me the next time he saw me."

I put a round into the floor between his feet. The gun made a popping sound, not loud at all. I doubted anyone in this neighborhood was likely to call the police because of a random gunshot. He jumped back, yelling in surprise. "What the hell?"

"Oops. I missed," I said, taking aim again.

"Hold on, mister. I'm telling you the truth." His voice had taken on a plaintive quality, begging, not the big man who chased a scared teenaged girl down an alley.

"I believe you," I said. "I'm going to ask you some more questions and if you lie to me I'll know it. I damn sure won't miss next time."

"Okay, okay."

"Who does Charlie work for?"

"I don't know his name. He's got a lot of money and lives out on Blood Island. He owns a massage parlor here."

"Where is Blood Island?"

"Down in the Mule Keys. He owns the whole island."

"Tell me about his massage parlor."

"It's over off Simonton. Near the Key West Bight. It's called The Heaven Can't Wait Spa."

"Crill, we never had this conversation. When I find Charlie, I'll know if you told him I was looking for him. If you do, I'll find you and kill you. Do I make myself clear?"

"Yes."

"Just forget about this evening and you'll have a longer life."

"I hear you. I never saw you."

I turned and walked out into the night.

CHAPTER TWENTY-FOUR

I had to cross the island and then head west to reach Simonton Street. Another two-mile trek. I started walking at a pace that would get me to my destination in thirty minutes. I was sweating in the evening heat, but at least I was wearing my walking shoes.

I was on Caroline Street approaching Simonton, when I noticed three men standing on the corner. One was elderly, and he seemed to be pleading with two young men, one black and the other white, who were standing on either side of him. As I got closer, I saw that the white man was one of the guys who backed up the thug with the pool cue at the Sharkstooth earlier that afternoon.

"What's going on?" I said.

"None of your business," said the black guy. "Move on."

The white guy stared at me for a moment. "Shit, that's the dude what kicked the shit out of Big Rick today. He's got a gun."

They turned and ran. I looked more closely at the shaken victim. It was Austin Dwyer, my seatmate on the bus from Marathon.

"Mr. Joyce," he said. "You're just in time."

"Are you okay?"

"Yes, thank you. Another minute or two and I might not have been."

"Glad I could help." I turned to leave.

"Ben," Dwyer said. "I was on my way to the Seaport Boardwalk for dinner. Will you join me?"

I looked at my watch. Nine o'clock. I hadn't eaten since Tampa Airport. Dwyer seemed anxious over his encounter with the thugs, and I decided to keep him company.

"Sure," I said. "I could use something."

Austin Dwyer was probably in his late seventies. He was a small man,
about five eight and couldn't have weighed more than one sixty. His ruddy
face reminded me of a happy leprechaun, a grin lighting up his features.
His head was covered in gray hair, and I could still see strands of the brown
that had been there in his youth. His accent was pure New England.

We walked the couple of blocks back to the boardwalk along the Key
West Bight, and took a table on the deck of the Turtle Kraals Bar and Grill.
Dwyer told me that he had been a history professor at a small college in
New Hampshire. When he retired, he moved to Key West, but when his
wife died, he moved back north, to Connecticut, to be closer to family. He
had taken the seniors' tour on a whim. It was sponsored by his alma mater,
the University of Rhode Island, and he thought it would be entertaining
as well as educational.

When our server came, I ordered conch chowder and blackened
grouper along with a Miller Lite. Dwyer asked for a salad and Chilean sea
bass.

"Did you ever hear of Blood Island?" I asked.

"Sure. It's down in the Mule Keys."

"Where is that?"

"Just a few miles west of here. They're part of the Key West National
Wildlife Refuge."

"Does anybody live there?"

"A couple of park rangers on Mule Key. That's about it."

"I heard that somebody lives on Blood Island."

"Maybe so. That's a private island that's not part of the refuge. I used
to fish out that way."

"What can you tell me about it?"

"Back in the Teddy Roosevelt administration the government decided that all the islands between here and the Dry Tortugas would be
part of a wildlife refuge. That includes the Marquesas Keys, which lie
between the Mule Keys and the Dry Tortugas. But, as often happens,
politics got involved. It seems that one of old Teddy's big financial supporters owned Blood Island on the western edge of the Mule Keys, out
past Boca Grande Key. It's about twelve miles from here, not far.

"A deal was struck, and the supporter was able to hold on to Blood

Island. It's the only island west of here that's not part of the Refuge," Dwyer said.

"That's an odd name for an island."

"Like everything down here, there's a story attached to it. Do you know about the *Nuestra Senora de Atocha*?"

"Sure. That's the Spanish treasure ship that Mel Fisher found."

"Right. But he wasn't the first to find it. She went down in a hurricane in September of 1622, near the Marquesas. Of the two hundred sixty-five passengers and crew aboard, only five survived, three crewmembers and two black slaves. Another ship, the *Santa Margarita,* grounded on a sandbar about three miles away, and a large number of her crew and passengers were rescued. The surviving fleet returned to Havana.

"A Spanish captain named Gaspar de Vargas found the *Atocha* within about three weeks of her sinking. Unfortunately for de Vargas, another hurricane hit in early October, and completely hid the wrecks of the *Atocha* and the *Santa Margarita*. He spent months looking for them and finally gave up.

"Four years later, a Spaniard named Melian found the *Santa Margarita*. He and his crew salvaged a great deal of its treasure and thought they knew where the *Atocha* lay. They set up camp on one of the Marquesas and worked for four years on the salvage operation. They never found the *Atocha*.

"Indians lived in the Marquesas in those days, and they sometimes helped the Spaniards and sometimes fought them. A crew in one of the small boats used in the salvage operation was blown east during a major thunderstorm in the summer of 1627. They ended up on the eastern side of what today is called Boca Grande Channel, and the sailors took shelter on a small island.

"A few days later, a search party located the beached boat and went ashore. They found the twelve men dead, their throats cut. They were lying on the beach, and their blood had soaked into the sand. They called the little island *Isla de Sangre*, Blood Island."

"That's quite a story."

"The Keys are full of grand and bloody stories," he said.

Over dinner, he regaled me with tales of bad men and good who had made the Keys what they are today. We finished our meal, and he thanked me again for helping him out of a bad situation. He stood to leave. I told him I'd stay for one more beer.

"Let me know if I can ever return the favor," he said, as we shook hands. "I'll be here another couple of days. We head north the day after tomorrow." He walked out the door with a group of people headed his way.

I sat quietly for a while, thinking about my day. My fear for Laura was escalating. I had to control that. I couldn't let my love for Laura and my fear for her safety cloud my judgment. This was just another battle in another war. I had to take charge of my emotions. I knew Laura wouldn't do anything foolish. She knew I was looking for Peggy. If she'd decided to take steps on her own, she would have let me know. She would never have left Jeff and Gwen alone and worried. Something bad had happened to her. Maybe Peggy was the key to Laura. I grabbed desperately onto that thought and banished the fear. For now.

I looked at my watch. It was nearing ten o'clock, and I still had to check out the massage parlor. I needed to find out who lived on Blood Island, and I thought I knew how to do that.

CHAPTER TWENTY-FIVE

I walked back toward Old Town, and on a little side street off Simonton, I found the Heaven Can't Wait Spa. It was housed in a Victorian mansion, its white paint gleaming in the reflected glow from the nearby streetlights. This was a more upscale part of town than where Crill lived, and the city had provided illumination more fitting to its wealthy citizens.

I walked up the wide front steps to the veranda that ran the width of the house. A porch swing hung from its chains attached to the ceiling. A discreet sign was fastened to the wall next to the door that announced the establishment's name and hours of operation. HEAVEN CAN'T WAIT SPA. OPEN UNTIL MIDNIGHT. Beneath the words was a logo of some sort, a Greek cross encircled by flowers.

I looked at my watch. Almost eleven. I could hear traffic a half block away on Simonton, not heavy this time of night, but steady. Cicadas hummed in the shrubs on either side of the porch steps. Otherwise, there was quiet. No noise escaped from the house.

I opened the door and stepped into a large foyer. The hardwood floors gleamed with fresh wax. Expensive Oriental carpets broke up the space. A wide curving stairway rose to the second floor. Off to my right I could see through open double doors to what must have been the parlor when rich people lived here. On my left was a formal dining room with a crystal chandelier hanging low over a long table surrounded by chairs with carved backs.

The foyer extended past the stairway into the back of the house. There was a Queen Anne desk sitting on a large Oriental carpet next to the stairs. A young blonde woman rose from behind the desk as I entered.

She was wearing a white gown of some light material. It covered her from neck to ankles. Her hair fell straight to her shoulders. She wore no makeup that I could see. Eyes of deep blue. Her smile was perfect. A typical white bread girl from the Midwest.

"Can I help you?" she asked in an accent of the Deep South. Alabama maybe, or Georgia. Certainly not the Midwest.

"I was told I could get a massage here," I said.

She wrinkled her pretty nose at me, assessing my shoddy attire and perhaps my less than optimal body odor. "Yes, but it's three hundred dollars for an hour," she said, her smile displaying less wattage than before.

I pulled three one hundred dollar bills from my pocket and lay them on the desk. "Okay."

She smiled again, a little less dubiously, I thought, and pointed toward the parlor. "Have a seat in there," she said, "and someone will be right with you."

"I've never been here before."

"I didn't think so."

"Is this the only place you have like this?"

"No, sir. We have branches all over the Southeast."

"What other cities?"

"Many of them. Please have a seat, sir," she said, pointing again to the parlor.

I sat. I was tired. It had been a long day, and the beers I had drunk over dinner were making me sleepy. My eyelids were drooping, and I startled myself awake. It wouldn't do to crash here.

In a few minutes another young lady came into the parlor. She was wearing the same gown as the receptionist, and looked so much like her they could have been sisters.

"Come with me, sir," she said. "I'm Sister Amy."

Sister Amy? What was this?

I followed her up the stairs, getting another smile from the receptionist as we passed her desk. Sister Amy led me into a large bedroom, with a massage table on one side. A king-size bed with a canopy took up the other side of the room. I saw a large mirror attached to the underside of the canopy, angled to give the occupants of the bed a bird's-eye view of themselves.

A door, recessed into the wall near the massage table, led to a bathroom. Sister Amy pointed toward it.

"You may take a shower, if you like," she said.

"I think I'll pass for now."

"Would you like to pray?"

"Pray? No." This was weird. "Why would we pray?"

"This is a Christian house, sir."

"No. No shower and no prayer."

"Suit yourself," she said, and undid some sort of fastener on the gown. It fell to her feet, and she stepped out of it. She was completely nude. She stood quietly, as if waiting for inspection. I complied.

She was beautiful. Her breasts were full, but not large, her stomach flat, tapering down to a thatch of blonde pubic hair. Her body was without scar or blemish, except for a small tattoo at the top of her left breast; a Greek cross in a circle of flowers.

There was something not quite right about the way she looked at me. Her blue eyes seemed dilated, and were fixed on a spot above my head. Her face and voice were devoid of animation. It was almost as if I were talking to a robot.

"Do you really want a massage?" she asked. "We can just fuck if that's what you want."

"I really don't want either," I said.

"You don't like me?"

"It's not that. You're beautiful, but I'm really looking for someone else."

She frowned slightly, as if not sure what to make of this.

"There are other girls," she said. "I'll tell Sister Barbara to send someone else up."

"No. I don't want any services."

"But Sister Barbara said you asked about a massage."

"Sister Barbara?"

"The receptionist."

"I'm looking for a girl named Peggy Timmons. Do you know her?"

"No. Is she in the Circle of Lilies?"

"Circle of Lilies? I don't understand."

"Who are you, sir?"

"I'm just a guy trying to find his daughter."

She bent to pick up her gown and wrapped it around her. I had enjoyed the scenery, and I was a little disappointed that it was now covered up.

"I'll see what I can find out," she said, and walked over to the bed and sat down. She was still, her hands folded in her lap, as if waiting for something.

I stood there for a minute, wondering what to do now. The door from the hall burst open, and a man rushed in. He was about my height and had a shaved head. He was barefoot and wore a pair of chinos and a white T-shirt that clung to his muscles. He was a weight-room freak. Probably worked out several hours a day. I wasn't in the mood for another fight.

I pulled the pistol from my pocket and pointed it at his face. He stopped in his tracks, his momentum almost pushing him forward onto his stomach. He put a foot out to catch himself. He was about six feet from me.

I said, "I don't know who you are, but you'll be dead if you take another step."

I backed up so that I had a view of the girl and the bruiser. She'd apparently activated some kind of emergency call button that had brought a bouncer on the run.

Sister Amy hadn't moved. "Bruce, he's looking for his daughter," she said.

Bruce looked at me. "What's her name?"

I shook my head. I didn't want anybody getting rid of Peggy because I was trying to find her. Bruce looked at Sister Amy.

"He said her name, but I forget," she said in that flat tone she'd been using all evening.

I lowered the pistol so that it was pointing at Bruce's chest. "Forget it pal. Just move out of the way so I can leave."

"That's not going to happen, buddy. You won't shoot me."

I shot him in the foot. He screamed in pain and fell to the floor, grabbing his bloody foot.

"Wrong," I said, and ran for the door.

As I reached the stairs, doors to other rooms were opening. Men and women in various stage of dress peered out. I took the stairs two and three at a time. As I got to the bottom, another weight lifter came out of the parlor. I pointed the gun at him, and he backed up, holding his hands in the air. I hit the front door, bounded down the porch steps, and ran toward Simonton.

I heard footsteps on the sidewalk behind me. At least two people were chasing me. I was running flat out, hoping to reach the major thoroughfare before they caught up with me.

I was fit from running on the beach, but they were in better shape. The footsteps were getting closer. I was breathing hard, used to jogging, not sprinting.

The sound of a pistol shot cracked the air. A bullet gouged a chunk of cement from the sidewalk near my left foot. I dove to my right, into the hedge that lined the sidewalk.

I could see my pursuers through the leaves of the bushes in which I landed. There were two of them, the one from the parlor and another brute. They were still coming, running. I had the .38 in my hand. I raised it and shot the parlor guy. He grabbed his gut and fell to his knees. His buddy dove into the shrubs less than twenty feet from me. Lights came on in the house behind the bushes.

I took off again, rounding the corner onto Simonton, where I saw two bicycles propped against a low wall. A young couple was sitting on the nearby grass, holding hands, talking quietly. I grabbed the closest bike, a girl's model, jumped aboard, and pedaled off. The young man hollered at me, but I didn't look back. I didn't think he'd leave his girl to chase me.

I headed southeast on Simonton, riding the sidewalk, staying in the shadows of the trees lining the road. I was passing city hall when a police cruiser pulled into my path. I came to a stop as the patrolman got out of his vehicle. I waited, straddling the bike. He walked toward me, his hand resting near the gun holstered on his equipment belt.

Oh, shit, I thought. *Oh, shit.*

CHAPTER TWENTY-SIX

The cop walked up to me. "Good evening, sir," he said. "Are you visiting with us?"

"I am."

"Then you're probably not aware of the city ordinance against riding a bike on the sidewalk."

"I'm sorry, Officer," I said, breathing a sigh of relief, "I wasn't."

"That's why we painted a bike lane on the major streets," he said, pointing to the now obvious bike lanes that ran on either side of Simonton. "We don't want you running down our old folks."

"You're right. I'll stay off the sidewalk."

"Have a good evening, sir," he said, and climbed back into his patrol car.

I moved into the bike lane and a couple of blocks later, turned left off Simonton and rode to within a couple of blocks of my rooming house. I left the bike on the side of the road leaning against a pole topped by a bus stop sign. It probably wouldn't be there in the morning. I felt bad for the kid who owned it, but sometimes one has to improvise.

I went to my room, got my shaving kit, and walked down the hall to the bathroom. Nobody was using it. I climbed into the shower stall and turned on the water. A trickle of cold rust colored liquid sputtered out of the showerhead. It'd have to do. I was too tired and dirty to worry about what kind of crap had taken up residence in the old pipes.

I crawled into bed, but couldn't sleep. The mattress was lumpy and the pillow hard as a rock. My mind was churning with images of young blonde nudes and shot-up bad guys. I hoped the one on the street didn't die, but I'd taken the only shot I had. I wondered what the hell Peggy had gotten herself into.

What was the connection between a high-class whorehouse in Key West, a place called Blood Island, and a student at the University of Georgia? What kind of joint called their whores Sister and prayed before copulation? Did Sister Amy's tattoo have any significance? It must have, since it was identical to the logo on the front door sign. Was any of this connected to the deaths of Wayne Lee and Clyde Varn? To the shootings at Coquina Beach and Hutch's? To the vulture pit guy? To Laura's disappearance?

I fell into a fitful sleep and dreamed of dead Spaniards and sunken ships and tattooed blondes.

CHAPTER TWENTY-SEVEN

I awoke the next morning, still tired. A dream lingered for a moment in my consciousness and then slipped away, as elusive as a handful of fog.

Sunlight was streaming through the dirty window into my room. I'd left it open during the night to catch what little breeze came by. I could hear birds trilling in the trees of the backyard, and the blasted chickens clucking on the grounds. In the distance, a rooster crowed, perhaps calling his hens for a little morning delight.

I stumbled to the bathroom just as a desiccated man was coming out. I washed my face and brushed my teeth, went back to the room and dressed in fresh clothes. It was a little after seven.

I stopped by the desk on my way out and gave the elderly woman thirty dollars for another night. I passed the bus stop where I had left the bike the night before. It wasn't there.

I walked a block to a small café that hunkered under a gumbo-limbo tree, its reddish bark the color of a tourist too long in the sun. There was a small grocery store attached to the restaurant, and I went in.

In Key West every kind of store carries nautical charts and gear. I bought a large-scale chart that covered the Lower Keys out to the Dry Tortugas, and a book of aerial photos of the Keys. I also picked up a copy of the local newspaper. I took them with me into the restaurant and ordered breakfast. I scanned the paper for any news of the shooting at the Heaven Can't Wait Spa, but there was nothing. My breakfast came and I ate while studying the chart.

I found Blood Island just where Austin Dwyer said it would be, out on the edge of the Boca Grande Channel. It was small, perhaps a half mile square. It was shaped like a crab, with a lagoon almost enclosed by arms of the island encircling it on either side. The water around the island was very shallow, and the only deep channel was the one that ran from the channel into the lagoon. The controlling depth was twenty feet in the protected area of the lagoon and less than ten feet in the entry channel. A big boat couldn't make it in without running aground.

I opened my book of photos and thumbed to the pictures of the Mule Keys. There was one that took in Woman and Boca Grande Keys and Blood Island. The colors of the water were stunning, showing all the shades of a tropical sea. I compared the photograph with the chart, and could see the turquoise shallows fading to the azure colors in the deep channel.

Blood Island had no beach, except in the lagoon. Several varieties of palm trees and Australian pines blanketed the island and mangrove forests ran right down to the water. They would be almost impenetrable to anyone trying to sneak ashore.

I finished breakfast and left the café. I called Debbie as soon as I got to the street.

"You've got to start sleeping later," she said, as she picked up the phone.

"I know, babe, but I need you."

"Yeah, you say that now, but not when I'm awake and horny."

I chuckled. Debbie was about as interested in me as she was in Logan, which wasn't much. She was a good friend.

"See what you can find out about a place west of Key West called Blood Island. Who owns it, what goes on there, etcetera. I also need to know who owns a piece of property in Key West." I gave her the address of the Heaven Can't Wait Spa.

"When do you need this?"

"Now."

"How do you know I don't have a playmate in bed with me this morning?"

"I know you, Deb. You're too picky for the local guys."

She laughed. "Don't be too sure," she said, and hung up.

I called Jeff Timmons. Nothing new on Laura. He was beginning to lose his equanimity, to panic. I could hear it in his voice, the quaver that hadn't been there before. She'd been gone for the better part of three days, and there had been no sign of her. The police still weren't excited about it. I told him I didn't have any more information for him on Peggy, but that I was still looking.

Peggy was important to me, but that was mostly because she was important to Laura. On the other hand, I had loved Laura for a long time, and the thought of not having her somewhere in the world, alive, breathing, and thinking occasionally of me, was stoking my fears for her safety. Where the hell was she? If I could find Peggy, maybe she would hold the key to Laura. That thought added a layer of urgency to my already revved-up intensity. I had to find the women.

It was time to get a better look at Blood Island. I walked over to Garrison Bight and rented an eighteen-foot Grady-White boat with a 150-horsepower outboard hanging off the transom. I only had to go twelve miles to Blood Island, but sometimes the seas in these latitudes kick up without much warning. If that happened, the Grady could take it without breaking a sweat.

I gave the attendant Ben Joyce's credit card and showed him the ID. He asked me a couple of questions to see if I knew how to handle a boat, and handed me the keys.

I bought a fishing rod and some bait from the tackle shop next door, and climbed down into the boat. I put the rod in its holder, cranked the engine, and motored out of the entrance to the bight. I passed the waterfront homes of the Naval officers who manned the facilities at the military installations that remained at the end of the continental U.S., and turned left into the main channel.

The seas were flat that early in the morning, and I made good time on a westerly course. I passed the western-most of the Mule Keys and eased up to Blood Island. I rode around it, seeing nothing but mangroves hugging the water. As I came to the eastern side I saw the deeper water of the cut leading around the island from Boca Grande Channel into the lagoon.

I stopped the boat and let if drift, the engine idling quietly. I put a frozen shrimp on my hook and dropped it into the water. I could see the bottom at any depth along the island. Farther out, in the Boca Grande Channel, the water turned a dark blue, indicating deep water.

My VHF radio came to life.

"The small boat off Blood Island. Please be advised that this is a private island. No trespassing is allowed. Trespassers will be shot on sight. Do you copy?"

I keyed my mic. "I copy Blood Island. Thanks for the warning."

"Remember it," the radio squawked.

Nice people, I thought. I pulled in my line and completed a circle of the island. The only place to land was in the lagoon. I was sure the approach was watched, so the radio message seemed a little superfluous. Maybe they just wanted to make a point.

I came back around to the east side, near the channel to the lagoon, and drifted. I picked up the binoculars that were part of the boat's equipment. I scanned the area around the passage into the lagoon. The island, like all the keys, was flat. There were large trees covering the spits of land that surrounded the lagoon. There was a dock protruding into the water from the main part of the island. Two go-fast boats were tied to either side, bows facing out.

I scanned carefully, but couldn't see any sign of life. Then, a glint of metal in one of the trees near the mouth of the lagoon. I focused on it, moving my vision on and off the target area, just as the Army had taught me long ago.

Then, I saw it. A slight movement, and another glint of sunlight off metal. I could make out a man sitting on a platform high in the branches of a large tree. He had a rifle cradled in his arms and was scanning with his own binoculars. I couldn't make out his features, but he was occupying what seemed to be a guard post. It had rails around the edges and a ladder reaching down to the ground. It had a roof from which rose a radio antenna, almost hidden by the tree branches.

I put my binoculars down and picked up my fishing rod. If he was looking for me, I didn't want him to see me looking for him. I fished for a few minutes, paying no attention to the island. I could feel the guard's eyes on me.

Twenty minutes or so elapsed before I put the engine in gear and slowly motored over the shallows. As I reached deeper water, I brought the boat on plane and headed back to Key West.

CHAPTER TWENTY-EIGHT

I went back to Garrison Bight and moored the boat at the rental company's dock. I told the attendant that I wanted to try some night fishing, and paid him for another day. He told me to keep the keys and take the boat when I wanted it.

I walked a couple of blocks to a dive shop I'd passed earlier in the day. I picked out a complete outfit, including a neoprene wet suit with hood, dual tanks, regulator, buoyancy compensator, weight belt, fins, mask, gauges, and computer. I took it to the counter and asked a young man with a surfer hairdo to fill the tanks for me.

"I need to see your certification card," he said.

"I don't have it with me."

"I can't fill the tanks without the card."

"Look," I said. "I'm buying, what, three grand worth of equipment here? It's of no use to me without air in the tanks."

"Sorry, I just work here."

"Suppose I called the purchases thirty-five hundred even, the last five hundred in cash. Would that get me some air?"

"That it would, my man."

He took the tanks and disappeared into the back of the store. I could hear an air compressor crank up and chug along for a few minutes. Soon, he was back.

I hooked the gauges to the tanks to make sure they were full, and gave him five one hundred dollar bills plus Ben's credit card.

"Can you hang on to the equipment for me until this evening?" I asked.

"Sure, but we close at seven."

"I'll be back by then. Thanks."

It was nearing noon when I called Debbie. "Got anything?" I asked.

"Some. The island is owned by a Bahamian corporation which in turn is owned by a Cayman Islands corporation whose shares are held by a Cayman bank."

"That sounds familiar," I said, remembering what Bill Lester had found out about the owner of Varn's condo. "What's the name?"

"Circle Ltd."

"Do me a favor and call Bill Lester when we hang up. Find out the name of the corporation that owned Clyde Varn's condo. I'll bet it's the same one."

"Will do. There wasn't a whole lot on the island. The Monroe County property records show that the Yates family from New York owned it for about a hundred years. They sold it to Circle three years ago."

"What was the price tag?"

"Two million bucks."

"Anything else?"

"A house was built on the island about fifty years ago to replace one that burned down. I downloaded the plans from the building department. It's a big house with a cistern on the roof to catch rainwater.

"About twenty years ago, the Yates family got a permit to install a diesel generator on the property and to build six guest cabins for family members. Not much other than that."

"What about the spa?"

"The property's owned by a Bahamian corporation. It's the same one that owns the island."

"Thanks Deb. Let me know what the chief says about Circle. Can you fax me a copy of the house plans?"

"Yeah. I'll also send you the plat on the permit to build the cabins. Give me a number."

"Send it to the Key West Police Department with a cover sheet to Detective Paul Galis, and ask him to hold it for me."

"Will do. I'll get back to you on the corporation."

"I'll call you back later this afternoon. While you're at it, find out what you can on a Reverend Robert William Simmermon."

"Sure thing, old pal. Anything else? Like the Yankee box scores for 1947?"

"Nobody loves a smart-ass, Deb," I said, and hung up.

I called Paul Galis and told him I was on my way over and to watch for the fax from Debbie.

I was tired of walking, and I had about decided that I was being a little silly in my precautions. If anybody was watching me, they knew by now that I wasn't destitute.

I took a cab from Garrison Bight to the Monroe County Sheriff's Office. It was a modern three-story building next to the jail on Stock Island. I showed my identification, my real one, at the front desk and was given a visitor's pass to clip to my shirt collar. I was still wearing running shoes and my cargo shorts from the day before, but with a clean golf shirt. A woman in civilian clothes escorted me to Galis's office.

The detective division was housed on the third floor. Galis had enough seniority to warrant a small office with a view over the water to the Naval installation on Dredger's Key.

He stood as I entered his office. He was a couple of inches shorter than I and had a head full of brown hair parted on the left. I guessed his age as late forties or early fifties. He was wringing his hands, wiping them together as if he were washing them. A small metal logo of the U.S. Army Special Forces was pinned to the lapel of his suit coat.

"I see that you used to wear a green beanie." I said.

"Right. I heard you did too."

"I did."

"David Sims told me a lot about you. I figured we Special Forces guys have to stick together. I told him I'd give you whatever help I could."

"I appreciate it. Were you in Nam?"

"At the tail end. How about you?"

"About the same time," I said.

"I've got a fax for you that came in a little while ago."

He handed over the sheets of paper. We were finished talking about the war. Some things just don't need to be examined too closely. Who needs the pain?

The first sheet of paper had a note scribbled on it. "The same corporation that owns Blood Island also owns Varn's condo." I wasn't surprised.

"Tell me what I can do for you?" Galis said, dry washing his hands.

He noticed I was looking at his hands. He smiled a little sheepishly and said, "Nervous habit. I'm a worrier."

"What are you worried about?"

"Nothing. Everything. I think it comes from working for the government too long. How can I help you?"

"I'm looking for a girl who disappeared from Longboat Key about four weeks ago. Two days ago her father, Jeff Timmons, got a call from a bar here called the Sharkstooth."

"Bad place."

"I agree. The caller hung up before Jeff got to the phone, but his caller ID captured the number. He called it and got the pay phone in the bar. There were a couple of murders up my way that had connections that led to Key West. The murders and the phone call all pointed to here, so I thought I'd come down and see what I could find out."

"Sims brought me up to speed on the murders. Any luck?"

"Some guys at the Sharkstooth told me about Crill and, after you gave me his address, I paid him a visit."

"Wait a minute. The people that hang out in the Sharkstooth aren't the kind to tell tales."

"I'm pretty persuasive sometimes."

"You're the one who took out Big Rick." It wasn't a question.

"Maybe."

"He's been pushing people around for years. About time somebody laid a hurting on him."

"How is he?"

"In the hospital. He'll live, but his reputation as a hotshot took a beating."

I changed the subject. "What can you tell me about Blood Island?"

"What do you want to know?"

"Who lives there?"

"No idea. It's technically in our jurisdiction, and I guess if there were ever a crime committed out there, we'd look into it. But it's a quiet place."

"Never had any trouble at all?"

"None. There aren't many people on the island. I think the owners come in occasionally, but the only year-round residents are the caretakers."

"How many of them?"

"Don't know. Never had a reason to find out."

"What do you know about the Heaven Can't Wait Spa?"

"You mean the whorehouse?"

I chuckled. "You know about that, huh?"

"Sure. But it's a clean operation, and I've never heard of any trouble there. No complaints from the citizens. We'll leave it alone unless somebody starts raising hell about it."

"Do you know who owns it?"

"Some corporation based in the Bahamas is all I know. God knows who owns the corporation."

"Did you know that Blood Island is also owned by a Bahamian corporation?"

"No, but I'm not surprised. There've always been a lot of Bahamians in and out of Key West. They're bound to own some property."

I told him about Clyde Varn and that the same corporation that owned Blood Island also owned Varn's Tampa condo. I explained all the connections that seemed to converge on Key West; the shooter at Hutch's, Varn, the phone call from the Sharkstooth Bar to Jeff Timmons.

"That's a lot of coincidences," he said.

"I don't put much faith in coincidences."

"Nah. Neither do I."

"Have you ever heard of an evangelist named Robert William Simmermon?"

"No. Who is he?"

"I'm not sure. Clyde Varn told me he left Peggy and her friends at an arena in Sarasota. Simmermon was preaching there at the time. Later, he came to Key West."

"One more coincidence," Galis said.

"Let me show you something." I picked up a pencil from the detective's desk and drew a reasonably accurate picture of the cross in the circle of flowers I'd seen on Sister Amy's breast and at the front door of the spa. I passed it over to him. "Does this mean anything to you?"

He looked at it for a moment. "No, I don't think I've ever seen it. What is it?"

I told him where I'd seen it.

"You mean," he said, "that you just went into that whorehouse and asked the first girl you came to if she knew Peggy?"

"Yeah. It wasn't the smartest thing I've ever done. But, I wanted to see if I'd get a reaction."

"And did you?"

"Oh, yeah." I told him what had happened, but left out the part about my shooting one of my pursuers. I didn't think he'd like that I was shooting up his town and stealing kids' bicycles.

"I outran them," I said.

"This is a strange town in many ways, Matt. We've got a lot of odd people, and some of them are just bone-deep bad. But most of the people who live here are decent law-abiding folks. My job is keeping the bad guys from taking over from the good guys. I need to know which you are. Good guy or bad guy?"

"I'm on your side, Paul. But if I get pushed, I push back. Like they taught us at Bragg."

"They taught us about war, Matt. Key West isn't a war zone. Not yet, anyway."

CHAPTER TWENTY-NINE

Galis offered me lunch and a ride back to Old Town. I declined both. I didn't want anybody to see me eating with a cop or getting out of a police cruiser. He called a cab, and I had it drop me a couple of blocks from the yacht basin at Garrison Bight. I didn't think anybody was looking for me, but I wanted to stay as inconspicuous as possible.

It was almost two in the afternoon, and I was hungry. I found a diner on Roosevelt Avenue that seemed to cater to the captains and crews of Charter Boat Row. I sat at the counter and ate a burger and fries. I finished, paid my tab, and walked out onto the street.

A black Lincoln Town Car sat idling at the curb. As I left the building, a large man in a dark suit got out of the front seat and approached me. I stopped. Wary, not expecting this.

"Mr. Royal," the man said. "Please come with me." He motioned to the car.

It took a moment for me to realize I'd been called by my real name. As far as I knew, no one in Key West, except Paul Galis, knew who I was. I started to deny that my name was Royal, when he opened his coat to show me a holstered pistol.

My gun was still in my pocket, but I couldn't imagine a shootout on a sunny street across from a busy marina. There were people all around, and someone would get hit. Galis was right. Key West shouldn't be a war zone.

The man smiled. "Cracker Dix sent me," he said.

Relief spread through me as my body relaxed. The adrenaline rush was subsiding, the bunched muscles loosening.

The man opened the back door and I slid into the car. An older man with receding gray hair was sitting on the other side of the back seat. His face showed the scars of a long-ago battle with acne. He was swarthy, and had a mouth full of large white teeth. He was dressed casually. He held out his hand. I took it.

"I'm Oscar Mendosa," he said. "I've been looking for you."

"How did you find me?"

"Cracker told me you might be using the name Ben Joyce. He also e-mailed us a picture of you." He held out a picture of me taken by Cracker on a recent fishing trip to Boca Ciega Bay.

Mendosa continued. "When you bought the diving gear this morning, Ben Joyce's name popped up in our computers. We talked to the young man at the dive shop, and he told us you were coming back this evening. I've had men here all day, and when one saw you go into the diner, he called me."

"Why were you looking for me?"

"I owe Cracker a great deal. If I can repay part of that debt by helping his friend, I'd like to do so."

"I appreciate it, Mr. Mendosa, but I don't really need any help."

"I think you do. Somebody is trying to kill you."

"Who?"

"I'm not sure. Somebody has put a bounty on you."

"A bounty? What are you talking about?"

"Pictures of you are circulating around town, and the word is that whoever calls a certain phone number with your whereabouts will get a thousand dollar reward. There are men in this town who would sell their mothers for a grand."

He held out another photo, a grainy black-and-white print. This one was taken of me at the whorehouse the evening before. I was standing in the entry hall talking to the receptionist. A security camera.

"Do you know who's behind this?" I asked.

"No. The phone number goes to an answering machine that tells the caller to leave his name and number and someone will get in touch. I left a number, and got a callback inside of ten minutes. I played dumb and hung up."

"Are you familiar with the Heaven Can't Wait Spa?"

"Oh, yes." He chuckled. "The religious whorehouse."

"Who owns it?"

"No idea. Our business does not deal in whores, so I never cared to find out. I've just heard stories about the place."

"I appreciate your bringing this to my attention, Mr. Mendosa. I'll be careful."

"I can give you some men to back you up."

"That's very kind, but I've got a lot to do in the next couple of days, and I have to do it alone."

He reached into his pocket and extracted a business card. He handed it to me. It had nothing on it but a phone number.

"This number," he said, "is answered twenty-four hours a day. Call it if you need anything."

"Thank you."

We shook hands, and I got out of the car. It glided silently into traffic and was gone.

CHAPTER THIRTY

It was mid-afternoon, and hot. The breeze off the water was negligible. Spring was beginning to turn into summer, and soon the days would all be hot and humid.

A few of the charter boats had returned from the day's fishing. A small group of tourists, a family perhaps, with too much red skin, was standing on the dock behind a moored boat. One of them, a teenaged boy, held a string of fish in his hands. The captain was taking their picture as they stood with goofy grins next to a sign advertising his services. A young man wearing only cutoffs was washing down the boat. A half dozen pelicans floated in the basin, waiting for the fish scraps they knew would be coming from the cleaning tables. Cars and trucks rumbled by on Roosevelt Avenue, leaving the smell of exhaust hovering over the docks.

I looked at the scene, picturing what the camera would catch, that instant in time when the family was together, happiness evident in their grins. The photograph would also hold the image of the boy cleaning the boat, and probably the pelicans lazing in the sun.

I wondered about that picture, about what would happen to it after it was admired and put away. Maybe one day an old man would pull it from a drawer, gaze at it, and remember when he was a teenager holding a string of fish, happy to be with his parents, now long dead. Would he wonder about the life lived by the boy washing the boat? Would he put the picture back in the drawer, never to be seen again? Life is fleeting, and when we near the end, we grab our memories and hold onto them with a ferocity that eluded us at the time of their creation.

I had a lot of time to kill. I couldn't do anything before dark, and I didn't want to go back to my room. If people were looking for me, they might have located the rooming house.

I stopped in a souvenir shop on Palm Avenue and bought a khaki-colored baseball cap with a sailfish and the words "Key West" embroidered on the front. I wore it out of the shop, keeping the bill low on my eyes. My dark sunglasses would help cover my face, and I didn't think a casual observer would recognize me.

I decided to visit the cemetery where the monument to the battleship *Maine* was located. The fabled ship, whose demise gave an excuse for the Spanish-American War, had sailed from Key West on its fateful journey to Havana Harbor. Many of its sailors were buried in this last piece of America they experienced.

I was walking idly down Angela Street when I saw a familiar figure cross the road in the next block. It was Michelle Browne, the lady who had introduced herself in Sarasota as the Reverend Robert William Simmermon's assistant. She was wearing a beige skirt, dark blue blouse, and sensible white pumps. Her auburn hair was in a ponytail, and her bracelets glinted in the sun.

She was walking at a fast clip, as if she were on an errand. I decided to follow her. I held back a half block and ambled along, looking at the houses that lined the street, trying for inconspicuousness.

She walked the four blocks to the Key West Bight and entered a waterfront restaurant. I followed, motioning to the hostess that I would take a seat at the bar. Michelle joined a man sitting at a table by the open deck overlooking the harbor. He stood as she approached. He was about six feet tall, slender, with white hair and a red face that looked as if he had spent too much time in the sun. The Reverend Simmermon, in the flesh. He was a lot younger than I'd guessed. Early thirties, probably. The white hair made him look older, but his features were that of a younger man.

The wall behind the bar was mirrored. I could sit facing forward and have a reflected view of Michelle and her companion. I ordered a draft beer and sipped it while watching my quarry.

They were sitting at the table sipping wine, talking quietly. Occasionally, one or the other would gesture or smile. The meeting and conversation had the look of two old friends enjoying the afternoon. After about ten minutes, Michelle sat back in her chair, a look of chagrin on her face. Then she moved in close, elbows on the table, her face a mask of anger, words coming fast. Simmermon tried to take her hand, but she jerked it back. He made a placating gesture, tried a smile, reached for her again.

Michelle stood, her napkin falling off her lap onto the floor. She said something I couldn't hear and walked out the front door. Simmermon stood, dropped some bills on the table, and left the restaurant.

I followed, hoping to get him alone. He walked quickly to the dock in front of the restaurant. There was a go-fast boat, similar to the ones I had seen moored at Blood Island, tied to a piling, its big engines idling. A large man wearing shorts, a white T-shirt, and a dark tan was untying the line as the evangelist clambered down into it and sat in the passenger seat. The other man took the helm seat, touched the throttles, and the boat pulled away from the dock, heading out of the basin.

I turned and ran for the street, hoping to catch sight of Michelle. As I rounded the corner of the restaurant onto Margaret Street, I saw her turning onto Eaton Street. I followed at a fast walk, catching up to her as she turned onto Simonton, and then quickly made another turn off the main thoroughfare. I knew where she was going.

I hung back now, letting her go. When I got to the next corner and looked down the side street, she was out of sight. In the middle of the block sat the Victorian mansion that housed the Heaven Can't Wait Spa.

CHAPTER THIRTY-ONE

I sat on the sidewalk, my hat pulled down over my eyes, my back leaning against a brick retaining wall in front of the house two doors down from the spa. Just one more of Key West's homeless, taking a siesta.

At four o'clock, I saw Michelle come out of the front door, accompanied by a man who looked vaguely familiar. She was talking and he was nodding his head. They stopped at the end of the walk, and he looked around briefly, surveying his surroundings. His face turned toward me, but his gaze didn't stop. I knew him. It was the truck driver Michelle had spoken to in Venice.

They shook hands, and the man returned to the spa. Michelle started walking along the street, going away from me. I got to my feet and followed at a safe distance. She turned at the corner and walked two blocks. I hung back, allowing her to put some space between us, but not enough to lose her.

In the middle of the third block, she opened a gate to a sidewalk leading to another Victorian house. I stopped, giving her time to get inside. She used a key to open the door.

I walked past the house, taking a good look. It was like every house in the neighborhood, old and beautiful, and probably modernized inside. I made a mental note of the address.

I turned the corner and, out of sight of the house, pulled out my cell phone. I caught Debbie just as she was leaving for work.

"This is getting to be a bad habit, Royal," she said. "What now?"

"I just called to hear your voice, sweet cakes."

"Right." She laughed. "I've got about five minutes to get to work. What is it?"

"I need the ownership of a house in Key West." I gave her the address. "And what did you find out about Simmermon?"

"Nothing yet on Simmermon, other than his Web site. I'll check deeper when I get off tonight. Keep your phone on. I'll call you back in a couple of minutes with the information on the house." She hung up.

I sat back down on the sidewalk, leaning on another retaining wall, hat pulled low. A profusion of jasmine flowers cascaded down the brick wall, their sweet smell somehow comforting. In a couple of minutes, my phone rang.

"Guess what?" Debbie said.

"The house is owned by a Bahamian corporation controlled by a Cayman bank."

"If you're such a genius, why are you bothering me?"

"Lucky guess. I wanted to make sure. Same corporation?"

"Yes. Circle Ltd."

"Thanks, kid. I owe you."

"Right. Take care of your sorry butt, Matt. I'd miss the big tips. I'm saving all those quarters you leave." There was a click, and she was gone.

I sat for a while, wondering if I should confront Michelle. I'd made a mistake going to the spa, questioning Sister Amy, and generally acting like an idiot. I hadn't done my homework on the place, and my search almost ended right there. By asking about Peggy, I may have put her in more danger. Time was critical. I had to know what was going on.

I walked onto the veranda of Michelle's house and rang the bell. She opened the door, wearing a big smile. She had changed clothes and was dressed casually in a pair of blue shorts and a halter top. Her hair was in a ponytail, and she was barefoot. Her lovely fingers were wrapped around the grip of a nine-millimeter pistol, pointed at my chest.

CHAPTER THIRTY-TWO

"Come in, Mr. Royal," Michelle said. "We've been expecting you."

Uh-oh. This couldn't be good. But, I'd never refused the offer of a pretty young woman, especially if she was holding a gun on me. I entered the house as Michelle backed into the foyer, gun pointed directly at my gut. I didn't doubt that she would gladly put one into my heart if I didn't do what she said.

She waved me into the living room off the foyer. "That was a pretty good picture our security camera got at the spa," she said. "I recognized you immediately."

The truck driver was sitting at ease in a recliner, no weapon in sight. He stood and frisked me. He took the .38 out of my pocket and put it on a table next to his chair. He sat back down, crossed one leg over his knee, and grinned.

He was a big man, with oversized muscles bulging out his T-shirt sleeves. His dark hair was cropped close, and his face wore the quizzical look affected by so many body builders who make up for their lack of brains with a lot of brawn. Three angry scratch marks ran the length of his left cheek. Peggy had taken a hunk out of his hide.

I wondered how he had gotten to Michelle's house without my seeing him, but then realized he could have come through the backyard.

Michelle nodded in the man's direction, and said, "Charlie recognized you on the street a few minutes ago. He thought you were following me."

"Mr. Calhoun, I presume," I said.

A momentary look of surprise crossed his face. "How do you know my name?" he asked.

"You're a famous street punk. Everybody tells me you're as stupid as you look. I wonder if that's possible."

He was coming out of his chair. "You smart-ass son of a bitch. You shot my buddies."

"Sit, Charlie," Michelle said, and like an obedient dog, he fell back into the chair.

"Minds well," I said.

"You might want to be careful, Mr. Royal. I might just let him loose on you."

"Please, call me Matt. We're all friends here."

"Sit on the sofa," she said, and took a chair directly across from me. I sat. There was a low coffee table between us, a large flat book of photographs of the Florida Keys lying on top.

"Why are you here, Matt?" Michelle asked.

"I'm looking for a girl. An eighteen-year-old college student named Peggy Timmons. The same girl old Charlie here was chasing a couple of days ago. I heard she just about took him. Looks like she marked him up pretty good."

Charlie started to rise again, a look of irritation on his face. "I'll kick your ass," he growled.

"Sit, Charlie," said Michelle, again.

"But, Michelle," Charlie said.

"Sit." Louder this time.

Charlie sat, but he didn't like it.

I looked at him and smiled. "You're a lot safer doing what the lady tells you, Charlie."

He started out of the chair again, but went back down at one look from Michelle. He wanted to tear my head off and, if I kept goading him, sooner or later he was going to take his shot. I was counting on it.

I heard a clock chime somewhere in the back of the house. Five o'clock. The light was slanting through the west-fronting windows now, little dust motes hovering in the beams. I heard a motor scooter pass on the street, and somewhere in the distance a ship's horn sounded. One of the cruise ships was leaving its dock, full of sunburned tourists heading for the next island.

I smiled at Michelle. "Are you going to tell me where to find Peggy?"

She smiled back. "No."

"What about her mother, Laura Timmons?"

"Who?" Michelle looked puzzled, as if she'd never heard the name before.

"Maybe I'll have to ask Reverend Simmermon," I said.

She and Charlie both laughed, quickly, snorts really, rather than laughter. "You think that idiot runs things?" Michelle asked.

"His picture is on Charlie's truck," I said.

She chuckled this time. "Yeah, I kind of let him think he's running things sometimes. It helps keep his ego in check."

"Is he on Blood Island?"

She looked mildly surprised. "My, my, you've been a very busy boy."

"Look, Michelle, I don't care what you've got going with the spa or anything else. I just want the girl."

"I can't let that happen, Matt. It's too late."

"Why is that?"

"She's seen more of our operation than is healthy."

"And Laura?"

"I don't know anybody named Laura. And if she's Peggy's mother, she'd be a little long in the tooth for our needs."

"I'm not sure I understand your operation. Do you kidnap these kids into prostitution?"

"Lord, no." She laughed. "These kids come from all over to find the light. They're all looking for something, and when the Rev gets through with them, they know they've found God. Or at least the Rev's idea of God."

"I don't get it."

"The Rev has a twisted view of Christianity. I'm not sure he believes it himself, but he sure can sell it to stupid people."

"What happens to the kids?"

"Most of them are girls. We sort of reprogram them and put them in the spas. They think they're hooking for Jesus. They're idiots."

I sat quietly for a moment, remembering the vacant look in Sister Amy's eyes. "You're drugging them," I said, my voice flat.

"Of course we are." Michelle let out a short laugh, like I'd just said something stupid. "How else are we going to keep them down on the farm? Or the spa?" She was enjoying herself.

I crossed my right leg over my left knee, swinging my foot rhythmically, feigning indifference to my situation. "How do you recruit them?" I said.

"Easy. The lost ones are always at the revivals. We do a preliminary look-see, chat them up, and, if they don't seem too smart, we put somebody on them to find out more."

"Like Jake Yardley," I said.

"Exactly."

"Then what?"

"We invite them down to Blood Island for a retreat. A few doses of certain drugs in their food, and they're ours. The Rev preaches to them, takes an interest in them, and tells them we love them. He usually screws the girls for good measure. Then we send them to the Heaven Can't Wait Spa. They've joined the Circle of Lilies. They think it's some kind of religious order."

"It's not?"

She laughed again. "I guess it's what the little bitches make out of it. When they've been there a while, and they're docile enough, we send them to our spas in other cities."

"And the boys?"

"They stay on the island to work and pray. They're fed and housed, and they're pretty happy. There're only a few guys."

"What happened to Yardley?"

"He got careless. For some reason, he put his name and address on the motel registration, and you found him. He had to be eliminated."

"Just like that? You kill a man over a mistake?"

"Happens sometimes," she said. "Just the cost of doing business. The fool called the Rev to tell him you were looking for one of the girls we recruited."

"Why leave his body on Longboat Key? And who killed Wayne Lee?"

"Bartel did that. He thought posing Yardley's body in that park was a work of genius. And he killed Lee to make sure he couldn't pass on anything Yardley had told him."

"And then Bartel tried to set me up at Hutch's," I said, a statement, not a question.

"That's right. And he blew it. I had to get somebody else to take out your buddy Hamilton."

"That didn't work either."

"No."

"Maybe you ought to start hiring better people."

"You have a point," she said, grinning.

"What happened with Peggy Timmons? She's not stupid."

"We found that out. That was another mistake Yardley made. He sent her three buddies on their way, but he gave Peggy to the Rev. That big idiot took her to his island and wants to keep her for himself. Thinks he's in love. He didn't count on her family hiring you to come looking for her."

"Is she on the island now?"

Michelle shrugged her shoulders. "It doesn't matter."

"You don't know where she is, do you?" I asked. "Maybe you don't have as much control as you think."

Charlie stirred in his chair. "I took her little ass back to the island," he said.

"Be quiet, Charlie," Michelle said.

"It's what the Rev told me to do," he said, a defensive tone creeping into his voice.

"Why didn't you tell me about this?" she asked.

"It just didn't come up," said Charlie.

Michelle glanced over at him with a look of incredulity, as if she were just now figuring out how stupid he really was. I used that moment to hook my right foot under the edge of the coffee table, and brought it up forcefully. The table went over, hitting Michelle in the knees. I was right behind it, grabbing her gun hand with my left and delivering a hard punch to her jaw with my right.

She crumpled like a spent balloon, the pistol falling to the floor beside her. I kicked it out of reach, and turned to Charlie just as he was reaching for me with his big ham hands.

I ducked, and Charlie grabbed a handful of air. I struck him under the chin with the heel of my hand. That rocked him back some, and I slipped under his flailing arms and got him from behind in a chokehold. I kicked him in the back of the knee, taking him to the floor. He was gasping for breath as I tightened my arm around his neck, his struggles decreasing. Then he was out. I checked. He wasn't dead.

I ripped the electrical cords from two of the lamps scattered about the living room and trussed my captives like a pair of hogs. I picked up my pistol and pocketed it. I pulled out my cell phone and dialed the number Oscar Mendosa had given me. An answering machine picked up and I left my name and number.

Less than a minute later, my phone rang. "Mr. Royal, this is Oscar Mendosa."

"Thank you for getting back to me, sir. I need a favor."

"What is it?"

"I have two people that I need kept on ice for a couple of days. I can't take the chance that they'll talk to their colleagues. I'd rather those people didn't know I'm coming for them."

"You could kill them."

"I know, but I'd rather not."

"I'll have some men there momentarily. Where are you?"

I gave him the address and sat back on the sofa to wait. My right hand hurt where I'd coldcocked Michelle. I was pretty sure her jaw was broken. She'd be eating soup through a straw for a while.

Charlie began to stir. I went over and chopped him with the butt of Michelle's gun. He was quiet again.

I sat on the sofa, Michelle's nine millimeter in my hand. I heard the hiss of an airbrake, and then the rattling of cans in the alley. Garbage men making a late afternoon pick up. The sunbeams were no longer coming in the windows, blocked now by other houses as the sun sank toward the Gulf of Mexico. The day was waning, and I still had a lot to do.

Thoughts were bouncing around in my head like errant cue balls on a billiard table. I'd done something stupid. Again. I had to stop walking through front doors without a plan. If Michelle hadn't been so intent on making me understand that she was in charge of this operation, I'd probably be dead by now.

At least the people on Blood Island wouldn't be alerted to my presence. If I could slip in without being noticed, I might learn something. I wasn't sure how I was going to get Peggy out, but a vague plan was beginning to take shape in the back of my mind.

I pulled out my cell phone and dialed Logan Hamilton's number. "Logan," I said. "Can you bring my boat down to Marathon first thing tomorrow?"

"Sure. What's going on?"

"I think I know where Peggy is, and I need the boat to get her out."

"I thought you were in Key West."

"I am. But I need the boat in Marathon. I'll explain later."

"Where do you want to meet me?"

"Go to Faro Blanco and wait for me to contact you. I'll be there by dark tomorrow. See if you can pick up a rifle and a shotgun to bring with you."

"I'll see you tomorrow," Logan said, and clicked off.

I heard a door open in the back of the house. As I was tensing up to aim the pistol, a voice reached me. "Mr. Royal, Mr. Mendosa sent us. We're coming in."

"Come ahead," I said, lowering the gun into my lap.

Two men came through the door, looked at the situation, and each picked up a body. The smallest one had Charlie. I was impressed.

The larger one looked at me and said, "Mr. Mendosa said for you to call when you don't need us to keep these two anymore."

"I will. Thanks, and please tell Mr. Mendosa I appreciate his help."

They went out the back door and I left by the front.

CHAPTER THIRTY-THREE

Michelle must have thought she and Charlie could take care of me. She apparently had not called in any reinforcements. Still, I was careful leaving, and made sure nobody was following me.

The sun was low, but there was still a lot of daylight left. It was a little after six, and soon the crowds would be gathering in Mallory Square for the daily sunset spectacle.

I had to get to the dive shop to retrieve the gear I'd bought. I walked the few blocks and turned into the door of the small store. The surfer guy was behind the counter and motioned me to the back of the shop. My new equipment was piled on the floor.

"I took all the tags off for you," he said. "That's a lot of gear to carry. Is your car close?"

"I don't have a car. I have a rental boat. We can put it in there."

"Are you going night diving? I can add some lights to the package."

"No. I'm going out first thing in the morning, at daybreak. I'll just store the gear in the boat."

"I hope the stuff's there when you get back in the morning."

"It will be."

He put the gear in a two-wheeled cart and followed me to the rental boat. He handed it down into the boat, and I covered it with a tarp I found under the center console. It wasn't hidden well, but it'd do until I got back.

I had some time to kill. I was headed for Blood Island, but I didn't want to arrive before midnight. The later, I thought, the better the chance that the island would be asleep.

I walked over to a restaurant in the Historic Seaport, which wasn't very historic, but provided a sense of fun for the tourists. I took a corner table and sat with my hat pulled low on my face. I'd picked up a newspaper at the entrance, and held that partially in front of my face while reading it. I was about as inconspicuous as I could be.

I ate dinner while planning my next moves. I was hoping to find Peggy during my planned foray onto Blood Island, and then figure out a way to get her out the next night.

I'd told Logan to take my boat to Marathon, about fifty miles above Key West. Michelle knew who I really was, and I had to assume that the other people who were looking for me knew that as well. I didn't want anyone to recognize my boat and raise an alarm on Blood Island. I didn't think anybody would be looking for me or my boat in Marathon.

I was tired and grubby from a long day in the sun. I considered going back to my rooming house for a bath and a change of clothes, but I didn't want to risk being seen. I'd head back there when I returned from Blood Island. It would be late enough that any surveillance would probably have been pulled off.

If I could locate Peggy on the island, I'd be in a position to take her off the next night. Logan and I could bring my boat in close and, hopefully, with surprise and a little firepower, we'd be able to evacuate the girl. It wasn't much of a plan, but it was the best I could come up with.

I pulled out the schematic Debbie had faxed me. It showed the layout of the buildings on the island. There was a large main house, with three cabins on either side, making a letter *C*, with the house in the middle of the crescent.

On my morning visit to the island, I had seen that it was heavily wooded with Australian pines and other hardy salt-water resistant plants. Palm trees were plentiful, and the ground cover was mostly palmetto, with some blooming tropical plants. Mangroves bordered the water.

The schematic showed a path leading from the large clearing where the house and cabins sat, down to the dock where I had seen the go-fast boats. Behind the house was a small building that I assumed was a utility shed of some sort.

I finished my meal and left the restaurant. The sun had given up the day, and darkness enveloped the key. I could hear the sounds of the nightly revelry from Duval Street, but I had no desire to join it. I walked the few blocks to the cemetery, found a bench, and took a nap.

CHAPTER THIRTY-FOUR

I stopped the boat near Blood Island's entrance channel and dropped the anchor. It was a few minutes after midnight. A new moon was dawning, and the sky was dark. A low cloud cover obscured the stars.

I'd run the last few miles at idle speed, running lights off, hoping that the noise of my outboard couldn't be heard on the island. There was an easterly wind blowing from the atoll, so I didn't think the sounds would carry from my position to the west of the channel.

I stripped down in the dark and began to pull the wet suit on. That done, I sat on the gunwale and pulled on the rubber booties and fins. I hooked up the regulator to the twin tanks, checked to make sure it was working, and swung the tanks over my head, settling them like a backpack. I put my gun, Reeboks, and a couple of granola bars into a waterproof bag, and hung it on my weight belt. I pulled the hood over my head, and seated the mask on my face. I was ready.

I slipped into the water and swam down the anchor line the few feet to the seabed. I set the anchor deep into the sand bottom. I didn't want to return and find my boat gone. The water seeping into the suit next to my skin was chilly, but as my body heat warmed the trapped water, it became comfortable.

I surfaced and took a bearing on the entrance to the little lagoon. I submerged and started swimming, pausing regularly to check the luminous dial of my compass.

In about twenty minutes, I surfaced to find myself in the middle of the lagoon. I could see the dock with the go-fast boats tied to it. The glow of a cigarette flared in the night. A guard inhaling. Then I saw the fiery arc of the butt as it was flipped into the water.

I submerged and swam to my right, making for the small sand beach I'd spotted among the mangroves. The bottom was coming up, and I stopped again, poking my head out of the water just enough to see. I was about a hundred yards from the dock and right in front of the little beach. I stayed there, kneeling on the soft bottom, quietly reconnoitering. There was no movement anywhere.

I knew there was a guard on the dock, but if there was anybody watching the beach, he was well hidden. I had to chance it. I crawled toward the edge of the sand, where it met the mangroves. As I lifted my body slowly out of the water, I tensed for a shout or a shot. Nothing.

I eased over to the mangroves, removed the fins, mask, and tanks and stowed them among the roots. I moved into the trees that came down to the beach. I sat and took off the booties and pulled my Reeboks from the waterproof bag. I took out the nine-millimeter Glock I'd taken from Michelle. It was loaded with a seventeen-round clip. I put the sneakers on and put the booties with the rest of the gear. I hung the waterproof bag on my belt.

There was a path leading off the beach. I followed it, moving quietly, remembering the jungle craft I'd learned a long time ago in a very different part of the world. A mixed choir of insects and frogs was hidden in the brush, singing loudly. Now and then, a small animal rustled the leaves as it moved about. I was just one more animal, a little bigger, perhaps, and more deadly, but at one with the jungle.

I neared a bend in the path, and became aware of the pungent aroma of a burning cigarette drifting on the breeze. I stopped, standing stock-still, not moving a muscle. I heard the rustle of feet walking the path, coming my way. I didn't want a confrontation that would arouse the island, and I didn't want anyone to know I'd made a visit. I ducked off the path into the bushes. In my black wet suit, I would be virtually invisible.

The steps moved closer, and I made out the shape of a man holding a rifle, walking carelessly along the trail toward the beach. A regular patrol, I thought. I hung back as he passed, and then slipped back onto the path.

I came to a clearing. I could see a large house in the middle, lights on in two of the upstairs windows, otherwise dark. Three smaller buildings flanked either side of the main house, forming a crescent, with the big house situated in the middle at the bottom of the figure. Just like the schematic from the Property Appraiser's Office. The guest cabins were dark. No lights in any of them.

I made my way to the first cabin on my right and stood quietly by the door. I didn't hear any sound from inside. Then, out of the darkness, a snort. Pigs? No, someone was snoring.

I turned the doorknob. It wasn't locked, and the door swung inward. I stepped quickly into the space and found myself in a bunkhouse. There was only one main room in the building, and a door at the far end that I assumed led to the bathroom. There were a dozen army cots spaced around the perimeter of the room, each one flanked by a tall metal wall locker. Lumps were in some of the beds, and an occasional snore erupted from one or the other of the bunks. I saw men's clothing hanging from hooks next to several of the lockers, and rifles leaning against the wall. This was the guardhouse.

I counted eight beds with occupants. The other four were empty, but not made. That probably meant that there were four guards stationed around the island. Two shifts were sleeping and would replace the others at whatever interval they used. I thought it might be like the old army guard regimen of two hours on and four off.

I softly closed the door and moved to the next building. Again, I stood at the door and listened. No sound at all. I tried the door. Locked. I peered into the nearest window. The place was similar to the first; twelve beds, all occupied. I didn't see any weapons. I moved to the next building. The door was standing open, and the building was empty.

I crossed the courtyard and went to the end building on the crescent, the one farthest from the house. A guard, carrying what appeared to be an M-16 rifle, rounded the far corner of the building just as I reached the front door. He was fifty feet from me. I dropped to the ground and rolled next to the foundation of the cabin, concealing myself in the weeds that had grown up there. He came toward me, and then turned and went to the front door. He couldn't see me in my black wetsuit and hood. He opened the door and peered inside, standing quietly for a few moments, as if listening. Closing the door, he moved off the way he'd come, back around the building.

I rose and moved to the door. I stopped and listened, but heard nothing. The cabin was quiet. The door was bolted from the outside, locking the inhabitants in. I only had to slide the bolt back to open the door. What I assumed to be the bathroom door at the far end of the room was ajar, and some light escaped into the larger room. I saw the same bunkhouse arrangement I'd seen in the other cabins, except this one seemed to house women. Was Peggy here? No way to tell. I didn't want to chance waking any of them and raising an alarm.

I turned to leave, and out of the corner of my eye, I caught movement. I turned quickly, and found a woman in a white gown coming at me like a wraith in the dark. I saw the glint of steel in the anemic light escaping from the bathroom. She held a small kitchen knife, raised in a stabbing position. I grabbed her arm, twisted it behind her back and covered her mouth with my hand, silencing her. The knife dropped to the floor. She kicked at my shins with her bare feet, trying to wiggle out of my grasp.

I whispered into her ear. "Quiet down. I'm here to help."

She slowed her movements and then stopped completely.

"I need to talk to you. If I let you go, will you be quiet?"

She nodded her assent, and I loosened my grip on her mouth.

"Where can we talk?" I asked in a whisper.

"Bathroom," she said, her voice mumbling beneath my hand.

We went toward the bathroom, my hand still held loosely over her mouth, her arm in a hammerlock. I pushed open the door and we walked into the lighted area. I let her go, taking a chance that she'd be quiet.

She turned to face me. "Hi, Peggy," I said.

"Who are you?"

"I'm Matt Royal. Does that name mean anything to you?"

"Laura's ex?"

"Yes. She sent me to find you."

"Can you get me out of here?"

"Not now, but I'll be back tomorrow night."

"How did you find me?"

"Long story. I'll explain later. Are they drugging you?"

"They tried. But I haven't eaten any of the food they've given me, so I think I'm okay. I've been feigning a drug stupor when they're around."

"What about the guards?"

"They're checking all the time. They tie me to the bed at night, but for some reason they forgot to do that tonight. I brought the knife back from Key West, and they didn't find it. The guards usually just look in the door, but sometimes they come inside. When I saw you, I thought you were a guard. I was hoping to get off the island again. I know where they keep the boats."

"I need you to stay put for one more day. Can you do that?"

"Yes. But I'm hungry. I haven't had anything to eat in two days."

I pulled the granola bars out of my waterproof bag and gave them to her. "Maybe this will help a little," I said.

"You've got to put a stop to this. Something big is about to happen, but I haven't figured it out yet."

"I know about the prostitution."

"It's much bigger than that."

"Any ideas?"

"No, but the Rev keeps bragging to me that he's about to do something bigger than anything he's ever done."

"Do you talk to him?"

"Mostly, I listen. He has me brought to the big house a couple of times a day. He wants to sleep with me, but so far I've held him off."

"How did you get to the phone in the Sharkstooth Bar?"

"One of the Rev's goons took me to Key West. They were going to put me in the whorehouse, but I got away."

"How?"

"I didn't eat anything the night before or at breakfast that morning. I had some sort of a stomach virus, I guess, and I couldn't keep anything down. The drugs wore off, but the goons didn't notice it. I scratched the guy taking me to the spa and ran. I tried to call my dad, but they found me and brought me back here."

"Did they hurt you?"

"No. They just gave me more drugs, which I didn't take because I didn't eat the food."

"We're going to get you out of this, Peggy."

"Please hurry. I'm either going to end up drugged again or starved to death."

"I have to go. The guard will be coming back soon. Stay put, and I'll be back tomorrow night to get you."

She kissed me on the cheek. "Laura always said you were one hell of a guy."

"She said the same about you," I said, turning for the door.

CHAPTER THIRTY-FIVE

I had been aware of a low hum since I came onto the island. I assumed it was from the generator that powered the lights, but I wasn't sure.

As I left the building in which I'd found Peggy, I tried to follow the sound. Thinking that any generator facilities would be behind the main house, I headed there. As I rounded the back of the house, the noise became louder. It was still faint, but I could tell the direction from which it came.

I followed the sound, careful not to alert any guards in the vicinity. I saw no one. In about a hundred yards, I came to a concrete-block house. The hum came from inside. Large-gauge wires ran from the small building toward the house and cabins. This had to be the generator shed.

I'd been on the island for more than an hour and didn't want to stretch my luck. I turned and moved toward the trail that led to the beach, stopping every few feet to listen for any movement.

As I approached the beginning of the path, a man with a rifle slung over his shoulder appeared out of the night. He was standing right where I needed to go. My watch told me it was almost two. If I was right about the guard schedule, there would be a new guard shift coming on in a few minutes.

I dropped to the ground and crawled silently along the edge of the jungle-like growth, creeping slowly toward the guard. Hopefully, he would be distracted while the new guard took his place, and I could slip by and be on my way.

I crawled to within ten feet of the guard, controlling my breathing, staying calm; using skills taught me long ago by an Army Special Forces instructor. I waited.

Minutes passed, and I heard a door slam. Voices came from the vicinity of the guardhouse. A man carrying a rifle slung over his shoulder approached and called out, "Al, I've got it."

"I'm on my way," said the guard named Al, and he started walking toward the approaching man. That gave me a split second's opportunity to move quickly onto the path. I took it, crawling on my stomach, propelling myself with my elbows, slithering as fast as I could without making a lot of noise. I made it into the cover alongside the trail, and as soon as I was out of sight of the guards, I began to walk toward the lagoon.

I got back to the beach to find that my equipment had not been disturbed. I quickly put it on and moved into the water, took a compass bearing on the opening to the sea and submerged.

I made it back to my boat without incident. I surfaced behind the boat, intending to put my gear on the small swim platform and climb up the ladder that hung into the water.

I undid the waterproof bag holding the nine millimeter and threw it into the boat. I didn't want to lose it or get it wet. My tanks, fins, and mask were on the platform when I noticed a small craft moving on the surface, just to the right side of my boat. I was still in the water, and my gun was on the floor of the boat.

I reached for the dive knife that was in the scabbard fastened around my ankle. If I could get into the boat, I'd use my pistol. If not, maybe I could take out the occupant of the boat coming at me. The knife wouldn't be a whole lot of protection, unless my assailant was in the water.

The craft materialized out of the darkness, like a ghost. It was a kayak. A black man was paddling toward the stern of my boat, where I hung impotently in the water. I had been discovered. I wondered why they didn't use one of the go-fast boats, but maybe they wanted to do this quietly.

The kayak came abreast of me, inertia pushing it forward. The black man was looking directly at me. His raised hand was holding the two-bladed paddle over his head. He was going to bash me with it, and I couldn't possibly get to him with the knife. Crap.

CHAPTER THIRTY-SIX

I started to submerge, thinking I might be able to swim away from my attacker. He held the paddle out toward me, and said, "Give me a hand. The current is strong."

"Who are you?"

"I'm Abraham Osceola. I can help you."

I had no choice. If he had a gun, he would have shot me by now. If I pulled him closer, at least I'd have a better chance to knife him if he proved to be hostile.

I grabbed the paddle with one hand, holding on to the swim platform with the other. I pulled him over until he reached out and grabbed the stainless-steel handhold on the back of my boat.

"Thanks," he said.

"What do you want?"

"Let's get into your boat, and I'll tell you a story." He grinned.

His voice carried the lilt of the Bahamas, a pleasing dialect of English that reminded me of clear water and gentle breezes. I pulled up on the ladder and took the painter from the bow of his kayak, tying it to the cleat on the stern of my boat. He climbed up after me.

I had the knife in my hand as I backed up to give him room to get into the boat's cockpit. He was wearing only a loincloth. He looked at the blade, grinned again, and said, "Not to worry. I'm a Seminole."

Crap, I thought. Those guys from Florida State never give it a rest. "I'm a Gator," I said.

He looked at me, puzzled. Then he laughed. "Ah," he said, barely able to contain his mirth. "The University of Florida. No, no. I'm a Seminole Indian. Part Tequesta, too. Let's get out of here."

Feeling a bit foolish, I cranked the engine and idled away from Blood Island, the kayak rolling in the little wake left by my boat's movement.

"I don't understand," I said. "You're a black Bahamian."

"I'm black, all right, but I'm a Seminole. And a Tequesta. Let me tell you my story." And he did.

Back in the dim reaches of history, probably about the time of Christ, the Tequesta Indians moved into South Florida and settled in present-day Miami-Dade and Broward Counties and in the Keys. They were likely subservient to the more numerous Calusa who dominated the Lower Peninsula for hundreds of years. Historians think their language was a Muscogean dialect spoken by the other tribes in the area. The Creeks of Georgia and Alabama also spoke a language related to Muscogean.

When the Spanish came to Florida in the early sixteenth century, the Tequesta welcomed them to their villages along Biscayne Bay. For more than two centuries, the Spanish and Tequesta maintained a tenuous, but mostly peaceful, relationship. Then, in 1763, the Spanish ceded Florida to the British. Most of the remaining Tequesta asked for, and were given, transport to Havana.

A small number of the Indians fled to the Everglades and sustained themselves as hunter-gatherers. Over the next sixty years, their numbers dwindled until there were only a few Tequesta left, eking out a subsistence living in the swamps where no white man ventured.

During the latter half of the eighteenth century, before the British assumed control of Florida, a group of Creek Indians from Georgia and Alabama began to drift south. They allied themselves with the local tribes of North Florida, intermarried, and soon separated from the Creek Nation and became known as the Seminoles.

Beginning in the middle of the seventeenth century, the Spanish encouraged slaves from the southern states to flee to Florida. Those who were successful were considered free, and they set up their own communities. The Seminoles became their protectors, and there was intermarriage between the two groups.

The black former slaves, and a number of blacks that had been living in Florida as free people for generations, known as Maroons, began to think of themselves as Seminoles, and, indeed, many of them had Seminole blood.

History records few of the black Seminoles, but one who rose to prominence was named Abraham. He was probably an escaped slave from Pensacola, who had joined the Seminoles in North Florida in the early nineteenth century. He married the part-black ex-wife of Billy Bowlegs, the hereditary Seminole chief, and they had a daughter.

Abraham became the chief negotiator for the Seminoles in their dealings with the United States. When the Second Seminole War broke out in 1835, Abraham was found fighting with the band of Chief Osceola. Most of the warriors in this famous force were black, and they were among the fighters most feared by American soldiers.

Osceola himself was not a Seminole, but the son of an English trader and a Red Stick Creek woman. History does not record how he came to fight with the Seminoles, nor does it mention that Osceola took Abraham's daughter as his mistress. A son was born of that union, and he was named Abraham Osceola.

My companion had finished his history lesson. We were now far enough from Blood Island that no one would hear or see us.

Abraham had been reciting as if he were in a trance. Now, his regular tone of voice returned. "I am descended from that son," he said, "and the Tequesta woman he married after the Seminoles retreated to the Everglades and absorbed the remaining Tequesta. Her father was the hereditary chief of the tribe. Later, at the end of the Second Seminole War, my ancestors and many other black Seminoles fled to the Bahamas. They did not want to be transported to Oklahoma. Who would?" He grinned.

"I'm happy to have learned something tonight," I said, "but how does this help me?"

"I grew up on the stories that form the oral traditions of my people, the Seminoles and the Tequesta. When I came to the States, I brought those traditions with me. I worked the fishing boats for many years, and now I'm retired. I'm almost eighty years old."

That was a shock. He could have passed for fifty. He was a powerful man, with no flab about his body. He was paddling a kayak on the open sea at midnight. I nodded my head, signaling him to continue.

He said, "What you call Blood Island was once a sacred place for the Tequesta. We called it by a different name, but even the name is sacred and can only be spoken to others of the tribe. They buried their caciques, or chiefs, there, and the warriors would often visit to commune with the spirits of those gone before. When I retired, I searched the islands of the Marquesas and Mule Keys. One day I found the burial grounds of my ancestors on Blood Island.

"I visited regularly, to pray with my ancestors, and to feel their spirits. One day, about three years ago, some rough men with rifles escorted me off the island and told me I'd be shot if I returned.

"I had to find a way on and off the island that would not alert the owners that I was there. The burial mound is on the northwest corner of the island, and there is a way to get in there by boat if you know how. I can show you."

"Why would you do this?"

"I heard you talking to the girl, Peggy."

"How?"

"I often wander the island in the night. I feel the spirits of the Tequesta there and I know I'm among my kinsmen. Tonight, I saw you sneaking around and followed. I couldn't imagine what a guy in a wet suit was after. I was at the open window of the bathroom when you were talking to the girl. I've been suspicious for a long time that something bad goes on there, but I've never been able to prove it. I would have gone to the authorities if I had any proof. I think you are the man to get that proof."

"Why do you care?"

"Those are bad men, and they desecrate a land my people think of as holy. Do you have a chart?"

I spread out the nautical chart of the area, and in the glow of a flashlight, Abraham showed me the exact spot where I could land my boat.

"See," he said, pointing to the chart, "this shows very shallow water all around this area. But, there's a tall Australian pine here at the tip of the island. It stands above the others, so you should be able to spot it even at night. From the Boca Grande Channel, you want to line up at exactly eighty degrees true to the tall tree. Head straight in. There's a deep-water channel right up to the tree, but it's narrow. When you get close, you'll see a cut in the undergrowth. There's a path that leads toward the houses, but it peters out before it gets there. You'll be able to get far enough in to see the generator building, and you can take it from there. I don't think they know about that trail, because it's never guarded."

I penciled in the information I needed and charted an exact latitude-longitude position in the Boca Grande Channel from which I'd start my approach to the island. I rolled up the chart.

"Thanks, Abraham. Where can I reach you?"

"You can't, my friend."

With that, he pulled his kayak to the boat, slipped into it, and paddled into the night. He never looked back.

CHAPTER THIRTY-SEVEN

I motored back to the Key West Bight in a drizzling rain. I'd changed into my street clothes and put on a windbreaker I'd carried to the boat earlier. I belted the dive knife and scabbard to my arm under the jacket, and put the pistol in the pocket. I stowed the dive gear under the tarp in the bow. By the time I docked the boat, I was soaked, and it was nearing three a.m. I'd call the kid from the dive shop in the morning and ask him to retrieve my equipment and store it. I started walking toward my rooming house.

The light rain continued, leaving a thin sheen of water on the pavement. The streets were empty, the rain dampening the usual carousing on Duval Street. The colored lights that adorned the windows of the bars reflected off the wet streets, giving the appearance of many small rainbows. The smell of the sea tickled my nose.

I stopped at the corner, two doors down from where my rooming house loomed out of the darkness. I wanted to make sure there were no bad guys watching for me. The street was quiet and deserted.

I climbed the stairs to my room, key in hand. I saw light coming from under the door. I was sure I'd turned the lights off before I left that morning.

I pulled the nine millimeter from the pocket of my windbreaker. I eased up to the door, listening for any sound. I heard a thud, as if someone had kicked the wall, then quiet again. I tried the doorknob. It turned, and I pushed quickly into the room, my Glock held in front of me.

"Don't shoot, podner," said a familiar voice. "I'm a friendly."

Jock Algren was splayed out on my bed. A muscle-bound man was trussed up in the corner, a gag in his mouth. He kicked the wall with his bound knees, making the thud I'd heard from the hall.

"Who's your friend?" I said, lowering the gun.

"Says his name is Martin Holcomb."

"Is he telling the truth?"

"I think so. He wouldn't tell me at first, but with a little encouragement he fessed up."

Holcombe's little finger on his right hand was pointing at an odd angle. "What happened to his finger?"

"I broke it."

"Ah, a little encouragement."

"Yeah. He's a sissy."

"Who is he?"

"He works for an outfit called The Circle. Told me he lives in a place named Blood Island. I found him in your room when I came to visit."

I had met Jock Algren on the first day of eighth grade, and he became my best friend. We'd stayed close during the intervening years. Jock was an oil company executive, but unknown to most anybody, he moonlighted as an operative of our country's most secretive spy agency.

"What're you doing here?" I said.

"Logan called me this afternoon. I was in Miami and caught a commuter flight down."

I was glad to see Jock, but a little surprised that Logan had called him. "What did Logan have to say?"

"He said you'd called and wanted him to bring your boat down and to bring some weapons. He told me you were looking for Laura's stepdaughter. He wasn't sure what was going on, but asked if I could get out of Houston in time to come with him. I told him I was in Miami and that I'd check things out and get back to him."

I pointed to the man on the floor. "What're you going to do about him?"

Jock winked at me. "I thought I'd kill him."

The man squirmed and mumbled something from behind the gag.

"What did he say?" I asked.

"It's not important," Jock said. "Do you want to kill him here or wait until we get outside?"

The mumbles became louder, the squirming more intense.

"Let's see what he has to say," I said, walking toward the trussed up man.

I leaned down, holding my knife so that he could see it, and whispered into his ear. "If you do anything more than talk to us, I'm going to gut you like a fish. Understand?"

The man nodded, and I removed the gag. I recognized him as the man I'd seen drive Simmermon's boat away from the restaurant earlier in the day.

He licked his lips and worked his jaw, tried to speak, and tried again. This time a raspy voice came through. "Don't kill me."

"I can't see much reason for keeping you alive," I said. "Besides, you were going to kill me."

"No, I wasn't. I was just going to take you back to the island. The Rev wants to see you."

"Why?"

"I don't know. He just does."

"How did you know where to find me?"

"I showed your picture around, and the old lady who runs this place told me you were here."

"Okay. Give me a good reason not to kill you and the old lady too."

"I don't care about the old lady, but I can give you some information about what the Rev plans."

"Tell me."

"You won't get out of Key West alive. The Rev has people watching the airport and car and boat rental places. U.S. One is the only road out, and they've got men watching that."

"Okay, but that's not much. What kind of plans does Simmermon have?"

"You won't kill me?"

"If you lie to me, and I'll know if you do, you're dead. Understood?"

"Yes," he said. "The Rev is going to blow something up."

"What?"

"I don't know. He keeps talking about the big bang, and laughing. Says it'll change the world."

"Why do you think that means he's going to blow something up?"

"He's been bringing a lot of explosives to the island. C-4 and some dynamite. I've seen it, but I don't know what his plans are."

"You just told me you were going to tell me about his plans. Now you're telling me you don't know what they are? I think you're a dead man."

"No. Honestly. That's all I know. Man, I'm telling you everything I know."

I looked at Jock, who nodded. I replaced the gag and pulled out my cell phone. I dialed the number Mendosa had given me and left my name and number with the machine. In less than ten seconds, my phone rang.

"Mr. Royal, I'm calling on behalf of Mr. Mendosa."

"Do you know who I am?" I asked.

"Yes. Cracker Dix's friend. What can I do for you?"

"I've got another man I need put on ice."

"Where are you?"

I gave him the address and hung up.

Jock was sitting on the side of the bed. "What's that all about?"

"A friend of a friend. I'll explain later."

I motioned Jock to follow me out of the room. We stood in the hall, and in a low voice I brought him up to date on what was going on, and what I'd been up to in the two days I'd been in Key West.

"Laura's missing too?" he asked, when I'd finished.

"Yes. At least as of this morning, she was still gone. Her husband would have called me if she'd turned up. I'm worried sick about her. I think Peggy is okay, and with any luck we'll have her back home tomorrow. But what the hell happened to Laura? She didn't just wander off."

I heard steps on the stairway, and the two men who'd come to Michelle's house earlier appeared. I led them into the room, and they both picked up the trussed man and left. Neither said a word.

"I've got to make a phone call," said Jock. "Why don't you get a shower? You stink."

* * *

When I returned from the bathroom, Jock was sitting in the only chair in the room. "You look beat," he said. "Get a couple of hours of shut-eye. I'll watch the place."

"Are you going to stick around for tomorrow night's festivities?"

"Wouldn't miss it. I made a couple of calls. Logan is going to meet one of my colleagues at the dock at Moore's Stone Crab Restaurant at first light. He'll load the boat with some more firepower in case we need it. Logan will shove off as soon as the weapons are aboard. He said he should be at Faro Blanco by noon."

"I thought you'd retired from all this."

"I did, but I was called back on a special mission. One of our guys was killed in Sarasota. The agency found me playing golf in Australia, and told me to get to Miami. They've got some leads."

"Why you?"

"Because of you."

"I don't get it."

"You found our guy's body. My boss knows we're friends, so here I am."

"The man in the vulture pit?"

"Yes."

"You know where the body is?"

"Buried in his family plot in Iowa."

"The Sarasota cops know about this?"

"No," he said. "We take care of our own."

"So, that's the reason his fingerprints weren't on file."

"Yes. But when the local cops ran the prints, we were notified. We took it from there."

"What's in Miami?"

"Probably nothing. I was supposed to meet one of our agents tomorrow and get completely briefed. Until today, I didn't know what our man was doing in Sarasota, or what kind of case he was working on."

"Do you need to get back to Miami?"

"No. I needed to talk to you anyway."

"I really don't know anything, Jock. I just found the body."

"When I called to get Logan set up, I was told that you might have stumbled into something that's related to what our agent was looking into."

"What?"

"The Reverend Robert William Simmermon. Get some sleep. We'll talk more tomorrow."

I looked at my watch. Almost four a.m. "We can count on a two-hour drive to Marathon," I said. "The traffic is always terrible on U.S. One. Wake me up in a couple of hours."

He nodded his agreement.

"I'm glad you're here, old friend," I said, and fell onto the bed and into a deep sleep.

CHAPTER THIRTY-EIGHT

I was dreaming of Laura. She was in a casket, a white one with walnut trim. I didn't want to look at her. Jock was pushing me forward, telling me I had to say good-bye. I moved toward the front of the room where she lay. Lilacs were stacked around her bier, and the air was suffused with the smell of fresh vanilla. I could see her face, thin now, the color leached out of it, diminished by the absence of her soul. A single tear leaked from her right eye, and a smile played at the corner of her lips, as if her death were a sad joke.

I awoke with a start. Sun was cascading through the window, and the confounded chickens were clucking in the yard. Relief chased the agony of Laura's death from my consciousness. Jock was asleep in the chair, his pistol in his hand

I didn't want to startle him. I lay still for a moment, and then said softly, "Jock."

His breathing didn't change, but his eyes popped open. He surveyed the room without moving. His pistol was in his lap, safety off. He knew exactly where he was and what he was doing. Then he stretched in the chair and said, "Good morning, podner. Good nap?"

I looked at my watch. It was a few minutes after eight. I'd slept the better part of five hours, and I felt like a new man. I got up and padded down the hall to the bathroom. I washed my face and brushed my teeth. Life was looking up, but I couldn't shake the feeling of dread left by the dream. I hoped it wasn't a portent, some sort of augury seared into my unconscious by that part of me that was connected psychically to the woman I loved above all people. The thought of losing Laura was too much to bear, so I tried to put it out of my mind. I knew I'd be less than successful, and that the apprehension would ride with me until I found her.

When I got back to the room, Jock took my place in the bathroom. I called Debbie.

"Don't you ever sleep?" she said, mumbling into the phone.

"The sun's up, and I need information. What've you got on Simmermon?"

"You're going to owe me a lot of quarters. I found out a lot about him, but the story doesn't hang together too well. I don't understand it all."

"Talk to me."

"He was born in Troy, Alabama, graduated from high school there, and went to Troy State University. He dropped out during his freshman year, and then disappeared for a time.

"Two years later, he shows up living in Key West, working on a shrimp boat. Two years after that, he shows up in Boulder, Colorado. The odd thing is, there's almost nothing on him in Key West. He didn't have a phone, utilities, apartment, car, credit cards, none of the things we need to live. All I could find on him was some taxes withheld by a fishing company that's no longer in business. And, there's no record of a job in Colorado."

"What about his evangelical organization?" I asked. "When did he pop up with that?"

"About four years after he dropped out of sight in Key West, he began preaching in a small church in Anniston, Alabama. He preached at a number of small churches for about a year, but he never stayed in one place for more than a few weeks.

"About three years ago, he bought a big tent and began his revival meetings, traveling mostly in Alabama, Georgia, and Florida."

"Thanks Deb. I don't know what all that means, but I appreciate your getting it for me."

"You owe me, loverboy," she said, and hung up.

That was interesting information, but my first order of business was to get to my boat and Logan. I wasn't sure how we were going to get to Marathon. If I went back to the rental boat, somebody would probably be watching it. I'd rented it before my photo was broadcast around town, but they'd be watching all the rentals now. Jock could rent a car using one of the bogus IDs he always carried, but I'd have to ride in the trunk to be safe. That was probably our best bet.

Jock returned, and I told him what I was thinking.

"I don't know," he said. "Yesterday, when I came in, I asked the old woman who runs this place what your room number was. She's already ratted you out once, and now she knows what I look like. It wouldn't take much for Simmermon's men to put us together."

"I've got an idea. Let's get out of here."

I was dressed in typical tourist clothes, cargo shorts, Hawaiian shirt, and Reeboks. I put on the sunglasses and pulled the ball cap low on my forehead. Slinging my backpack over my shoulder, I led the way down the stairs and out the door. Thankfully, the old lady wasn't in sight.

Jock stood six feet and was lean and fit. He had a Houston Astros ball cap covering his bald head. The fringe of black hair that still clung to life was getting streaks of gray. He wore slacks, loafers, and a designer T-shirt. He was carrying a small suitcase that sported the logo of a Hawaiian Country Club. He looked a little too elegant to be with me, but people would probably think I was his valet or something.

"Where are we going?" Jock asked.

"Breakfast at the Hyatt."

"Isn't that a little conspicuous?"

"Not at all. I don't think Simmermon's people would be looking for us at a tourist hotel. Besides, we need to see somebody."

The hotel sat near the foot of Duval Street, next to the water. The superb views commanded a superb price from the guests, but the place was always booked.

We entered the lobby and went through to the restaurant. I saw a big table surrounded by senior citizens. Austin Dwyer sat among them, facing the dining room.

I asked the hostess to seat us at the table next to them. Austin looked up as we were escorted to the table and given menus. As soon as the hostess left, he came over.

"Ben," he said. "Nice to see you again."

I introduced him to Jock, who was sitting with a bemused look on his face, wondering, I thought, whether the old man was dotty or if I'd given a false name.

"Please sit down, Austin. I have a favor to ask."

He sat. "I owe you big time. What can I do for you?"

"I have a very delicate situation, and I need your complete confidence. Can you give me that?"

"Certainly. Mum's the word."

"First, my name isn't Ben Joyce. It's Matt Royal. I'm a lawyer from Longboat Key, and I've been doing some undercover work, trying to find a young woman who has been kidnapped. Jock here is an old friend who's lending a hand."

"Can't say I'm surprised, Matt. I thought you were too well spoken to be a transient. How can I help?"

"Jock and I need to get to Marathon this morning, and for reasons I can't go into, we can't rent a car. I was wondering if you might have room on your bus."

"We do. I'll make it right with the tour director. Get your breakfast. We're leaving as soon as everybody gets through eating. Our bags are already loaded."

I thanked him, and he went back to his table to finish his meal.

"Who is this guy?" Jock asked.

I explained how we met, and told him about the altercation two nights before. "We can trust him," I said. "And the bad guys aren't going to be looking for us on a senior citizen's tour bus."

"If you say so."

"Bring me up to speed on your agency's connection to Simmermon."

"Another agency, Alcohol, Tobacco, and Firearms was tracking some C-4 and other explosives that were stolen from a National Guard Armory in Macon, Georgia. Turns out that Simmermon was running a revival in the area at the time the stuff disappeared. Apparently, this wasn't the first time that weapons disappeared when he was in the area.

"It also looked as if Simmermon had ties to some pretty bad folks. He was connected to a bunch of right-wing nuts who want to overthrow the government, and maybe some Muslim groups with the same idea.

"My agency tried to put a man into Simmermon's organization. I don't know what went wrong, but somebody must have figured it out, because our agent ended up as buzzard food."

"Do you know who killed your guy?"

"We're pretty sure it was the jerk you shot at Hutch's."

"I don't get it. How did I get caught up in this?"

"You went looking for Peggy and turned over the hornet's nest. We think that when Simmermon's people heard that you had discovered our agent's body at Pelican Man's, they decided that you were one of us. They had to take you out."

Austin came back to the table. "You ready to go?"

We were.

CHAPTER THIRTY-NINE

The fifty-mile ride to Marathon was uneventful. Jock and I sat near the back of the bus. Austin sat in a facing seat. I explained to Jock that Austin had been a history professor and had once lived in Key West. I told Austin about my meeting with Abraham Osceola, and asked him if any of that made sense.

"Actually," he said, "it does. The Tequesta ruled the Keys for many generations, and we think they paid tribute to the Calusa, who substantially outnumbered them. The blacks who were part of the Seminole tribe were called Seminole Negroes by the whites in the area. Abraham is a historical character, and was part of every treaty effected between the Seminoles and the American government during the years between the First and Second Seminole Wars."

"What about the Tequesta connection?" I asked.

"Your friend has his history right. The remnants of the Tequesta intermarried with the Seminoles and became part of their tribe. The Tequesta, as a tribe, had ceased to exist by the middle of the nineteenth century. But their blood runs through a lot of Seminole veins today."

"The Abraham I met is a Bahamian. How did that happen?"

"Like he told you, at the end of the Second Seminole War, a large number of the black Seminoles migrated in dugout canoes to Andros Island in the Bahamas. Over the years, they became indistinguishable from the islanders in speech and looks, but they maintained their Indian culture and their Seminole names. They always, to this day, refer to themselves as Seminoles."

Florida is full of historical oddities, I thought. Maybe I'll turn out to be one of them.

At noon, we crossed the Seven Mile Bridge onto Vaca Key, the island that held the town of Marathon. The bus dropped us off at the Faro Blanco Resort. I gave Austin one of my business cards and invited him to visit Longboat Key. He said he would.

Jock and I walked past the restaurant to the marina. I saw Logan at the fuel dock looking out over Florida Bay as he filled my boat with gas. The boat was a Grady-White twenty-eight foot walkaround. It was made for fishing, with a large cockpit and wide gunwales, made so that the fisherman could easily walk around the cabin trunk to the bow if he had a fish on the line. It sported twin 250-horsepower Yamaha outboards that would push it through the water at almost fifty miles per hour. I had not scrimped on electronics, and it was equipped with the latest radar, chart plotter, fish finder, and radios. She was my love, and her name was *Recess*.

Jock and I walked down the dock toward the fueling point. Logan finished the fueling just as we reached him. He put the hose away and turned to greet us.

I stuck out my hand. "How was your trip, Captain?"

Logan grinned. "Smooth as glass. I made it in less than seven hours. How're you doing, Jock?"

"Good, Logan. I do believe you've gotten me into a mess, though. Did my man meet you this morning?"

"He did. I think he may have knocked over the National Guard Armory on his way to Moore's. I've got more weapons aboard than I've seen since I left Vietnam."

Jock laughed. "Better to be overarmed than underarmed."

I said, "Let's get some lunch and some rest before we head back to Key West. We've got a big night ahead of us."

We ordered lunch and a bag of sandwiches to go. That would serve as our dinner that evening before we launched onto Blood Island. It was going to be a long day.

I brought Logan up to date over lunch, telling him everything I knew. When we finished, I walked out onto the patio and called Jeff Timmons.

"Any news?" I asked.

"Not a word, Matt. I'm worried sick. She's been gone four days."

"I don't know what to say, Jeff. Has there been any activity on her credit cards, bank account, anything?"

"Nothing. Have you found out anything about Peggy?"

"Maybe. I'll know a lot more tomorrow." I didn't want to give the man any false hope. We had a dicey night ahead of us, and a lot of things could go wrong. "I'll call you tomorrow," I said, and closed my phone.

I turned to find Jock and Logan standing behind me. "Nothing on Laura?" Jock asked.

"No. This doesn't make any sense at all. I don't think her disappearance is connected to Peggy's, but it is one odd coincidence."

"And you don't like coincidences," said Logan.

I nodded my head, and we walked to the boat. We paid the fuel bill and boarded *Recess*. Logan hadn't been kidding. The cabin held three M-16 rifles with several extra clips, three shotguns, an M60 machine gun and tripod, a rocket-propelled grenade launcher, and a large box of assorted gear.

"You expecting a war, Jock?" I asked.

"You never know."

"Damn," said Logan. "I hope not. I hadn't seen an M-16 since Vietnam. When that guy loaded them aboard, I told him I thought I'd go back to helicopters. Damned if he didn't bring out the M60. Our door gunners used those."

Logan had been a helicopter pilot in Vietnam, but before he went to flight school, he'd been an infantryman, like me.

We motored out of the marina, under the Seven Mile Bridge and around to Boot Key Harbor on the ocean side of Vaca Key. We dropped anchor, opened the hatches and turned on the fans in the cabin.

There was just enough room in the small cabin for the three of us to sleep. We secured the boat, and took a nap.

CHAPTER FORTY

Hawk Channel runs in a generally westerly direction along the ocean side of the Keys. It is well marked and bordered on one side by the Keys themselves, and on the other by reefs.

At six o'clock, we weighed anchor and headed into Hawk Channel for the two hour run to our first destination. Sand Key lies just outside the Key West harbor on the Atlantic side. It's a popular dive spot, and on any given evening, there would be a number of boats anchored over the reef that surrounds the area. We'd be able to wait there until midnight, when we'd start our trip to Blood Island.

The run along the Hawk Channel was pleasant, the sea calm, the sunshine bright. Jock spent the trip taking the sun on the fold-down seat in the aft cockpit. Logan helped me navigate and groused good-naturedly about the lack of Scotch on board.

We arrived at Sand Key just as the setting sun painted the sea in red and orange. A slight wind was blowing from the Atlantic, just enough to cool us down without causing the sea to kick up. We spent the next three hours checking weapons and discussing a plan of attack.

We were eating our sandwiches when my phone rang. Jeff Timmons.

"Matt, I just got a call from the police. Laura's in a hospital. I'm on my way there now, but I wanted you to know. "

"How bad?"

"She's fine, I think. Thank God. She's been in a coma, and they couldn't identify her. She's awake now. Turns out her fingerprints aren't on file anywhere, and the Atlanta cops didn't make the connection between Laura and the woman in the hospital."

I breathed a sigh of relief. I felt like I'd been holding my breath since

I heard that she had disappeared. "That's great, Jeff. What happened?"

"She went out for a walk and fainted. She apparently hit her head on a curb and was knocked unconscious. Somebody called an ambulance and they took her in. When she came to, she told them who she was. I'm on my way to the hospital now."

"Is she going to be all right?"

"I think so. She's awake and lucid. I'll let you know as soon as I know something more."

"I'll be out-of-pocket tonight, Jeff. I'll call you in the morning."

A sense of relief swept through me. The dream wasn't an omen. She was alive and well and would probably be her old self soon. I'd get Peggy back to her, and her life would pick up where it had stopped dead with Peggy's disappearance. I would lose Laura again, but I had no claim to her. She had loved me, and I had driven her away. She'd found happiness with a good man, and that was more important to me than having her back. Hell, I'd probably just disappoint her again, and she deserved better. And now, after all these years, we'd be friends again. She would be just a phone call away, and I'd have to be satisfied with that. It was more than I'd had for the past ten years, and it would have to be enough. Love, I think, the real kind, the bone-deep, tissue-pervading emotion that perhaps only comes along once in a lifetime, is controllable, if the object of that love is happy. Even if her happiness includes me only on the periphery of her life.

At midnight, we were in the Boca Grande Channel, engines idling. We were west of Blood Island, looking for the tall tree Abraham Osceola had told me about.

Jock was rummaging around in the box of equipment brought aboard at Moore's. He handed me a pair of night-vision goggles. "Here. Try these."

I put them on, and the night turned green. There was no moon, but the sky was blanketed with stars. I saw the tree, and using my handheld compass, took a bearing. "We're not quite there," I said. "Logan, move us a little more to the north."

In a few minutes I could see the tree Abraham had told me about. "We should be at the entrance to the channel. Let's take her in quietly."

Logan made the turn and lined up on the tree. The depth sounder was reading fifteen feet all the way in. As we got closer, I could see a small opening in the dense mangroves that lined the island. I pointed it out to Logan, and he steered for it.

"Bottoms coming up," Logan said. "Five feet."

The boat could handle two feet, so we had a little leeway.

"Tides coming in." I said, "I'd rather be a little shallow than too deep. It'll be deeper when we come back."

The bow of the boat nosed into sand, and we stopped. The depth sounder was on the transom, so it would give us a reading at the stern. "What's your depth?" I asked.

"Three feet," said Logan.

"Let the anchor go."

Logan hit the switch on the console, and the electric windlass began to drop the anchor. Once in the water, I'd secure it deep into the sand, so the boat wouldn't float away.

We were all dressed in dark clothes provided by Jock's man at Moore's. We put camouflage paint on our faces, and black watch caps on our heads. Jock gave Logan a pair of night-vision goggles, and he hung another around his own neck. He passed out grenades. We attached them to the web belts we found in the equipment box.

I climbed over the transom, and water came up to my waist. The bottom was hard sand, and the footing was good. Jock handed over an M-16 and my nine millimeter. The grenades were attached across my chest and still dry.

Jock and Logan slipped quietly into the water, and we made our way to the bow of the boat. I used my feet to dig the plow anchor deeply into the sand. We were about ten feet from the shore. I went first, feeling my way with my feet, not wanting to fall into a hole.

The goggles provided us with a view of our surroundings, and I could see the narrow trail leading away from the water. We started out in single file, me in the lead and Jock bringing up the rear. We'd traveled about two hundred yards when I saw the outline of the generator shed.

The three of us had studied the schematic of the island that Debbie had sent. We knew exactly where we were.

"I'm going to blow the generator," Jock said. "Create a diversion."

"With what?" Logan asked.

"C-4," Jock said. "Courtesy of the guy at Moore's."

"Do you know how to use that stuff?" Logan asked.

"Oh, yeah," Jock said, and moved toward the shed.

In the green glow of the goggles, I saw something I'd missed the night before. There was a pipe running from the shed, along the ground and disappearing into the palmetto scrub that flanked the little building.

"What do you think this is?" I said, pointing to the pipe.

Logan looked more closely. "Gotta be the fuel supply. Probably runs to some kind of storage tank. It'd have to be near the water, so a barge could come in now and then to replenish the fuel."

I was concerned about starting a fire that would be between the boat and us when we started back. "If Jock blows that thing, are we going to have a fire on our hands?"

Logan shook his head. "I doubt it. That's diesel and it has a very high flashpoint. We should be all right."

Jock had broken the lock on the door of the shed and was inside. In a couple of minutes, he came out. "I've set the charge. It shouldn't do anything but cut off the electricity. I don't think it'll even make much noise, and it surely won't blow the place up."

We moved away from the area to a few feet from the back of the main house. Jock used some sort of device he had in his pocket to blow the charge. There was a loud pop, and the lights in the house went out. We moved quickly toward the cabin in which I'd found Peggy.

The guard from Peggy's cabin was running toward the guardhouse, his rifle strapped across his back. I saw another guard coming from the area of the trail leading to the little beach I'd found the night before. They seemed confused by the loss of power and were probably trying to find the guy in charge.

I unbolted the door to the cabin and went in. "Peggy," I said, loudly. "It's Matt."

"I'm here, Matt. I'm tied to the bed."

I looked around, peering through the goggles. I saw her across the room, straining at ropes that bound each arm to the bed. Other women were beginning to stir. I ran to Peggy and cut the ropes. She was wearing a white gown and was barefoot.

"Can you walk?" I said.

"Yes. But we have to get the Rev."

"Do you have any shoes?"

"Flip-flops. Under the bed."

"Get them, and let's go."

She reached under the bed and came up with the flip-flops.

I started for the door, leading her by the hand. Jock and Logan had taken positions on either side of the entrance, facing the courtyard, rifles at the ready. We left the building, and I bolted the door, keeping the drugged women in and out of harm's way.

"We've got to get Simmermon," Peggy said again.

"We don't have time to get him. We've got to get out of here before these guys figure out what's happening."

"Matt, Simmermon has some big plans about blowing people up. I don't know what they are, but it's about to start. We have to get him to tell us what he's doing."

I stopped at the door near Logan and Jock. "What do you know?" I asked.

"He took me to his room today. I tried to get him to talk to me about what he was going to do. He just said it was big, and rambled on about God telling him to blow up some people. He said that his disciples were going to change the world in a day or two."

"Is he crazy?"

"I think so. He must be."

"Did he hurt you?"

"No. Oh, you mean did he screw me? He tried, and I had to let him, but he couldn't, if you know what I mean. He said it was God's way of punishing him for not starting the bombings earlier."

Jock turned and said, "We'd better get him. Do you know where he is, Peggy?"

I said, "Peggy, meet Jock and Logan, my friends."

Peggy nodded. "I can take you to his room, but there're usually guards in the house."

"Let's go," said Logan.

We ran toward the main house, staying in the shadows of the two cabins that lay between the one where Peggy had been held and the house. The sound of a rifle rang out, and a small clod of dirt kicked up beside Logan's feet. I saw a rifleman on the porch of the big house, lining up another shot. Jock fired from the hip, on the run, and the man tumbled to the ground.

I looked up and saw another rifle beginning to poke out of an upstairs window. "Second story, on the right," I called out. Logan blasted away with his M-16, knocking the gunman back into the room.

We dashed for the front porch, Jock in the lead and me in the rear holding onto Peggy. She was running barefoot, holding her flip-flops in her hand. By the time I hit the steps leading to the verandah, Jock and Logan were flanking the door, rifles at the ready. A classic infantry approach.

As I reached the porch, Jock nodded. He stepped back and kicked open the front door. I had my rifle trained on the opening, but no one was there. I was looking at a traditional entrance hall, with a stairway reaching to the second floor. Living and dining rooms opening off the hall. Everything appeared green through the night-vision goggles.

Peggy whispered, "Upstairs, first door on the right."

"Stay here," I said.

I started through the door, Jock and Logan providing cover. A man appeared at the top of the stairs. I shot him, and he tumbled down, landing at my feet. I saw movement to my right, and turned to fire. A white gown seemed to float out of the living room. I realized it was a girl, her eyes wide, fear etched on her face. I grabbed her by the arm and flung her back inside.

"Take care of her, Peggy."

I started up the stairs. Logan and Jock took a quick look into the rooms flanking the hallway, and announced that they were clear. They followed me up the steps, climbing backward, rifles pointing downward. Mine was pointing toward the landing at the top.

I topped the stairs and Jock came up behind me. Logan planted himself on the second step from the top to guard the front door and entrance hall. Peggy and the girl were cowering in the living room, still in sight of Logan.

I kicked in the door to the bedroom Peggy had pointed out. A man was standing in the middle of the room with a pistol pointing at me. I shot him in the heart. Another man rose from behind the bed, his arms in the air. Simmermon.

"Don't shoot," he said. "I'm a man of God."

I waved the rifle toward the door. "Come with me, Reverend."

"Who are you?"

"I'm your worst nightmare." I'd always wanted to say that.

"Where are we going?"

"Never mind. You can come or I can just shoot you."

"I'm coming."

We went back down the stairs, Jock leading the way, Simmermon next, and then me, with my rifle touching his sorry back. We reached the hallway and started for the front door. A bullet whizzed by my head, burying itself in the steps behind me. Simmermon and I both dove for the floor.

Peggy had moved out of the living room. She slammed the door shut and dropped back to the floor.

"Where's the girl?" I shouted.

"She's under the sofa," said Peggy. "She's the housemaid. She'll be fine right where she is."

Logan had moved into the living room and was peering out a window. I joined him.

"The guards are getting into position in the front," Logan said. "I saw a couple more head for the back of the house."

A disembodied voice came out of the dark courtyard, amplified by a bullhorn. "You assholes are surrounded. Come out with your hands up."

There were probably fifteen men with rifles in kneeling firing positions in the courtyard. Not a very good tactical position. Amateurs. They were like the ducks in the shooting gallery at the carnival. Just waiting to be taken down.

Logan had gone to the back of the house. I heard him call out. "There're half a dozen armed men at the back of the house."

Jock said, "Oh, shit."

CHAPTER FORTY-ONE

"What now?" asked Logan.

"We attack," I said.

"Attack? Okay," said Logan.

"At Bragg, they taught us that when surrounded, we Attack! Attack! Attack!"

Jock grinned. "Sounds like a plan."

Peggy spoke up. "You're all as crazy as the Rev."

"Jock," I said. "Go out the back and use some of those grenades when I give the word. Logan, you stay with me. We're going to shoot the asses off those people. Peggy, you stay down."

I turned to Simmermon. "If you make one move I don't like, you're a dead man."

"I'm a man of God," he said again.

"I'm on my way," said Jock as he ran for the back of the house.

I shouted to the men in front, "We've got the Rev."

The bullhorn came back. "It don't matter. We've got our marching orders."

"I've also got Michelle Browne," I hollered.

"That don't matter none either," came back the bullhorn enhanced cracker voice.

Jock yelled from the back of the house. "I'm in place."

"Go when you hear the first shot," I said.

"Got it," said Jock.

I could see the guy standing in the middle of the courtyard with the bullhorn to his mouth. He'd turn to the side occasionally and spit. "If you don't come outta there, I'm gonna turn my boys loose," he said.

I shot him in the chest. I moved my sights just to his right and pulled the trigger again. Logan took out the one at the end of the firing line, and then the next one. I knocked another over and moved to the next one.

By then, they were getting the message. They'd gone prone on the ground, and were backing to the cover of the cabins. Five of them lay dead on the courtyard.

Just as I fired the first shot, I heard the first of a series of explosions. Jock was throwing the hand grenades with deadly accuracy. The explosions kept coming, one after the other. After the fifth one, there was quiet. Jock called out, "I think I got them all. Let's go."

Simmermon was still on the floor. He lay there, his arms shielding his head, whimpering. I kicked him. "Get up, you sorry bastard," I said.

"No. I'll die."

I put the muzzle of my rifle in his ear. "You're going to die if you don't get your sorry ass on your feet."

He came to his hands and knees and then to his feet.

I took Peggy by the hand and led her to the back of the house, nudging Simmermon with my rifle. Logan kept firing out the window at the fleeing guards. As I got to the back of the house, I called for Logan to join us. He came on the run.

I put Peggy's hand in Jock's. "Take her back to the boat. Logan, you bring up the rear, and take care of Simmermon. I'm going to stay here for a minute or two to make sure none of the bad guys are still up for a fight."

They went out the back door. I stood in the darkness, staring through the night vision goggles. A wave of disgust washed over me. I'd just killed several men and scared the piss out of some others. I wondered if they were just young men caught up in this in the same way Peggy was. I hoped not. I wanted them to be really bad guys. Maybe I'd feel better about killing them.

I didn't see any movement. I headed out the back of the house, found the trail, and walked carefully toward the boat. As I got close, I heard Logan say in a loud whisper, "Matt?"

"It's me," I said. "I'm coming in."

Logan had stopped about a hundred feet from the water, guarding the rear, giving Jock and Peggy time to get onto the boat. He'd tied the preacher's hands with some twine and stuffed a handkerchief in his mouth as a gag.

We eased our way toward the shoreline. Jock and Peggy crouched in the bushes near the water. Jock turned and put his finger to his lips.

We crawled up to where Jock was hiding. He put his finger to his lips again, and then pointed toward the boat. There was a figure standing in the water at the bow. In the green glow of the goggles, I saw the man standing in knee-deep water, talking into a handheld radio. Then I saw movement at the stern. Somebody was trying to board *Recess*.

I touched Logan on the shoulder and pointed to the man at the bow. I pointed to myself and then to the figure at the stern. Logan's old infantry training kicked in. He raised his rifle, pointing at the man at the bow. Just as he fired, I shot the man on the stern. Both bodies crumpled into the water.

"Let's go," I shouted.

Jock boosted Peggy up onto the boat while Logan and I stood watching the shoreline.

"Okay," Jock said, "I've got it. Come on aboard." He was scanning the shoreline, rifle at the ready.

I reached down and tugged at the anchor, loosening it in the sandy bottom. Logan shoved Simmermon up the ladder and into the cockpit. I climbed up the stern after Logan, got to the helm, and used the windlass to retrieve the anchor. I cranked the big Yamahas, turned the boat on its axis, and came on plane as I ran the reciprocal course of the one we'd come in on. If I ran aground, we'd be in big trouble. Simmermon was lying on the deck, and Jock and Logan were putting new clips in their rifles.

We roared into the turn into the Boca Grande Channel, and set a course for Naples. I wasn't going back to Key West that night. As we came around the northern end of Blood Island, I heard Logan curse. I turned to see what the problem was. Two go-fast boats full of riflemen were rounding the head of the island, heading straight for us.

Jock spotted them. "Oh, shit," he said.

CHAPTER FORTY-TWO

I pushed the throttles all the way forward. The boat jumped, flattening out on the water as it gained speed. I doused the running lights that I'd turned on as we came into Boca Grande Channel. The go-fast boats could outrun me, but maybe they couldn't see me in the dark. If they had radar, we were in trouble.

I kept the boats in sight on my radarscope, their blips making steady progress toward us. I realized they were on a course to intercept me. They knew exactly where I was. They had radar.

Jock disappeared into the cabin, and in a moment was back, lugging the M60 machine gun and its tripod. He laid it on the deck and went back down into the cabin. He returned with the rocket-propelled grenade launcher. We were loaded for bear.

Logan took the launcher, caressed it softly, smiling. "Man, I haven't used one of these in years."

Jock looked up from where he was assembling the tripod for the machine gun. "Do you remember how to use it?"

"Bet your ass," said Logan. "Bet your *sweet* ass."

I took another look at the radar screen. "They're closing on us," I said. "They'll be in rifle range in a few minutes."

Logan pushed Simmermon from his sitting position onto the floor of the cockpit. "Peggy, get in the cabin," he said. She did.

Just then, I saw winks of muzzle fire from the lead go-fast. "He's firing on us," I said. "He's too far away to do any damage, but they'll both be in range in a couple of minutes."

Jock had the M60 tripod braced on the gunwale near the stern. "I see them," he said, working to get the gun ready.

He settled in, quickly threading the cartridge belt into the chamber. He pointed it in the direction of our pursuers. I heard the heavy retort of the M60 override the sound of the straining outboards. Jock was firing steady streams of tracers. The lead go-fast had closed to within a thousand yards of us, when it veered off its course, turning away. Jock must have gotten some hits.

Logan was standing, feet planted wide apart, riding with the movement of the boat. He had the RPG launcher on his shoulder, his eye to the optical sight, the breech pointing overboard. He pulled the trigger, and the rocket shot from the barrel, the back-blast rolling harmlessly across the water.

The lead boat exploded. In the bright light of the blast, I could see shards of fiberglass shooting like flaming arrows into the dark water. The boat was gone in an instant, and a burning patch of gasoline was already dying out.

Logan let out a howl of elation. "Bring it on!" he shouted, shaking his fist at the scene of carnage.

The other go-fast made a wide arcing turn at high speed, bouncing in its own wake. I could hear the roar of its engines as it sped back the way it had come, tracers from Jock's M60 chasing it.

"Should we look for survivors?" I asked.

"There won't be any," said Logan. "Let's find out what Simmermon has to tell us."

I eased the throttles back to neutral. We drifted on the dark Gulf waters. No other boats were in sight, and my radar screen was empty. The quiet of the night was broken only by the slap of small swells hitting the side of the boat.

Logan pulled Simmermon up by his shirtfront and sat him against the bulkhead. He removed his gag and said, "You want to tell me who you're going to blow up?"

"The world."

"When?"

"It's started already. You can't stop it."

"Can't stop what?" Logan asked.

"The bombers. Some have already left the island, and the others are leaving today."

"What are the targets?"

"The ones God picks."

"You can do better than that, Rev," said Logan.

"God talks to me, you know. He tells me what to do. I am his earthly right arm."

Peggy had come up on deck. "I think he's schizophrenic," she said. "Once, when he had me in his room, he got quiet, and then started talking. It was like he was having a conversation, but I could only hear his side of it. He told me it was God talking to him."

"Voices," said Jock. "He's crazy as a loon."

Logan kicked Simmermon in the hip. "I want to know what you're going to blow up," he said.

"It's not what, it's who," Simmermon said. "You'll see. God is going to cleanse the world of heathens."

"How?"

"Suicide bombers," said Simmermon, a look of pleasure crossing his face. "We're going to set the world right."

CHAPTER FORTY-THREE

Jock was talking into his satellite phone, facing astern, nodding his head, writing on a piece of notepaper he'd pulled from his pocket.

He closed the phone and turned to me. "We need to meet a Coast Guard boat. They'll take Simmermon off our hands." He read the coordinates off his notes.

I dialed them into my GPS. "We're only about ten minutes from the rendezvous point," I said. "Did they give you a time to meet?"

"A forty-one footer is on its way now."

I flipped on my running lights and brought the boat up on plane, turning onto a course that would take us to the Coast Guard boat. Logan was squatting on the deck, still talking to Simmermon. I couldn't hear them over the roar of the engines. Jock stood on the deck holding the stock of the M60, still on its tripod.

As we approached the rendezvous point, I slowed the boat. My radio came alive.

"*Recess, Recess,* this is the United States Coast Guard. Request that you turn your running lights off and then on."

"This is *Recess.* Wilco," I mumbled into the mic as I flipped the lights off and then on.

A spotlight hit us, its beam piercing the dark and pinning us to the black water. "*Recess,* this is the Coast Guard. We have you in sight. I'll approach from your port. Don't shoot."

"Coast Guard, this is *Recess.* I copy. I have you in sight. We're standing down."

The white boat with the red striping and the Coast Guard emblem appeared out of the darkness. Its spotlight was trained on an area off my bow, not blinding us now.

The Coastie coxswain eased his boat alongside us. A woman in blue fatigues threw fenders over the side, and a young man in the same uniform threw me a line. Jock went to the bow to catch another line, and we secured the boats together.

One of the Coasties said, "Permission to come aboard?"

"Come ahead," I said. "We're glad to see you guys."

A uniformed man, who looked to be in his mid-twenties, climbed aboard *Recess*. "I'm Petty Officer Bob Postel," he said. "I was told to meet you and take charge of a prisoner. Which one of you is Mr. Houston?"

Jock stepped down into the cockpit and said, "That would be me."

The Coastie threw a sloppy salute. "I was told to meet you, sir, and put myself and my boat under your command."

"That won't be necessary," said Jock. "I do need you to take charge of a prisoner and keep him incommunicado at your station until I get there."

"I understand, sir. I'll need to put a life jacket on him. Can I untie his hands for that?"

"No problem."

"Sir, just so you'll know, we've thrown a cordon around Blood Island. I don't know what's up, but I was told to let you know that."

"Thank you, Petty Officer. Would you ask the commander on the scene to contact me on the VHF?"

The Coastie untied Simmermon's hands, put a life jacket on him, and then used handcuffs to restrain his arms behind him. He and another man helped the Rev onto the Coast Guard boat, and they were gone into the night, their stern light receding into the darkness.

"Mr. Houston?" I asked.

"One of many names," Jock said, and grinned.

"What now?"

"We're going to meet the Coast Guard commander. We may need to get back on the island, and then we need to talk to Simmermon and the people you've got stashed."

The radio beeped, and then a voice came over it. "*Recess, Recess,* this is the Coast Guard cutter *Intrepid.*"

"This is *Recess, Intrepid.*"

"I'm in command of the operation at Blood Island." He gave his co-ordinates, and said, "Can you come to me?"

I looked at Jock who nodded his head. "Roger that," I said. "We're on our way."

I dialed in the new coordinates and we headed west.

The *Intrepid* was a 210-foot Reliance-class cutter, carrying a crew of seventy-five and sporting a 25-millimeter chain gun and two 50-caliber machine guns. These guys were serious. The chain gun could fire two hundred rounds per minute and was accurate to a distance exceeding one mile. It would blow anything less than a warship out of the water.

The cutter was lit up like a downtown square. Deck lights bathed the white ship in a brightness that would let anyone within miles know she was there. She was hove to about a mile from Blood Island, staying to the deep water of Boca Grande Channel. I could see the running lights of other smaller Coast Guard vessels hovering on all sides of the island.

I radioed the cutter as we approached, identified myself, and was told to come alongside. Lines were thrown down from the deck along with a rope ladder.

Jock grabbed the ladder and told me he'd be right back. Logan and I let go the lines, and I backed *Recess* off several yards.

In a few minutes, a Coastie on the cutter's deck waved me back in. Jock came aboard, and I backed off again.

"We're going in," Jock said.

"In where?" I asked.

"Back to Key West, to the Coast Guard station. A Delta Force team out of the Hurlburt Field in the panhandle is going to drop on Blood Island in about an hour. In the meantime, the Coasties have the place bottled up tight. Nobody's going to be leaving."

Logan said, "From what the Rev just told me, I think he's planning to hit some mosques. Called it divine retribution for what's going on in Israel."

"He could start a war," Jock said.

"I think that's his intention," Logan said.

CHAPTER FORTY-FOUR

It would be daylight soon, and we were all tired. We still had a lot to do, and we had to make arrangements for Peggy. She was sitting next to me at the helm. "Peggy, you need to call your dad," I said. "And I'd like to talk to him too."

I handed her my cell phone and she dialed the number. In a moment I heard her say, "Daddy, I'm with Matt. I'm okay."

They talked for a minute, and she handed the phone to me. She was crying loudly, sobbing, her head buried in her hands. Logan came to the helm and put a hand on her shoulder, just letting her know he was there.

"Matt," Jeff said, "how can I ever thank you?"

"Don't worry about it, Jeff. We're practically family. We're on our way to the Coast Guard station, and I'm sure the local cops will want to talk to Peggy. They'll be in touch and arrange to get her home. What's going on with Laura?"

His voice was low, strained, flooded with emotion. "It's not good," he said. His voice caught, a sob stifled. "She's very sick. Some sort of virulent form of leukemia. She's been aware of it for some time, but she didn't tell anybody. Didn't want to worry us."

"Prognosis?"

"Terrible. She's close to death. I think she's been holding on to see Peggy. I'm not sure how I'll live without her."

Pain ripped through my soul; shock and despair gnawed at my brain. No. Not possible. Laura was dying. That just couldn't be. She had been awake and lucid just a few hours ago. She was going to be fine. I had banished my fear with the relief that came with that knowledge.

I knew we'd never have a life together, but as long as she was alive, there was always that glimmer of hope. When she'd needed help finding Peggy, she called me. And I knew that if I needed her badly enough, I could just go to Atlanta to see her. The despair I'd felt during the dream of her funeral bore down on me, dark and hopeless. My mind could not comprehend a world without Laura. Darkness was closing in, shutting down my emotions, drawing me into a pit from which I would not emerge. But Peggy needed me, and Laura needed Peggy. I willed the cloying dread back into its rotten corner, back there where the memories of dead soldiers hide in the shadows and lurch occasionally into my nightmares.

I choked back my emotion. "How long, Jeff?"

"Today, tomorrow, a couple more days at the most."

"I'm sorry, my friend, so goddamned sorry."

"I know. Me too. Thanks for finding my little girl. I'm sure you know how much this means to Laura. She'll go peacefully, now." I heard a sob as he hung up the phone.

I turned to Peggy. "He told you about Laura?"

"Yes. Oh, Matt, I've got to get home."

"We're on our way, honey," I said, and pushed the throttles all the way forward.

I hailed the Coast Guard station on my radio as we approached their docks. Two men came to meet us, took our lines, and pointed us to the building housing the administrative staff.

On the way in, I'd told Jock and Logan about Laura's condition. Logan stood next to Peggy during the entire trip, his arm around her shoulder, cradling her head in the crook of his elbow, giving support to a young lady who was losing a mother for the second time in her short life. A somber air hovered over our little group as we climbed out of the boat onto the cement piers.

Peggy was quiet, her face showing no expression. She was still dressed in the white gown, now streaked with dirt. Her flip-flops slapped the pavement as we walked. She was holding Logan's hand.

"What about Peggy?" I asked.

"She'll come with me," Jock said. "We'll get her some clothes and send her home to Atlanta. I think the local cops will want to talk to her first."

"Call Detective Paul Galis at the sheriff's office. He's aware of the situation."

At the door to the station Jock stopped. "Can you get to those people you've got under lock and key? We need to squeeze them for any information about suicide bombers."

"I think so. Let me make a call."

I dialed Mendosa's number and identified myself to the answering machine. A moment later, my cell phone rang.

"This is Matt Royal. I'd like to meet with the people you're holding for me."

"Hold, please," the voice said.

He came back on the line. "Where are you?"

"I'm at the Coast Guard station on Trumbo Road."

"Stand out front. A car will be there in five minutes."

"I have a friend with me."

"Hold, please."

Then, "Mr. Mendosa says if you vouch for him, bring him along." He hung up.

"They'll be here in a couple of minutes," I said.

Jock nodded. "I'll leave it to you then. I have some talking to do to the Reverend Simmermon." He walked into the building, leading Peggy by the hand.

"Who are the people on the phone?" Logan said.

"They're friends of Cracker Dix's."

Logan laughed. "That doesn't sound good."

"They're solid people, and they owe Cracker. He called in part of the debt to help me."

"Good ol' Cracker," said Logan, a wry grin softening his face.

The sun was trying to rise out of the Atlantic. The sky was brightening over the little city, the harbinger of the sun's rays, signaling another day for the revelers who come to Key West to drink and party. I thought it was going to be a beautiful morning. I wondered what was happening on Blood Island. I hoped it wasn't going to be a blood bath.

The black Lincoln Town Car glided to a stop in front of us. The same driver who'd met me on Roosevelt Avenue was behind the wheel. He got out and said, "Good to see you, Mr. Royal."

"Good to see you again. This is Logan Hamilton. Also a friend of Cracker's."

They shook hands, and Logan and I got in the backseat. We headed northeast, out of the city. We came to a sign announcing that we were on Big Coppitt Key. We turned off U.S. 1 onto a residential street. We stopped in front of a large house at the end of the street. A garage door opened and the Lincoln eased into the space and stopped.

"We're here," said the driver.

We got out and followed him into the house, through a large kitchen and into the living room. One wall was mostly windows, giving a view through a stand of trees down to Florida Bay.

The house sat on a large lot, much larger than you would expect to find in the Keys. The trees all around gave it a sense of seclusion.

Mendosa was sitting in an easy chair sipping coffee, the morning paper on his lap. He rose as we entered the room. I introduced Logan, and said, "I need to talk to your guests. It's very important."

"Certainly. I'll take you to them, but they may not be in a mood to talk. Perhaps we should have a plan in case they won't cooperate."

"Aren't you interested in why we're here?"

"Of course I am, but it'd be rude to ask. I don't need to know. Probably don't want to know." He grinned.

I nodded. "You're probably right."

We talked for a few more minutes, and then Mendosa led Logan and me down a hallway to a bedroom. The room was bare except for a bed. A large window looked out over the backyard. I could see beyond the trees to the bay, shimmering in the early light. The backyard was a study in shadows cast by the rising sun. Michelle was lying on the bed, fully clothed and wide-awake.

"Good morning, sunshine," I said.

She looked at me, hate darting from her eyes like lightning. "Asshole," she said through clenched teeth. "You broke my jaw."

"Sorry. I'd like you to meet my friend Logan."

"Another asshole."

Logan smiled. "Nice to meet you too, ma'am."

"I've got a few questions," I said.

Michelle turned her head away from me. "I've got nothing to say."

I looked at Mendosa. "Would you be kind enough to ask Mr. Calhoun to join us?"

He left and returned with one of his men holding Charlie Calhoun by the arm, his hands cuffed behind his back.

I said, "Good morning, Mr. Calhoun. I'd offer to shake hands, but you seem a little distracted."

He stared straight ahead. "Fuck you, Royal."

"Charlie," I said, "I'm going to ask you some questions. You get one try at answering truthfully. If you don't, you pay the consequences."

Michelle mumbled through her clenched jaw. "Don't say a word, Charlie."

I looked at Charlie. "You've got one chance. Don't blow it."

"Fuck you, Royal."

I smiled at him. "You've got a limited vocabulary. Tell me what the Rev is going to blow up."

A look of puzzlement, or maybe just stupidity, crossed his face. "I don't know what you're talking about."

"Charlie, don't be stupid. If you help me, you'll be helping yourself."

"Go to hell, Royal."

I turned to Mendosa. "Would you be kind enough to take this cretin out back and have him shot?"

"Certainly," said Mendosa, and nodded to the man who'd brought Charlie to us.

Charlie looked at me with a knowing grin. He didn't think we'd do it. People who lurk on the edges of civilization know that their greatest protection from the wrath of society is the unwillingness of good people to do bad things. Sometimes, the lurkers misjudge.

CHAPTER FORTY-FIVE

Logan followed Charlie and his keeper out of the room. They reappeared on the lawn outside the window. Mendosa's man moved out of my line of sight, leaving Charlie and Logan standing alone on the grass.

"You might want to watch this," I said to Michelle.

Logan was standing behind the handcuffed Charlie. He raised a pistol to the back of Charlie's neck. The sound of a gunshot rattled the glass in the window. Charlie dropped loosely to the ground, like a bag of potatoes. Logan turned and walked out of our view.

Michelle screamed as the gunshot sounded. "My God! You shot Charlie."

"You're next, Michelle," I said. "I'm tired of fooling around. Tell me what I want to know and you live. Lie to me, you die. It's that simple."

She was sitting on the side of the bed, hands in her lap. They were shaking. Her face was twisted in a rictus of fear. Tears were sliding down her cheeks. Reality had come home to Michelle, and she didn't like it.

"I don't want to die," she said.

I sat on the bed beside her. I reached out and took her hand. "I don't want you to die either. Tell me what Simmermon is doing."

She caught her breath, swallowed a sob. "I'm not real sure. He's been crazy lately. Says God's talking to him and telling him to kill the heathens."

"How does he plan to do that?"

"I think he's got some of those kids convinced to use themselves as suicide bombers. He's planning to blow up churches."

"Churches? Christian churches?" I said.

"Yes. He thinks if he sends the bombers into Christian houses of worship, the Muslims will be blamed. He wants what he calls another Crusade to free the Holy Land."

"How does he figure to do that?"

"He says that the bombings will cause such a groundswell of public outrage that the U.S. will have to bomb the Muslims out of existence."

"All one and a half billion of them?" Incredulity strained my words.

"That's what he says, starting with the ones in our country."

"He's not squeamish about sacrificing his brother Christians in return for killing Muslims?"

Michelle rolled her eyes. "He says the Christians who are killed are going to heaven anyway, or most of them, and they'll be better off."

"He's not planning to be among them I take it."

"No. He says God wants him here on earth to help turn everybody else into Christians, to save them."

"And if the Jews or Buddhists or whoever don't want to be saved?"

"I don't think he's worked that one out yet," she said.

"How long has he been planning this?"

"I'm not sure. He just told me about it a couple of days ago at lunch. I think he's been working on it for a long time though. He said the plan is already in operation."

"How did a string of whorehouses come to this?"

"I don't know. I met the Rev a few years ago at a tent revival in Alabama. He understood what I was going through, and I joined his organization. I'd worked in a house in Birmingham, and when I realized all these little sluts were looking for salvation, we came up with the plan for the spas. It was a good deal until he went nuts."

"Not such a good deal for the girls."

"Not a bad deal either. They have a nice place to live, food on the table, and a medical plan. Most of them don't want to leave."

"But you keep them drugged."

"Only for the first month or so. Then they can either leave or stay on at one of our other spas in a different town."

"So, Key West is where you break them in."

"You could say that."

"What happens if the girl doesn't want this kind of life?"

"The Rev takes them back home I guess. I don't really know."

"I thought you ran things."

"I thought I did too."

"Where is he sending the bombers?"

"I honestly don't know. I didn't even know there were bombers until a couple of days ago."

"Okay. You're going to stay here for a while. One of your other guys is here too."

"Who?"

"Martin Holcomb."

"He's one of the Rev's thugs. I hardly know him."

"I'll have Charlie brought back to his room."

"His body?"

"No, Michelle. Charlie's not dead. Sane people don't kill just to make a point."

"But I saw your buddy shoot him."

"Yes, but with a dart gun. The gunshot came from a pistol fired into the ground. Charlie will have a headache but that's all."

"You can't prove anything."

I pulled a tape recorder out of the pocket of my shorts. "I think I can," I said.

"You son of a bitch," she said. "You rotten son of a bitch."

CHAPTER FORTY-SIX

The driver took Logan and me back to the Coast Guard station. I thanked the driver and told him I'd be in touch about his guests.

The Coastie on the front desk took us to a room in the back of the building. Jock was there, sitting at a small conference table. Paul Galis sat on the other side, nervously rubbing his hands together. A compact man in Army battle fatigues was at the end of the table.

Jock introduced Logan to Galis, and both of us to Major John Lockman.

"The major is in command of the Delta Force team," said Jock. "They've secured the island and have all the remaining men under arrest."

"What about the girls?" I asked.

Jock shook his head. "They're bringing them in on a Coast Guard boat. They'll be treated for drugs, and then we'll see what we can do about them."

Galis said, "My people raided the spa, and we have three men in custody. The girls are being held for medical treatment."

"They're all on drugs," I said.

"We know," said Galis. "I doubt they'll be much help to us in making a case against Simmermon."

I shrugged. "I've got three of his people under wraps and a recorded statement from Michelle Browne, his top assistant."

A look of surprise crossed Galis' face. "Where are they?"

I grinned. "I don't think you want to know. But I'll get them for you later today."

Galis laughed. "Good enough."

I turned to the major. "Did you lose anybody?"

"No, sir," he said. "There were only a half dozen armed men left, and they gave up quickly. We found several bodies with gunshot wounds and five who died from what looks like grenade shrapnel."

Jock put his elbows on the table, leaning in. "That sounds about right. Matt and Logan are old infantrymen."

The major looked at us. "Army?"

Jock said, "Matt was Special Forces, and Logan was in the 82nd until he got out of the mud and learned to fly helicopters."

"Airborne," said the major, just loud enough to be heard.

"Airborne," Logan and I repeated. It was the mantra of those who jump out of airplanes in order to take care of the rest of us. George Orwell once wrote something to the effect that people could sleep peaceably in their beds at night only because rough men stand ready to do violence on their behalf. I was looking at one of those rough men, and I was glad he was on our side.

I said, "Did you find any explosives, Major?"

"Yes, sir. We found a big stash. There were also vests, like suicide bombers use."

Logan spoke up. "Did the people you took prisoner know anything about suicide bombers?"

"Yes, sir. We've got several who keep talking about wanting to die for God. They told my intelligence people that they were supposed to leave the island today and fan out across the country. Apparently something big was planned for this Sunday."

Jock said, "Simmermon is as crazy as a run over dog, but he keeps talking about the ones who went out yesterday."

"How many?" I asked.

"Only three, he says, but who knows."

"Did he say where they're going?"

"Yes. One is here, another is going to Atlanta, and the third is headed for Orlando."

Logan said, "Today's Saturday. Are we talking about tomorrow? That's not much time to stop this."

"Tomorrow," Jock said. "We've got to move fast. I've alerted the FBI. Their counterterrorism force is working on it. Galis will have men at every church in Key West on Sunday. I don't know about Atlanta and Orlando. Too big. Too many churches."

The phone on the table rang. Jock picked it up, listened, and hung up. He looked at me. "Peggy's about to leave. She wants to see you."

Galis stood up. "I'll take you to her, Matt."

I followed him out the door and down a hall to another small conference room. Peggy was there, dressed in slacks and a blouse. Another woman, a tall blonde in her mid-twenties, was with her.

Peggy stood and hugged me. "Thanks for saving my life."

I hugged back. "You're worth saving. Laura told me so."

"Come to Atlanta with me. Laura will want to see you."

"How is she?"

"Bad. Very bad. Daddy said she perked up when he told her you found me, but she doesn't have long."

"I can't leave right now, honey. We've got a big problem on our hands with Simmermon."

"Matt, if you don't come now, you may not get to see her."

I knew that, and I also knew that I wasn't needed in Key West. But I thought Jeff and Peggy and her sister, Gwen, should share what little time Laura had left. I'd long ago forfeited my right to those last precious hours of her life.

I kissed Peggy on the top of her head. "Tell Laura I'm thinking of her."

Peggy started to cry and wrapped her arms around me. "Come see me in Athens, Matt. Promise me."

"I will. Soon."

Galis introduced me to the good-looking blonde. "Matt, this is Deputy Karen Senkbeil. She's going to Atlanta with Peggy."

We shook hands. "Take care of my girl, Deputy," I said. I turned and walked out the door, hurrying before I started crying. Paratroopers aren't supposed to do that. Not in public, anyway. Not even for Laura.

CHAPTER FORTY-SEVEN

I rejoined the meeting. Coffee had been delivered and each man had a mug in front of him. I poured myself one and sat down next to Logan.

Jock said, "We've worked out a plan of sorts. Blood Island is secure, and Major Lockman is going to leave a platoon there to make sure it stays that way. He and the rest of his men are headed back to Hurlburt. I'm going to sweat Simmermon some more, and see if I can get something else out of him. We're also going to be interrogating the other people from the island. Maybe somebody heard something or knows something."

"What about other governmental agencies?" I asked.

"The FBI is on it, and because of the explosives, ATF is joining them. The president is being briefed, and if we can't stop the bastards, he'll be prepared to make a statement to the nation on Sunday evening, explaining what happened."

"Not a great plan."

Jock looked at me. "No, it's not," he said, "but unless you've got a better one, I don't know what else to do."

"How do Logan and I fit into this?"

"You don't, officially."

"Unofficially?"

"I'd like for you to go to Orlando today. Make contact with your buddy at the U.S. Attorney's Office. He'll be expecting you. He's been told that you'll be coordinating our efforts up there and acting as liaison with me."

"That sounds pretty official."

"There'll be no record of it. Parrish knows that."

David Parrish was the chief assistant U.S. attorney for the Middle

District of Florida. He'd been my law school classmate and good friend for many years. We'd worked together before.

"Okay," I said. "Can Logan take my boat back to Longboat Key?"

"No. The Coasties will take care of your boat. I want Logan to go with you. You'll be met at the airport by one of our men. He'll drive you to Parrish's office and leave you a car. Check in with me when you get there."

"What about the people I'm holding?"

Galis stirred. "I'd like to have them in custody," he said.

Jock looked at me. "How quick can you get them here?"

"Pretty quick. But I've got to go get them."

I called Mendosa's number again and waited for the callback. It came quickly.

"I need to pick up my people and deliver them to the cops," I said. "If it's all right with Mr. Mendosa, I'll drive out and pick them up. Nobody has to know where they've been."

"Hold on."

I waited.

He was back on the line. "Mr. Mendosa said to come on out."

Logan and I took a government car and drove back out U.S. 1, taking the turnoff on Big Coppitt Key. The garage door opened as I pulled into the driveway. A space was waiting for me. I pulled in, and the door slid closed. A man was standing at the doorway leading into the house. He waved Logan and me in.

Our three guests were standing in the kitchen, hands cuffed behind them, blindfolds over their eyes, their mouths gagged. Nothing was said by anyone.

We guided the three into the backseat of the car, and I backed out of the garage. We returned to the Coast Guard station on Trumbo Road and turned them over to Detective Galis.

CHAPTER FORTY-EIGHT

Orlando. My old hometown. It was a city that lived up to its nickname, "The City Beautiful." It was dotted with over a hundred named lakes, and its suburbs had many more. It was a city of gracious homes and tall office buildings. Condos were sprouting downtown and the city center was a vibrant place to be on a weekday. On this Saturday, it was quiet.

"I'll leave the car for you," said our driver, tossing the keys to me. "Somebody will pick me up in a few minutes."

He'd parked in the public lot beneath I-4, across the street from the federal courthouse in downtown. "Better leave your weapons in the car," he said.

Logan and I had flown up from Key West in a business jet owned by some federal agency. We didn't have to surrender our weapons. Each of us had a nine millimeter, and I still had a dive knife strapped to my ankle.

Before we left Key West, Jock had dispatched a Coastie to retrieve my dive gear from the surfer guy who ran the shop. It would be stashed aboard *Recess*.

A Coastie had directed us to an area where we could shower and shave. Logan and I were both dead tired. We hadn't slept since we took the naps while anchored at Boot Key the afternoon before. We grabbed a couple of hours of sleep, and then dressed in new clothes provided by a grateful government. We both were wearing slacks and golf shirts, with light windbreakers to hide our pistols.

We landed at Orlando Executive Airport shortly before noon, met our escort, and were driven to the courthouse.

We left our weapons in the trunk of the government sedan, cleared courthouse security, and were escorted to David Parrish's office. He was waiting for us, a big blond man whose hair was now mostly gray, a slight paunch hanging precariously over his belt.

"Matt," he said in his Georgia accented baritone, "it's good to see you."

I introduced him to Logan, and said, "I'm told you know why we're here."

"Not exactly, but I got orders from Washington to, as they say, show you every courtesy. That means I'm to do what you tell me to do."

"I like that," I said. "How about getting me a cup of coffee?"

"Go to hell, Royal," he said, grinning. "There are just some things I won't do for my country. Can you tell me what's going on?"

We had taken seats in a small conference room. David sat at the end of the table, and Logan and I flanked him. The seal of the U.S. Justice Department hung on the wall behind Parrish's head, and black-and-white photographs of the present and former U.S. attorneys general lined two other walls. The final wall was glass, providing a view of I-4.

I leaned into the table. "David, we're in a hell of a fix. Somebody is going to blow up a church here on Sunday."

"Whoa. What's going on?"

I filled him in on what we knew and what we didn't know. It was sketchy at best, and not very enlightening.

Parrish leaned back in his chair, hands under his chin, fingertips touching. "What are we supposed to do?"

"I don't know. I need to call Jock and see if he has any more information."

A look of mild surprise crossed Parrish's face. "Ah," he said, "I should have detected the fine hand of Mr. Algren in all this. He has a lot of juice in Washington."

Jock, David, and I had worked together before.

"He seems to," I said.

David looked at Logan. "Where does Logan fit into all this? Are you government too?"

Logan laughed. "Not since I got out of the Army. I got shanghaied into this mess by our friend Matt. I'm not sure what I'm supposed to do here, other than hold Royal's hand."

I stood up. "I've got to make a call," I said, and stepped into the hallway, pulled out my cell phone.

Jock picked up on the first ring.

"Anything more?" I said.

"Not much. We've helped the Rev's memory with some drugs, but what we're getting is pretty disjointed. He seems to be living in the past somewhere and talking about somebody named Albert Thomas and another guy named Colin Edinfield. I don't know who they are, and the government computers tell us they're both dead. I can't make any sense out of it."

"Anything else?"

"Nothing. He keeps mumbling something about Arlington. That doesn't make any sense either, and the people he's named aren't buried there."

"Let me know if anything comes up."

"Okay. You should have some FBI and ATF types getting to Parrish's office within a few minutes." He hung up.

I rejoined Logan and David, and in a couple of minutes two men in suits were shown into the room. David stood and made the introductions. FBI and ATF agents.

David sat back down and asked, "Do you guys know anything about why you're here?"

The FBI agent spoke up. "We've been briefed about a possible church bombing in the area. That's all we know."

"That's about all we know too," I said.

The FBI agent turned to me. "Tell me just exactly who you are."

Parrish fielded the question. "Mr. Royal is in charge. Mr. Hamilton is assisting him. That comes from the very top, and that's all you need to know for now."

I could tell the two federal agents didn't like that. "Gentlemen," I said, "I don't like this any better than you do. I've got my assignment though and, if it'll make you feel better, I'm taking my orders from somebody who works for the government and outranks almost everybody in the world. If and when I give an order, I'll simply be conveying it from my principal. Clear?"

"Not really," said the AFT agent, "but I know how to take orders."

"Good." I then told them everything I knew, including the garbled information Jock was getting from Simmermon.

The FBI agent shook his head. "That's not much to go on. I know we've got all our people and ATF's people ready to go to work. Our counterterrorism guy is in charge. We just don't know what to do."

My cell phone rang. It was Paul Galis.

"Michelle tells me they have a whorehouse in Orlando," he said. "There's one in Atlanta too."

"Where's the one in Orlando?"

He gave me an address and hung up.

I looked at the men gathered at the table. "We may have a starting place." I explained how the Heaven Can't Wait Spas operated, and their ties to Simmermon.

The ATF agent looked up from the table. "That might be their staging area. I can get some dogs in there that'll find any explosives in a matter of minutes."

I shook my head. "If the bomber isn't in the house, a raid will spook him. He'll go to ground, and we'll be sitting here wondering where he is when a church goes up."

Parrish leaned forward. "Any suggestions?"

I nodded. "Let's send somebody in undercover. See what we can find out before we go breaking down doors."

"We can send in an agent," said the FBI.

"I'll go," I said. "I may have a better sense of what we're looking for. I've been in one of these places before, and I might see something that's out of the ordinary. Something someone else might miss."

"That could be dangerous," said Parrish.

"I know," I said.

I just didn't realize how dangerous.

CHAPTER FORTY-NINE

The day was winding down as Logan and I left the courthouse. It was almost four o'clock. Light traffic was passing by on I-4, tires singing on the asphalt. Two blocks to the east the bars and clubs along Orange Avenue were already starting to fill up with the young people who every night made downtown Orlando their own.

"Let's find a hotel," I said. "We can grab a few winks before I go whoring."

We'd decided to wait until late that evening to approach the spa. The federal agencies were doing everything they could, and it wouldn't matter if we put off our visit. The bomber would either be there or he wouldn't. The feds already had somebody watching the place, and if anyone who didn't look like a customer entered or left, we'd know about it immediately.

Our plan was for Logan and me to drive to the spa at about ten that evening. Logan would stay with the car, fully armed, and be in constant contact with me via a small radio attached to my body. If I gave a code word, he'd notify the federal agents surrounding the place, and they'd come running. It was a good plan—in theory.

We found a hotel near downtown, checked into separate rooms, and went to bed. I woke up at eight, and immediately thought of Laura. I don't think I was dreaming about her, but she was the first thought that entered my mind as I regained conscious thought. She was dying, might already be dead. Her death was going to be a permanent part of my life, and I wondered if I would spend the rest of it waking to regret and loss.

I shook off the grim thoughts, showered, shaved, and ordered hamburgers from room service. Logan joined me, and we talked over the plan again. I made a call to make sure the feds were in place around the spa. No one had seen anybody enter or leave the place other than the typical middle-aged client. There was nothing else for us to do.

Logan drove. The spa was only a few blocks away in an area of Orlando known as Thornton Park. It was a trendy part of town, peopled mostly by young urban professionals who owned the condos in the towers that lined East Central Boulevard and spread out south of Lake Eola. Many of the old houses in the neighborhood remained. Some had been turned into art galleries or restaurants. One, a beautiful three-story brick Federal mansion, had become a spa. An upscale whorehouse.

When I'd lived in Orlando, the building had housed a firm of lawyers. Some would say that the business of the place hadn't changed, just the occupants.

We circled the block several times, looking for a place to park that would give Logan quick access if I needed him. I didn't see any sign of cops or feds, which was good. If I didn't see them, nobody else would.

Finally, as we rounded a corner, a car pulled out of a space right in front of the spa. Logan parked and turned off the engine. He put an earpiece in place and said, "Let's make sure this thing is working."

I got out of the car and walked a few feet. I turned to look back, and tested the mic. "You know, as much as you keep grousing about not getting laid, you could be doing this."

He grinned and held up his right hand, forefinger and thumb circled in the OK signal. I turned and walked toward the front door.

The porch was not large, more of a stoop. Several steps led up from the street. I crossed to the front door. There was a small sign attached to the brick next to the entrance. It was identical to the one at the spa in Key West.

I opened the door and walked into a large entry hall. A small desk was set in the middle, and a woman of about thirty, wearing a business suit, sat behind it.

"May I help you, sir?" she said, smiling.

"I'd like a massage," I said. "Do you have someone available?"

"Certainly, sir. Just have a seat in the living room."

She pointed to an arched doorway leading to a room off the entrance hall. I sat on a reproduction Chippendale sofa and waited. The whole drill was reminiscent of my visit to the spa in Key West. If something worked, why change it? McDonald's and Burger King used the same concept. Sort of. I wondered if I would be greeted by a wiser and older version of Sister Amy.

In a few minutes, a young lady entered the room. She was wearing a sundress in a bright floral pattern, pulled low on her shoulders. I could see the swell of her breasts under the fabric, but it was a dress that wouldn't have been out of place at an afternoon tea party. Her blonde hair was done up on the back of her head in some sort of a twist. Her feet were encased in high-heeled sandals, her toenails freshly painted light pink to match her perfectly manicured fingernails.

As I stood, she held out her hand, palm down, an old-fashioned lady handshake. "I'm Marta Sweeney. I'll be your hostess this evening."

I shook her hand and introduced myself as Miles Leavitt.

"Have a seat," she said. "Have you been here before?"

"No. First time. I'm a little nervous."

"Where're you from?" She was trying to put me at ease.

I was going to say Nahant, Massachusetts, just because nobody had ever heard of the place, but I was sure my accent would give me away. "Atlanta," I said.

"Here on business?"

"Yes. I had to stay over the weekend."

"Well," she said, favoring me again with her smile, "let's see if we can make it a positive experience. How did you find your way to me?"

I told her the name of the hotel where Logan and I had rooms. "The bell captain mentioned this place."

"Oh, that would be Jaime?"

"I don't know his name. He's a Hispanic gentleman."

I'd noticed the man when we checked into the hotel. I was hoping he had a tie-in to this place, or at least he wasn't someone the management would be suspicious of. Apparently, I'd made a good guess.

"Would you like to come upstairs?" she asked.

"This is a beautiful house," I said, trying to buy some time. "Do you live here?"

"Oh, yes. I live on the third floor with some of the other girls. The second floor has our public rooms." She giggled. "Although, they're very private, if you know what I mean."

If Marta had ever had a regional accent, she kept it well hidden. Her diction was just about perfect. She was a well-trained young lady. In another time, she would have been described as a courtesan.

"Ah," I said, stumbling a little over my words, "what about payment?"

"You can give Ms. Young at the desk a credit card, if you like, and settle up when you leave. The card will show that you spent some money at an upscale restaurant in downtown Orlando. You ordered a couple of bottles of wine for your business associates." She giggled again.

"I don't have a credit card. How about cash?"

"You can leave a five hundred dollar deposit with Ms. Young. I think that'll be sufficient, don't you?" She made a small moue, kind of cutesy, and out of character for a whore.

This was certainly a different place than the one in Key West. This must be what happens to the girls after they get used to their new lives and get the drugs out of their systems. They transfer up the line into better and better houses. Michelle and Simmermon had put together an assembly line of whores, turning them into newer and better models of their old selves. I wondered what happened to the girls when they got too old for this line of work.

I pulled five one hundred dollar bills out of my pocket and gave them to Ms. Young. Marta led me upstairs, and into a room dominated by a four-poster bed. A large man sat on the bed, shirtless, his abdomen swathed in a bandage. He was pointing a .22-caliber pistol at me. The last time I'd seen him was on a Key West street three nights before. When I'd shot him.

CHAPTER FIFTY

"Ah," the man on the bed said, "I can see that you're surprised to find me here."

"A bit," I said. I knew Logan was listening, but he wouldn't panic and send in the troops unless I said the magic word. I wanted to hear what this muscle-bound ape had to say.

He grinned. "We have wonderful security. Our video cams are high resolution. I recognized you as soon as you came through the door. I owe you something, I think." He waved the gun around a little for emphasis.

I had to let Logan know what was going on. "So, you're the guy I shot in Key West."

"You got that right, asshole." He wasn't smiling anymore. A slight grimace of pain crossed his face.

"Still hurting? I'm surprised you could travel."

"A doc on our payroll in Key West fixed me up, and the boss sent me here to recuperate. I sit and watch the fucking video screen all day. It ain't a lot of fun."

Marta had stood silently during our conversation. I turned to her. "Marta, you brought me into the first room at the head of the stairs. Is this where you always stash your friends with .22 pistols?" Logan needed to know exactly where I was and what kind of firepower he was facing.

She giggled. I think it was a habit she'd developed. An annoying habit in a whore.

"Well," I said, "recess is over."

Recess was the magic word. The cavalry would be on its way. I turned back to the man on the bed.

"I think you need to know," I said, "that in about two minutes this place is going to be swarming with cops and federal agents."

"Right," he said, and laughed. "And I'm supposed to let you go."

"That'd be the smart thing to do."

I heard a loud voice from downstairs. "Federal agents. Put your hands on your head." Then, heavy boots bounding up the stairs.

"See?" I said.

Marta giggled.

"Shit," said the man, and put the gun on the floor.

The door burst open, and Logan dove into the room, his nine millimeter in his hand. Another man wearing a bulletproof vest was right behind him, a shotgun pointing into the room.

"Hell of an entrance, Logan," I said.

He rolled to his feet. "I thought you'd like that. Learned it in the Army."

The man on the bed had his hands in the air. His face was impassive. Marta was crying softly, tears running down her pretty cheeks. Their lives had just taken a big detour.

Two Orlando police officers came into the room, handcuffed Marta and the gunman, and took them out. I went to the door of the room and saw other cops leading more women down the stairs.

Logan said, "They'll be searching the place with explosive sniffing dogs. Let's go to the command post."

A pickup truck was parked in the street in front of the house, a large box trailer attached to it. Truck and trailer sported the logos of the Orlando Police Department. Cops and their handcuffed prisoners were milling around, waiting for transportation to the county jail.

The FBI agent we'd met in Parrish's office was in the trailer talking to the police commander. He invited us in and introduced us to the cops on duty. A radio receiver sat on a table attached to one wall of the trailer. It was crackling with information from the officers and agents inside the house.

We sat, sipping cups of coffee poured from a large thermos, listening to the radio reports. They were all negative.

After about ten minutes, the FBI agent said, "That's the last one. No explosives."

"What about the people in the house?" I asked. "Any other men?"

"I'll check." He went outside to talk to one of the officers.

Logan asked, "What do we do if we don't get anything out of this?"

"I don't know. We may have a bunch of dead people on our hands tomorrow."

"Shouldn't the authorities warn people not to go to church in the morning? Wouldn't that at least stop the carnage?"

"I would think so. Let's see what happens."

The FBI agent returned. "Other than the guy holding the gun on you, we found two other bouncer types. Both are in their thirties. They don't fit the profile of the young men Simmermon has brainwashed."

"No," I said, "they don't."

A uniformed police officer came into the trailer. "Mr. Royal?" he asked.

"I'm Royal."

"I'm with the bomb squad, sir. We didn't find any explosives, but my dog did get a little crazy at one point in a room on the third floor."

"What do you think that was all about?"

"We searched the room completely. I think the dog may have smelled explosives that had been there and were moved. I can't prove that, but my boss said I should let you know."

"Thank you, Officer," I said.

I turned to the FBI agent. "Will you find out how the gunman got here from Key West?"

"Sure," he said, and left the trailer.

"What are you thinking?" asked Logan.

"I'm not sure, but the explosives may have come from Key West with the idiot I shot."

The agent returned and brought the gunman with him. "He won't talk," the agent said. "Wants a lawyer."

The prisoner's hands were cuffed behind his back. His face was an impassive mask, but his darting eyes gave away a level of nervousness about his surroundings.

I directed the agent to let the man sit in a chair, and asked him and the officer manning the radios to leave. It was just Logan, the gunman, and me.

Logan went to the door and locked it. I brought my chair over to the handcuffed man and sat facing him. "You know we're not cops," I said.

He nodded his head.

"Then you know we don't have to play by the same rules the cops do."

His mask cracked a little, his mouth twitched, he blinked twice, rapidly.

"Okay," he said. "So what?"

"I'm going to ask you some questions, and, if I don't get honest answers, I'm going to hurt you. Understand?"

"Okay."

"What's your name?"

He grinned. "John Smith."

I punched him in the stomach. He screamed. Blood began to seep from his bullet wound and a flower of red took shape on the bandage.

The door rattled, and then a knock. Logan opened it slightly, said something to the person outside, and shut it again. He turned the lock and nodded at me.

"See?" I said. "Nobody's going to save you. What's your name?"

"Peter Johnson."

"Okay, Peter. That's better. Where do you live?"

"In Key West. At the spa."

"What's your job?"

"I'm security."

"Ever been to Blood Island?"

"Yes, to pick up the girls sometimes."

"How did you get to Orlando with a bullet wound?"

He hesitated. I drew back my hand, a threatening gesture.

"Okay," he said, "okay. Michelle got a private plane to bring me here. She said it wasn't wise for me to stay in Key West."

"Was anybody with you?"

"Just the pilot."

"Did you bring anything with you?"

"Just some clothes, and a suitcase for the Rev."

"Did Michelle give you the suitcase?"

"No. The pilot had it. Said one of the guys from the island brought it to the plane and told him to send it here."

"What was in the suitcase?"

"I don't know. It was locked."

"What did you do with it when you got here?"

"I gave it to Ms. Young."

"The receptionist?"

"Yeah. She runs the place."

"Did you ever see it again?"

"No. Man, I'm bleeding bad."

The bandage was getting redder. I was finished. Logan opened the door and the FBI agent came back inside.

"He needs a doctor," I said.

"On it," said the agent, and grabbed Peter by the arm, lifting him out of the chair.

"His name's Peter Johnson," I said.

"Come on, Peter," said the agent. "We'll get you fixed up."

"Can you find Ms. Young and bring her to me?" I asked.

"Sure thing," the agent said and led Peter Johnson out the door.

The agent came back with Ms. Young. She was still in her business suit, dark hair in a bun, subtle makeup on her face. Except for the handcuffs, she could have been on her way to a business meeting.

The agent pointed toward the chair Peter had vacated and told her to sit. I took the other chair as the agent left the trailer. Logan made a big show of locking the door.

"I have some questions for you, Ms. Young," I said. "I'm not a cop, but I need honest answers quickly."

"I have nothing to hide," she said.

"Tell me about the suitcase Peter brought you."

"Peter came in late yesterday. I'd gotten an e-mail from Michelle the day before, so I was expecting him."

"The suitcase?"

"He had it with him. He said I'd be told what to do with it. About an hour later, I got an e-mail from the Rev telling me that somebody would pick it up today."

"Did somebody pick it up?"

"Yes. Late this afternoon."

"Tell me about it."

"Nothing to tell, really. Some fat guy showed up, told me the Rev had sent him for the suitcase. I gave it to him, and he left."

"What time was this?"

"Around six, I think."

"Did you know what was in the suitcase?"

"No. I didn't ask.

The FBI agent took Ms. Young out and returned. I told him what I'd learned, and that I thought we were at a dead end.

"What about the surveillance photos?" he asked.

"What surveillance photos?" I said.

"We took pictures of everyone entering and leaving the house since we got set up here."

"What time was that?"

"Everything was in place by five o'clock."

"Then we probably have a picture of the fat man."

"Probably, for whatever good it'll do us."

He left to retrieve copies of the photographs.

CHAPTER FIFTY-ONE

I looked at my watch. After eleven. Time to call Jock. He sounded tired. I told him what had happened.

"I've got some good news," he said. "We rolled up the Atlanta bomber."

"That is good news. How?"

"We got lucky. The Atlanta police have been tracking a group of nuts that want to take over the government. A surveillance team caught the leader coming out of the Heaven Can't Wait Spa carrying a suitcase. They followed him to a sleaze-bag hotel on the south side where he met with a young man. They arrested both.

"The suitcase had a suicide bomber vest already rigged to explode. The young man confessed to having come up from Blood Island yesterday. They haven't yet figured out how the suitcase got to the whorehouse, but they're interviewing the girls now."

"What about Key West?" I asked.

"Nothing yet, but the island is full of cops looking for the bomber."

"Did you find out anything from any of the other people on the island?"

"Not much. We're pretty sure we got all the bombers except the one here and the two headed for Orlando and Atlanta. The guards didn't know anything, and the girls were pretty much drugged up the whole time."

"Were there other bombers?"

"Yes. They're really sick kids. Simmermon did a number on them. They actually believe he's God's chosen prophet and that they're doing the Lord's work, blowing up good Christian people."

"Jock, don't you think it's time to warn people about this and keep them out of church tomorrow?"

"Can't do it, podner. I already suggested that. The people who make these decisions are afraid an announcement would cause a huge panic, and a lot of folks won't get the message anyway."

"So, we just let a lot of good church-going folks die?"

"Not my call. I agree with you. We've just got to find these bastards before they set off the bombs. Keep plugging." The phone clicked off.

I dialed Debbie's number.

"It's late, Royal, and I just got home from work," she said.

"What ever happened to 'hello'?"

"Caller ID. I don't feel like being nice to you."

"Sorry, babe. I need some more help."

"You still in Key West?"

"No. Orlando."

"I don't even want to know why."

"No you don't. I need you to see what you can find on two people who're dead. Albert Thomas and Colin Edinfield."

"And you need this when?"

"Now would be good."

"Geez, the things I do for quarter tips." She hung up.

I told Logan what Jock had said about Atlanta.

"Glad to hear that," he said. "But if the government can't find anything on Thomas and Edinfield, how do you expect Debbie to?"

"Maybe she won't find anything more, but it's worth a try. She's good, and it's about time we had a little luck."

The FBI agent came back, his hand full of black-and-white photographs.

He laid two on the desk. "This is the fat guy coming in at 5:48 and leaving five minutes later. He's carrying a suitcase coming out."

I studied the pictures. The one of the man leaving the house caught his face straight on. It was high resolution and clear as a cloudless sky. I felt my heart skip a beat, my pulse quicken. This was the last thing I expected. I knew the man with the suitcase.

CHAPTER FIFTY-TWO

"I ain't believing this," I said.

"What?" asked Logan.

"You ever go to Hutch's over on Cortez Road?"

"The place where you almost got killed? No. Why?"

I pointed to the face on the photograph. "This is the guy who runs the place. Fats Monahan."

"You're kidding. I thought that guy Bartel tried to kill him along with you."

"It could've been a set-up. Cracker was pretty sure the voice on the phone telling him to get me to Hutch's that morning was Fats."

"Wasn't Fats upstairs shaving when you got there?"

"Yeah, but he probably meant for Bartel to get me down in the bar. It was awfully dark in there. A perfect place for an ambush. Maybe he was late getting there, or I was early."

"What's Fats doing mixed up in this?"

"I don't know, but we'd better find out soon."

The FBI agent had been following our conversation. "What's this all about? You guys know this man?"

"Yeah," I said. "I think he tried to kill me recently."

"Fill me in," the FBI guy said. "This could be important."

"Let me make a call first."

I dialed Detective David Sims's cell phone in Bradenton.

"Hope I didn't wake you," I said. "This is Matt Royal."

"No, I'm watching the tail end of a Devil Rays game. Pretty bad. What's up?"

"Have you talked to your buddy Paul Galis in the last couple of days?"

"No. Why?"

"Long story, but I'm working with the government on a potential bombing in Orlando. You can call Galis to verify. It looks like our old buddy Fats Monahan is involved."

"Fats? From that bar out on Cortez Road?"

"The same one. We picked him up on surveillance with what we think is the bomb in question."

"What do you need from me?"

"Anything you can get on Fats or his bar. We're in a very short time frame here. Call Galis and get up to speed."

"I'll do that, Mr. Royal. You seem determined to screw up my life."

I laughed. "Not intentionally, I assure you." I hung up.

I called Debbie.

"Almost finished," she said. "I need another few minutes."

"Keep digging. I want you to also check into a guy named Fats Monahan and Hutch's Tavern."

"The place over on Cortez Road?"

"Exactly."

"Well, I don't have anything else to do at midnight. Except sleep." She hung up.

"She needs to find a boyfriend," I said.

"Deb?" said Logan. "I don't know. She's pretty picky."

I filled the FBI in on what we knew about Fats and told him about Sims's role in this.

He turned to leave. "I'll get our computer people onto chasing Fats," he said. "Maybe they'll turn up something we can use."

"Tell them to hurry," I said, as he went out the door.

I called Jock to tell him about Fats. "I'm not sure how he fits into this, but he's got the explosives."

"I'm fresh out of suggestions. Keep me informed." He hung up.

"Logan," I said. "Got any ideas about the connection between Fats and Simmermon?"

"Beats me. Both of them have a history in the Keys, but that's about all I can see that would tie them together."

"That and Varn. Fats knew Varn from his days with the drug lords, and Michelle had Varn killed. I didn't think to ask her if Simmermon knew about his killing."

I dialed Galis' number.

"Paul," I said, "any luck with the bomber down there?"

"No, but I just got off the phone with David Sims. Sounds like you might have stumbled onto something."

"Yeah, but we'll play hell finding Fats in Orlando tonight."

"I've been in contact with Atlanta PD. They tell me the bomber there was going to hit a large Baptist church near downtown. I don't know if that could be a pattern, but we're not pulling any of our people off all the other churches down here."

"Do you have Michelle Browne stashed somewhere close?"

"Yeah. She's in isolation in the county jail, about a hundred yards from my office."

"I need you to ask her about Fats. I also need to know if Simmermon knew about the hit she put on Varn or Yardley or whatever they called him."

"I'll see what she can tell me."

"Don't be gentle, Paul. A lot is riding on this."

"I gotcha. I'll get back to you in a few minutes."

I didn't know what else to do. I had to wait for calls from Debbie and Paul Galis, and hope they had some information that would lead us toward our bomber.

The night was passing by with the speed of an out-of-control freight train on a downhill grade. Every minute, every second, moved us closer to a catastrophe that could change the world. Even if the president's address to the nation stopped the reaction Simmermon hoped for, a lot of good people would die on a quiet Sunday morning in Orlando. We had to stop this madness, but damned if I knew how.

I was tired. I dozed in my chair, waiting for a phone call. My head fell to my chest and woke me up. I looked around the room, my brain slowly coming into focus. Logan had nodded off in his chair, his head tilted at an uncomfortable angle. A snore escaped from his open mouth with every breath. I got up to get another cup of coffee. My phone rang, its irritating jangle waking Logan.

"Matt," said Paul Galis, "I don't have much for you. Michelle says that Simmermon is the one who put the hit on those guys in Bradenton. She didn't know who he used."

"She told me she knew about Bartel and even had to get somebody else to take a shot at Logan."

"Now she's saying that she only knew what Simmermon told her. She never met Bartel. She did agree with the Rev that there was a dangerous situation in Longboat Key because of Peggy, and thought that taking you guys out was the best way to solve the problem. She also wanted to take Peggy out, but Simmermon was falling in love and put the kibosh on that idea."

"That sounds a little out of character for the Rev, doesn't it?"

"Michelle said that he falls in love regularly. Usually the girls he goes for end up in management. The affairs don't last long. Michelle was one of them. It turns out that the woman running the Orlando operation was too."

"Okay, Paul. Thanks. I'm betting that Simmermon and Fats have been in this together for some time. Did Michelle say any more about the bombings?"

"No. She stands by her story that she only found out about it the day you grabbed her. She thought it was just more of Simmermon's craziness."

"And she doesn't know Fats?"

"Says she never heard of him." He hung up.

I looked at my watch. One o'clock. We weren't going to make it.

CHAPTER FIFTY-THREE

A picture of Fats had been given to every law enforcement officer in the Orlando area. Off-duty police officers had been called in. It was the greatest manhunt in the city's history, and the cops weren't being told why they were looking for Fats. The powers in Washington didn't want a panic.

The various law enforcement agencies had finished with the whorehouse, and we'd moved the command post to the Orlando police department headquarters on Hughey Street, just south of the Federal Courthouse.

We were housed in a small room that had been set up for emergencies. There was a conference table flanked by executive desk chairs, a sideboard with coffee and water, and an array of radio gear at one end of the room.

We sat, and we waited. The police officer manning the radio was back with us. The droning of ordinary police calls filled the small space. At two thirty a.m. my phone rang. Sims.

"Matt," he said, "Fats Monahan is a ghost. He came to Manatee County about three years ago and started working at Hutch's. He doesn't own it, but I'll have to wait until the county courthouse opens to find out who does. He's got no record or warrants out for him. I can't find anything on him prior to his coming here. I'm betting Fats Monahan isn't his real name."

"Thanks, Detective. We're getting more pieces of the puzzle."

"Galis tells me you've got a big problem up there. Let me know if you need anything else." He hung up.

Ten minutes later, Debbie called.

"Tell me you've got something good," I said into my phone.

"I'm not sure what I've got, but it's interesting."

"Tell me about it."

"Colin Edinfield was born in Troy, Alabama, at about the same time as Simmermon. He went to Troy State, dropped out when Simmermon did, and then showed up in Key West about the same time as Simmermon. I can find no record of Edinfield working during the three years he spent in Key West, but he had utility bills, credit cards, a bank account, the whole nine yards."

"Maybe Edinfield and Simmermon are friends."

"Or maybe there're the same person," said Debbie.

"Go on."

"Edinfield drops out of sight at the about same time that Simmermon shows up in Colorado. Edenfield's bank account was closed and he stopped paying rent and utilities. He just disappeared. There's no record of him anywhere after that."

"Are you sure?"

"I've mined every database there is. He's gone."

"I hear a 'but' in there somewhere."

"I did find a record of Edinfield spending two years in a state mental institution in Alabama. The two years after he dropped out of Troy State."

"What do you make of it?"

"Either Edinfield is dead or Simmermon is dead and Edinfield has taken his identity."

"Simmermon is probably a schizophrenic," I said. "Maybe Edinfield was in the institution because of schizophrenia, and when he got out he hooked up with Simmermon."

"Or maybe," Debbie said, "Edinfield is Simmermon."

"Why do you think that?"

"There's a pretty good record on Edinfield from his birth until he leaves Key West. Then, nothing. The record on Simmermon during the same years is very spotty and doesn't make a lot of sense. How did he live in Key West with no rental or utility history? Or in Colorado, without a job?"

"Maybe he lived with Edinfield."

"Maybe," she said, "but I don't think so. There's no record of Simmermon ever living in Key West except for the pay records from a defunct company. That's real easy to doctor up. He's got rent and utilities, credit cards, and all that in Colorado, but no job."

"What high school did they go to?"

She gave me the name.

"What did you find on Albert Thomas?" I asked.

"This is a strange one too. He was a certified public accountant in Miami. Seemed to have a good practice, married, owned a home in Kendall. Turns out he was working for some drug dealers. He was charged with an assortment of financial crimes and turned state's evidence. He testified in the same trial Varn did, and then he disappeared. No further record of him, except that his wife divorced him."

"That's got to be Fats. He told me part of this."

"Well, I've got some stuff on Fats too."

"Let me guess. He showed up as the owner of Hutch's, and there's no record of him before he appeared in Bradenton."

Debbie laughed. "You're almost right. Actually, he doesn't own the property or the liquor license. He just works there. Guess who the owner is?"

"Circle Ltd."

"You got it, kid. Have fun doing whatever you're doing." She hung up.

I asked Logan to go find the FBI while I called Jock.

"Jock, things are happening up here." I told him what I knew. "I'm beginning to think these guys, Simmermon, Fats, and Varn are all alumni of the Witness Security Program."

"Sounds plausible. See what you can find out about that. I'm on my way to the airport. I'll be in Orlando in about an hour. There's nothing else I can do here. We may have gotten a break. Galis is following up on it."

"What?"

"One of the girls from the island finally got coherent enough to talk to us. Said she and her boyfriend were believers, and joined Simmermon's entourage when he was in Jacksonville. The boyfriend's not one of those we took into custody and he's not one of the dead. We think he might be one of the bombers, either in Orlando or here. We've got the name of the bomber in Atlanta, and he's not the boyfriend."

"Any idea where the boyfriend might be?"

"The girl says he has an aunt in Key West. Galis is on his way there now. He'll let me know what he finds. Gotta go. I'm at the airport."

The FBI agent walked into the room, Logan following behind. I told him what I'd learned about Simmermon, Thomas, and Edinfield. "We need to get to somebody in the school administration in Troy and find out what we can about Simmermon and Edinfield," I said.

"I'll get right on it," the agent said. "We'll have to get some people out of bed."

I explained my theory about the Witness Security Program. "Can you find out if these guys were part of it?"

"That's run by the U.S. Marshals Service. They don't like to give out information on the people in the program. Not even to law enforcement."

"Make some calls. Get me some information."

"I'll try." He turned to leave.

"FBI man," I said, the edge to my voice bringing him up short. "Do it. We're about out of time."

CHAPTER FIFTY-FOUR

At three thirty, Galis called. "We got the bastard," he said, without preamble.

"The bomber? Where?"

"The little shit was sleeping in his aunt's guest room over on Thompson Street. The suicide vest was under the bed."

"Have you questioned him yet?"

"Oh, yeah. He was planning to do the Lord's work. The kid's a real believer."

"What was his target?"

"A Baptist church near downtown. It's our biggest. Would've gotten a lot of press around the world."

"And killed a lot of people."

"Yeah."

"Have you talked to Jock Algren?" I asked.

"Just hung up. He's on a government jet en route to Orlando. What's going on up there?"

I told him what we'd learned. "I'm wondering if we can narrow down the targets here. The bombers in both Atlanta and Key West were after big Baptist churches near downtown. That could limit our scope if we focus on the two or three Baptist churches in the Orlando downtown area."

"And it could be dangerous, Matt. The Atlanta and Key West targets could be just coincidental."

"You're right, and I don't like coincidences. I'll let you know what happens."

"I hope I don't see it on the news."

"Me either," I said, and closed my phone.

• • •

At four o'clock, Jock walked into the room. He looked tired, his face drawn and haggard, his clothes rumpled.

"Hey, podner," he said, "how're we doing?"

"Waiting," I said.

Logan was reared back in his chair, feet on the conference table. "You look whipped, Jock," he said.

"Yeah. Where's the coffee?"

I pointed to the large thermos sitting on the sideboard. "It's probably mostly mud by now."

"If it's got caffeine, I can use it."

The FBI agent came in. I introduced him to Jock. "Mr. Algren is the overall commander of this effort," I said. "He's the one I report to."

The agent took stock of Jock. "What agency are you with?"

"That's not important," Jock said. "But I talk directly to the president."

"I guess that's important," the agent said. "Maybe you can get the Marshals Service off its duff. They won't give me anything on the Witness Security Program. I've alerted my supervisor and he's working up the chain of command to see if our director can talk to the Marshals director."

Jock gave the agent that cold stare that I knew had intimidated stronger men than the FBI man. "You called your fucking supervisor?" he said, his voice rising. "Why didn't you go straight to the top?"

The agent wilted a little. "We have to follow protocol on these things," he said. "We do have a chain of command, you know."

Jock exploded, the hours of frustration bursting out of him like a Roman candle. "You bureaucratic pissant," he said, his voice low. "Don't you realize that people are about to die?"

"Protocol is important, Mr. Algren," the agent said.

"Fuck protocol," Jock said. His voice was low and strident. "And fuck your chain of command."

Jock pulled his cell phone from his pocket and hit one button. In a moment he said, "Mr. President, this is Jock Algren." Silence. "Not yet, sir, but we're making progress." Silence. "Yes, sir. I need you to call the director of the U.S. Marshals Service and have him get somebody to talk to me about the Witness Security Program." Silence. "As soon as possible, sir. I need names, addresses, and a lot of information on some of the protected witnesses." Silence. "Thank you, sir. I'll keep you posted."

Jock closed his phone and turned to the agent, who looked as if he wanted to cower in the corner of the small room. "That's done. Now get the hell out of my sight."

The agent turned for the door. "Wait," I said. "Did you find out anything from the folks in Troy?"

"Yes, sir," he said. "The high school principal is retired, but it was a small school, and he remembers most of the kids. He never heard of a student named Simmermon, but he does remember Edinfield. Says he was a troubled boy, and thinks he ended up in a mental institution."

"What about records?"

"There is no record of a student named Simmermon."

"Thank you, Agent. I appreciate your help," I said.

"Agent," Jock said. "I apologize for my behavior. Chalk it up to a lack of sleep."

"Apology accepted, sir," the agent said as he left the room.

"Shit," said Jock. "The guy was just doing his job."

I told Jock about the connection I saw to the churches in Atlanta and Key West. "I wonder if we ought to concentrate our assets on similar churches in Orlando."

"If we do that, and the bomber takes out an unprotected church, we're going to look like the world's biggest idiots. Plus, I'd have to live with the slaughter of a lot of innocent people because I got stupid."

"You're probably right. At least we can put a little protection around all the churches. Maybe we'll get lucky."

Jock was pacing now, his face a mask of pain. "We're going to lose them, podner. I'm about to get a lot of good people killed."

"Calm down, buddy. We're making progress."

"Yeah," said Jock, "but is it enough?"

CHAPTER FIFTY-FIVE

It was four thirty when Debbie called. "Matt," she said, "I couldn't sleep. I went into the newspaper archives for northern Alabama, and came up with something that I thought you might be interested in."

"Shoot."

"A couple of years ago, when Simmermon was really getting his revivals into the big time, he got into a pissing match with a Methodist minister in Birmingham."

"What about?"

"Mostly theological issues. The minister didn't think Simmermon was staying true to the Bible. Said he was preaching hate wrapped up in Christian principles. The preacher took the position that Christian principles are about forgiveness, and Simmermon said that they were about exclusiveness. In other words, if you want to go to heaven, you need to listen to Simmermon."

"How does that fit into the problems we're facing?"

"Well, you haven't exactly told me what problems you are facing. I know you're in Orlando, and you're there because of Simmermon."

"Sorry, babe. That's all I can tell you."

"Well, anyway, the connection I see is that the minister from Birmingham is now the pastor of the Lakeside Methodist Church in downtown Orlando."

"Uh-oh. What's the minister's name?"

"Carlton Tarlington."

"I'll be damned. Thanks Deb. Get some sleep."

"Yeah, right." She hung up.

I turned to Jock and Logan. "Jock," I said, "when you had Simmermon drugged up, could he have been saying 'Tarlington' instead of 'Arlington'?"

"Maybe. Why?"

I relayed Deb's findings.

"That could be it. Do you know the church?"

"Yeah. It's a big one. The sanctuary probably seats a thousand people."

"That's got to be his target," said Logan. "Can't we warn Tarlington and get his people out of harm's way?"

Jock shook his head. "We can't take that chance. The bomber would just hit another target. We've got to take him out."

Jock's phone rang, and he stepped outside to take it. When he came back, he was smiling. "That was the director of the Witness Security Program. He was at home and plugged into his agency computers. Amazing what wonders a little juice will work in bureaucracies."

"What did he find out?" I asked.

"Not enough. He's going to dig a little deeper and call me back. But, Edinfield and Thomas were in the program. So was Clyde Varn. They set Edinfield up with a new name, Robert William Simmermon, and tried to manufacture a past for him. It was pretty good, and would have been enough if Debbie hadn't gotten curious."

"What about Varn and Thomas?" Logan asked.

"Varn was sent to Topeka and became Jake Yardley. About a year ago, he disappeared. The Marshals say it isn't that unusual. The witnesses get bored or miss their old life and just leave the program. The government doesn't spend a lot of manpower looking for them."

"That's about when he showed up in Bradenton," I said. "Is there any evidence that he knew Edinfield in the program?"

"Some. While Edinfield was in Key West he was working for some pretty bad folks. He was crazy, but he somehow got tied in with the same drug-running group that Varn was associated with. Edinfield worked on some fishing boats, and apparently he was bringing drugs into Key West.

"The Marshals think he might have met Varn there. Varn was muscle for the drug importers that Edinfield worked for. When the whole thing fell apart, Varn and Thomas testified, but Edinfield was too crazy to be a witness. They put him in the program anyway, and manufactured the Simmermon persona. The three of them spent some time together in a safe house the marshals maintain in Miami."

"That's probably the connection," I said.

Jock nodded his head. "Probably. The Marshals didn't expect their man to find the Lord and become an evangelist. There wasn't anything they could do about it though. He dropped out of the program and became a little bit famous."

"What about Fats?" I asked.

"He was the accountant for the drug mob. He went into the program too, but the director is going to have to get back to me on him. There was some sort of computer glitch. They're working on it."

My phone rang.

"I'm sorry to wake you, Matt." It was Jeff Timmons.

"No problem, Jeff. I wasn't asleep."

"There's no other way to say this," he said. "Laura wanted me to tell you how much she appreciated your finding Peggy. She said to tell you she loved you. She died about ten minutes ago."

I was expecting it. When I heard Jeff's voice on the phone, I knew it had happened. But nothing really prepares you for the death of a loved one. Tears welled in my eyes. I choked down a sob. "Shit, Jeff," I said. "I'm so sorry."

"I'm sorry too, Matt. She loved both of us, you know. I always knew that, and I've always been okay with it. You gave me back my daughter. Peggy was with Laura at the end. I'll never be able to thank you enough for that. Please stay in touch." He hung up.

I put the phone in my pocket. Tears were running down my cheeks. I knew it, and didn't care. The radioman was out of the room, so it was just my two best friends and me. They'd understand.

"Laura's dead," I said, and walked out of the room.

I left the building and stood on the front steps. The city lights partially obscured the night sky, but I could see stars shining through the glare. Maybe Laura was one of them.

An elevated highway, Interstate 4, ran in front of the police head-quarters. Traffic was light, a few late-night revelers headed home. I heard a dog bark nearby, a lonely sound in the wee hours. Soon, another dog took up the conversation. In the far distance, I could hear a siren, its faint wail gently caressing my ears.

My mind was flooded with memories of Laura. The day I met her, our wedding day, the day she left me. Mostly, I saw her that morning ten days earlier on the deck of the Longboat Hilton, staring at the Gulf, her face squeezed by worry. Her smile, her embrace, her teasing banter. I'd give the rest of my life to go back to those minutes beside a placid sea, drinking in the essence of my life's love.

I wiped my eyes. I didn't have time for grief. There were a lot of people in Orlando who were about to be grief stricken. We had to stop the bomber. There was enough pain in the world brought about by events beyond human control. We didn't need to add to that by letting the crazies loose on an unsuspecting nation.

I said good-bye to Laura, and walked back into the building.

CHAPTER FIFTY-SIX

Jock looked up as I walked into the room. "You okay, podner?"

"I will be," I said.

"I'm sorry," said Logan. "She must have been special."

"She was. Anything else on the bomber?"

"Maybe," said Jock. "The Witness Security Program director called back. It seems that Mr. Thomas lived in Orlando under an assumed name while he was in the program. He disappeared three years ago."

"Was Monahan the name given him by the feds?"

"No. He was Jared Buckhorn then."

"Where did he live?"

"He had a house on Primrose Street. He sold it when he moved. That's all the Marshals have on him. He dropped out of sight completely."

"Who did he sell the house to?"

"No information on that."

"Do you have an address?"

"Sure do," said Jock, and gave it to me.

I called Debbie again. She wasn't going to like this, but it was quicker than getting the county property appraiser out of bed.

"Babe?" I said. She had obviously been asleep.

"Oh, great, Royal. What time is it? Oh, five thirty. Forty-five minutes sleep is all I need. What now?"

"One more search. I think I know the answer, but I need you to confirm it."

"All right. What's the question?"

I gave her the address and told her I needed the ownership of the house.

"You want to take a bet on it being Circle Ltd?" she said.

"Nope. I'm guessing that's what you'll find."

"Don't hang up."

I heard her tapping on a computer keyboard. Then, "It's Circle Ltd."

"Does the corporation still own it?"

"Yes."

"Thank you, dear. Sleep tight."

"Go to hell, Royal," she said and hung up.

I returned the phone to my pocket. "That address is owned by the same corporation that owns the whorehouses and Blood Island. Fats may be there."

"Let's round up the troops and find out," Jock said.

Thirty minutes later Jock, Logan, and I were sitting in a government sedan in front of the Primrose Street house. The FBI agent was with us. An Orlando police SWAT team, dressed in combat gear, was about to enter the house. ATF agents with explosive sniffing dogs would follow them in. An Orlando fire department ambulance was parked down the street.

We waited. The night was easing into day. It was six a.m., and dawn had replaced the darkness. A light showed in the window of the house next door. The smell of brewing coffee wafted across to us. A cat ambled across the lawn, paying no attention to the strangers encroaching into its territory. Newspapers, thick with the Sunday ads, were lying on front sidewalks. People were sleeping in, but soon they would be up and coming outside for their papers. We needed to be finished before then. Nosey neighbors could easily get hurt if there was a shootout, or worse, an explosion.

The SWAT team moved with an unexpected suddenness. The front door was battered open by a ram held by two officers. The men crowded into the house, yelling "clear" as they went from room to room. Two ATF agents and their dogs went through the door at a fast walk. The whole operation took about a minute.

The SWAT commander came out of the house, looking relaxed, and walked over to our car. "The house is clear," he said. "The ATF guys say there're no explosives in the house. We found a fat guy asleep in the master bedroom."

Jock smiled coldly. "That's good news, Captain. We'll talk to him in the house. Restrain the fat man, and clear all your guys out."

"I'm the team commander," the officer said. "I can stay if you like."

Jock shook his head. "That might not be good for your career. Get your men out."

The captain went back to the house, and soon the entire group was huddled on the sidewalk across the street. Lights had come on in more of the houses, and uniformed Orlando police officers were going door to door, reassuring the residents that everything was under control.

Jock, Logan, and I went into the house. Fats Monahan was sitting on a sofa in the small living room, his hands cuffed behind his back, head down, staring at his lap.

"Morning, Fats," I said.

He looked up, surprise written on his features.

"Matt," he said. "Thank God. These officers have me mixed up with somebody else."

I laughed. "I want you to listen to me very closely, Albert Thomas," I said.

He blanched at the sound of his name. Blood drained from his face. He knew at that moment that his life was finished. He'd spend the rest of it in jail.

I knelt down in front of him, my face even with his. "We're not cops," I said. "We don't care if you live to walk out of here or die where you sit. Understand?"

"Yes."

"Tell me who and where the bomber is."

"I don't know what you're talking about."

I pulled my dive knife from its scabbard at my ankle and stabbed him in the shoulder. He screamed. I heard boots hitting the sidewalk at a run. One of the cops on his way.

Jock moved to the door to intercept the officer. He crossed his hands, plams down, like a baseball umpire signaling safe. "We've got everything under control," he said.

Fats was groaning, looking at me, his face wrinkled in terror and pain.

"Fats," I said, "I'm going to butcher you alive right in this room if you don't start talking."

"Okay," he said, his voice strained. "I don't know where Joshua is."

"Is Joshua the bomber?"

"Yes."

"When did you see him last?"

"At midnight. He came here to get his vest."

"What's his target?"

Fats stared at me, his eyes a bit glazed. "Listen, don't stop this. We're going to save Western Civilization."

"By killing Christians?"

"They'll be martyrs. They'll go to heaven immediately. It's God's way."

"I don't get it," Logan said. "Why kill your own people?"

"We're just going to kill enough to get the government off its ass and start killing Muslims. We need to root out the heathens."

"You're as crazy as the rest of them," said Logan.

"Fats," I said, "I'm going to stab you again. You can pick the spot."

"No, Matt. Don't you see? This is for us, for America."

I pulled back on the knife. "Where do you want it?"

"No, don't stab me again. I'll tell you."

"Martyrdom's not for you, huh?" I said.

"It's not my time."

"What's the target?"

"Lakeside Methodist Church."

"When?"

"Nine o'clock. The early service."

"Describe Joshua to me."

"He's about twenty years old, blond hair, six feet tall."

"What's he wearing?"

"Beige suit and blue tie."

"Where are the explosives?"

"A vest. Under his suit coat. My shoulder hurts like hell."

"Fats," I said, holding the bloody knife under his nose, "if you aren't giving me the right description of this idiot, I'm coming back for you. Your martyrdom is going to be preceded by more pain than you can imagine."

"I'm telling you the truth. Can I get something for this shoulder?"

Jock said, "Fats, did you kill the man Matt found at Pelican Man's?"

"I had to. He was some kind of government agent."

"How did you know that?" Jock asked.

"I didn't for sure, but we had to be careful. It's better to sacrifice one of our own than to take a chance on the whole thing going down the drain."

"Why did you leave him in the vulture pit?" I asked.

"That was Bartel. He liked to make a statement."

"Where did you find Bartel?" I asked.

"I didn't. The Rev sent him to me. Said he'd do whatever I needed done."

"That day in your bar? What the hell was that all about?"

"I knew you were going to talk to Wayne Lee. I tried to stop him before you found him, but he got by me somehow. I saw you and Logan go into the bar with him, and I saw you two leave. I waited until Wayne left to take him out. I didn't know what he'd told you, so I had to get you too.

"The next morning, I called Cracker and told him to get you to my place. Bartel was supposed to kill you in the bar downstairs, and then get out of there. He was late."

"And it cost him his sorry life," I said.

"Yeah," said Fats. "Another martyr. I'm really hurting here, Matt."

I waved at Logan, and he left to get the paramedics.

"Fats," I said, "the paramedics are going to help you out here, but if you've lied to me, they're going to give you back to me."

Fats just nodded his head.

"We've got less than three hours to find this guy," Jock said. "Any suggestions?"

The three of us were standing on the sidewalk in front of Fats's house. The SWAT team had loaded up in their black SUVs and gone back to wherever they came from. A few Orlando police officers had stayed in the area to calm the neighbors' fears. The ambulance had taken Fats for treatment at a clinic where the doctor wouldn't ask a lot of questions. He'd be held there until we were finished.

I felt sick to my stomach. I'd just stabbed a defenseless man, and I'd have done it again if he hadn't given me answers. Fats was a bloody and dangerous man who'd tried to kill me and my friend Logan. He'd killed poor helpless Wayne Lee, and he had no compunctions about killing a church full of decent people.

He had information that could save a lot of lives, and I knew that harsh tactics were called for—and even condoned. Especially by the people who would have died or lost loved ones if I hadn't acted. I did what was necessary, and I knew I would do it again.

In the process, I had found the beast that lived within me, and I wasn't happy to meet him. It didn't fit with my own view of myself. I'd killed men before, but every time, it was when they were trying to kill me. I had been a soldier in a war and, as terrible as that is, you can always justify your actions as discharging your duty to your country or just trying to survive.

This was different and, while necessary, I didn't think I'd ever have the same benign view of myself again. It was like losing a close friend. The Matt Royal I knew, the fun-loving beach bum lawyer, had died over the past few days, and had been replaced by a monster who was perfectly willing to shoot and stab people. I wondered if I'd ever find my old self again. I was glad Laura would never have to know this new version of the man she'd loved when she was young.

"Joshua could be anywhere," said Logan, bringing me out of my pitiful self-loathing reverie, "or nowhere."

Jock shook his head. "I don't think Fats lied to us. He was too scared of Matt's knife."

"Why don't we concentrate our forces at Lakeside Methodist," Logan said. "As thin as we are, we won't do much good for the other churches. It'd be too easy for the bomber to slip by. Are you familiar with the Lakeside Church, Matt?"

"Yes," I said. "In another lifetime, Laura and I were married in that church."

"Shit," said Logan. "I'm sorry, Matt."

Jock said, "What if we put our troops just around the big churches downtown? If the bomber smells a rat at one, maybe he'll just move on to the church in the next block. If we're wrong, we're going to lose a church any way you cut it."

"What do you think, Matt?" Logan said.

"Sounds like a plan. I think we should be at Lakeside. We can put sniper teams around the square. If we approach him, all he has to do is punch a button or something, and all hell breaks loose. We've got to get him before he has a chance to react. Are your sniper credentials still good, Jock?"

"Unfortunately, yes," he said. "So much for retirement."

CHAPTER FIFTY-SEVEN

I stood beside Jock in the bell house atop the steeple of the Lakeside Methodist Church. A German made Heckler-Koch PSG-1 sniper rifle rested on a tripod placed on the edge of the half wall that surrounded the small space. The bells weren't used anymore, and loudspeakers placed around the room played a recording of somebody else's bells clanging the faithful to worship. The din made normal conversation impossible.

We had rearranged our forces to cover the big downtown churches. Orlando had once been called the City of Churches, and almost every corner along Rosalind and Magnolia avenues boasted a house of worship.

It all made sense. If Simmermon was going to blow up a church, why not take out his spiritual nemesis in the bargain? He and Tarlington had struggled against each other for the allegiance of the faithful. In Simmermon's crazed mind, Tarlington was the anti-Christ and had to be killed for the good of the faith.

So we had climbed the stairs to the steeple to do a job I had no stomach for. Yet, here I was, ready to kill a boy who had been taken in by a crazed charlatan.

I held a pair of high-powered Zeiss binoculars to my eyes, scanning the crowd below. Other sniper pairs, a shooter and a spotter, were scattered about the area. The first one to catch sight of the bomber was to take him out. I hoped none of the snipers would mistakenly take out an innocent person, but these guys were well trained, among the best in the world, and I thought we'd be okay.

The church was large, and had been built when Orlando was a much smaller city. Office buildings and retail outlets now crowded in on either side, but the large square in front of the church was intact. It was a gathering place for the faithful and the hangers-on, a place to see and be seen on Sunday mornings.

The only entrance the church used for Sunday services was the front door. This was a tradition dating back many decades. It forced the members to mingle on their way to church. It also meant that the bomber would have to come across the square.

If Fats had given us the wrong information, a lot of people were going to die in the next few minutes, including Jock and me. We had volunteered for the bell tower, since it was our decision to place our resources here. If we were wrong, another church would die this day, and if we were right and let the bomber get by, we would die with this church.

It was nearing the nine o'clock hour. The sun was hot, shining from an almost cloudless sky. The water of the nearby lake was flat, and the tall buildings surrounding it reflected off its surface. The crowd in the square was getting bigger as people stopped to chat with one another.

The radio receiver plugged into my ear buzzed with static. I mentally tuned it out, but then I heard Logan's voice. "Matt, I saw somebody who could be our target," he said. "He's standing almost in the middle of the square. He's alone, wearing a beige suit. Can you see him?"

Logan was moving about the crowd, a roving spotter on the lookout for the bomber. We were all wired into a tactical radio network, so that when one of us spoke, all the members of our team could hear.

I scanned the crowd with the binoculars. Jock put his eye to the Hendsoldt scope fastened to the top of the rifle. He had it set for 100 meters, a distance that was a little longer than a football field.

I saw the figure Logan was talking about. I looked closely, and I knew Jock's scope gave him a closer look than I could get. I wasn't sure if this was our guy.

Jock removed his eye from the scope and said into my ear, "Not him. This guy is in his thirties."

"You sure?"

"Yes. I'm about to kill somebody's son. I've got to be sure."

"Whoever he is, Jock," I said, "he's not the son his parents knew. He's been brainwashed. He's a robot."

Jock nodded, but I knew he didn't believe me. He was going to do what he had to do, but it didn't sit well with him.

I spoke into the mic. "It's not him, Logan. Keep a sharp lookout."

"Ten-four," came the reply.

Jock was scanning the square with his eye to the scope. "There," he said. "On the edge of the crowd, over by the lake. Take a look."

I turned the binoculars to where Jock was pointing. This could be the guy. He was in a beige suit, blue tie, and he was about the right age. His coat was unbuttoned. If I gave Jock the word, this was a dead man. What if I was wrong?

"Steady," I said. "Let's be sure."

"He's moving," said Jock.

The man was striding across the square, not looking to either side, headed for the front door of the sanctuary. A gust of wind came off the lake. For just a second, it lifted his coat. I saw the vest. "Do it," I said.

The rifle recoiled at the instant I heard the shot. I held the binoculars to my eyes, watching the boy in the beige suit. Time slowed to a crawl, like in a movie run in slow motion. The back of his head blew out from the force of the bullet entering his brain. Bone and tissue splattered the sun-washed bricks of the square. He dropped with no effort to catch himself. He was dead before he hit the ground. Jock had drilled him through the forehead with a 7.62-millimeter round.

The sound of the rifle caused panic in the square. People were looking around for the origin of the blast. Some dropped to their stomachs, others simply began running. Several people closest to our target were standing over the body, frozen, looks of horror straining their facial features. I saw Logan, moving at a dead run, cross the square. He reached the body, squatted beside it, pulled the coat back, looked up at us and pumped his arm in a victory gesture. His voice came over my earpiece. "Got the bastard, Jock. You got the crazy bastard."

CHAPTER FIFTY-EIGHT

Longboat Key is a place to heal the soul. The summer brings a quiet time for the year-round islanders. The snowbirds are back in the north, the tourists are gone, and the key slows to a pace that could be considered glacial.

A month had gone by since the death of a young man on a sun-swept church square in the beautiful city of Orlando. The headlines told of a plot to assassinate the mayor of Orlando, who attended the church, and of a police sniper who killed the would-be assassin. There was nothing about bombers or crazed religious freaks or, for that matter, whores.

The Heaven Can't Wait Spas in several cities were quietly closed down, and the working girls told to leave town. The Reverend Robert William Simmermon was locked in a small cell in a mental institution, and would probably spend the rest of his life there.

Michelle Browne was cooperating with law enforcement, helping them piece together the empire and find the girls who wanted to go home. Most didn't. They liked being whores, and were looking for other high-class venues in which to ply their trade.

Michelle's goons, Charlie Calhoun and Martin Holcomb, were being held on assault and battery charges and would spend some time as guests of the state of Florida.

The girls taken by the Army from Blood Island were drying out in treatment centers in South Florida and would be given the opportunity to rejoin their families. Paul Galis told me that most of the families were so dysfunctional that the girls didn't want anything to do with them. Social Service agencies were being brought in to help the young women.

The Key West bomber would probably spend the next twenty or so years in a federal penitentiary. He had been brainwashed, but he wasn't crazy. Hopefully, by the time he got out of prison, he would have shed his demons.

Fats was going to be in jail for the rest of his life. His wounds had been treated, and he was spending some quality time in the Seminole County jail, a federal prisoner awaiting trial. He kept trying to tell anyone who would listen that a crazed lawyer from Longboat Key had stabbed him, but the FBI assured the reporters that Fats had been hurt in an altercation with a drug dealer.

Jock Algren was back in Houston, playing golf and trying to convince his agency that he really was retired. He reported that the bosses kept nodding in understanding, but he was sure he'd get another call in the future.

Me? Aw, hell, I was doing okay. Peggy Timmons was visiting, with her dad's blessing. She had adopted me as a kind of uncle, and I liked the role.

She was a tough gal, and wouldn't let her ordeal on Blood Island ruin her life. She had arranged to reenter the University of Georgia in the fall, and had plans to follow her dad to medical school. She missed Laura, as did I. It was good to have someone I could talk to about her. I was learning a lot about the life Laura had as a Timmons, and I was glad to know that it had been a good one.

My boat was still in Key West, watched over by the Coast Guard. Logan and I were going to get it the following week. We'd take our time getting back to Longboat Key. The tarpon were running in Boca Grande Pass, and we meant to bag our share. We planned to stay over a few days on Sanibel Island and find out what those people did for fun. I'd heard there was a new restaurant there, named for a fictional character conjured up by one of the local islanders. The food was reportedly outstanding.

So, on a tropical evening in early June, Logan and Peggy and I sat on the patio of Café on the Bay, enjoying a dinner of fresh seafood and white wine. Debbie was tending bar at Moore's and hadn't been able to join us. We'd stop by for a nightcap later. Peggy had become quite fond of her, and we all appreciated Debbie's help in rooting out what we had come to think of as pure evil.

A freshening breeze blew off the Gulf, bringing the smell of the sea, and rustling the branches of the banyan trees under which we sat. The lights on the patio were subdued, and Peggy's face was in shadow. She was beautiful, and, I knew, tough as nails.

"What I don't understand, Peggy," said Logan, "is how you got tied up with that bunch of nuts in the first place."

"I'm not sure either, Logan," said Peggy. "I wasn't ready for the freedom I found when I went off to college. My mother died when I was five, and Laura married my dad and raised me from the time I was eight. She was a wonderful mother, but she and Dad were pretty strict about what I could and couldn't do. When I got to Athens, all the restraints came off, and I went a little crazy."

"How did you get hooked up with Simmermon?" Logan asked.

"My boyfriend and I and a couple we lived with in Athens came here for spring break. We had all dropped out of school and were doing drugs and hanging out in Athens. It seemed like a good idea at the time, even if we didn't have any money. We met Jake Yardley on our first day here, and he seemed like a godsend. He took us in and paid for everything for several days. We lived on the beach and ate and drank well. He even had some weed for us. We couldn't believe our good luck."

I'd heard the story before. Peggy had spent part of our week together trying to explain to me, and probably to herself, the disconnect from reality that led her to Blood Island. "Tell Logan about meeting the Rev," I said.

"Yardley kept telling us about this man of God who had a place in his organization for people like us; people who didn't have any other place to go. I was the only one of us with any kind of family, and the other three thought we ought to meet Simmermon.

"Yardley took us to the Rev's motor home over at Robarts. He was a smooth talker; offered us sanctuary," she said, using her hands and fingers to indicate quote marks. "He said we could go with him to a tropical island and live a life of ease. Said God would bless us with everything we needed or wanted. I didn't realize then that the punch he served us was laced with some kind of drug. We were all floating on the Rev's benevolence.

"The next thing I knew, I was on Blood Island, and my friends were gone. The Rev told me they had abandoned me, but that he was going to save me. That all sounded good, until I got sick and got the drugs out of my system. Everything's a little fuzzy about that time, but I must've been on the island for a couple of weeks before they tried to take me to the whorehouse."

We sat quietly, sipping our wine, savoring the evening. Peggy was pensive on this, our last evening together. After a while, she said, "Matt, I don't really understand why you came for me. You hadn't seen Laura in years, and you'd never met me."

"I came because I loved Laura," I said, "and I would've done anything she asked of me."

"Why then, did Logan come? He'd never met Laura. And Jock?"

"They came," I said, "because they're my friends."